TEARS OF STRATHNAVER

SHEENA MACLEOD

MACMOR BOOKS

Published by MacMor Books

Text copyright © 2021 Sheena Macleod

Cover design by Michelle Arzu

Tears of Strathnaver is a work of fiction. Names, characters, organisations, places, events and incidents are either products of the author's imagination or are used fictitiously.

ISBN- 978-1-7398664-0-2

DEDICATION

To my father

. . . and the clansmen will flee from their native country before an army of sheep. . . . the people will emigrate to islands now unknown in the boundless oceans
The Brahan Seer (17th century Highland Prophet)

SET OF SAVAGES

The Highlands of Scotland
Strath of Kildonan
January 1813

The removal notices burned to ash in the woman's hand; the grey flakes fluttering to the frozen earth like moths from a flame. As the factor glowered at the woman, standing in the front row of tenants facing up to him, a pulse in his temple beat out an angry rhythm.

His horse snorted and stepped sideways. He steadied the grey mount and held up a gloved hand, instructing his men to stay where they were. 'Let the auld witch burn them. The law is on our side.'

The woman thumped her fists onto her hips. Bright eyes peered from a face engrained with peat dust. 'To Hell, you will go for this, Mister Sellar,' she said in Gaelic, and the rows of tenants roared their agreement.

After translating her words, the minister addressed the crowd. 'These men will be back with new notices of removal. This time, obey those that He has placed above you. To disobey their order to move is to go against the will of God. Accept what is happening as just punishment for your sins.'

The factor met the tenant's angry looks with a fiery glare. What a parcel o' beggars. How they told each other apart, he didn't know. His eye caught on one difference, and he scoffed. Concealed in the front two rows of women were three men in dresses.

He laughed and pointed to each of the men. His face lost its smile. 'You! Step forward. Explain yourself.'

No one moved.

The factor waited. Liquid dripped from his nose. He had been teased about his large, beaked nose for as far back as he could remember and had long since learned not to let it show that he cared. He tilted his chin upwards, sniffed and directed his anger at the lines of tenants now daring to defy him.

Rows of men stood behind the women as if forming a second line of defence. 'Pah! Look at you. I was led tae believe there were good fighting men in the straths. Yet here you a' are, hiding behind the skirts o' your women an' leaving them to fight your battles for you.'

The factor's men roared with laughter, and the tenants called back in anger. A woman shouted and waved a letter at the minister, who leant down from his horse and took it from her soil-encrusted fingers.

The factor turned to the minister. 'What is that woman babbling about?'

'Their men have been taken from them.'

'What?'

'She said that you are trying to remove them from their homes while their men are fighting in the war.' The minister handed him the letter.

The factor studied the contents and laughed. He turned his attention back to the baying tenants. 'Silence! This letter o' entitlement tae land in return for furnishing soldiers expired five years syne.' He raised his eyebrows, tilted his head and smirked. 'If you had taken the time tae learn tae read or tae speak English then you would have known this.'

A red-haired woman spat on the ground. 'So you are saying, but this is our home and we are not leaving. We will hold this land until our men are returned to us.'

'Home,' the factor said and glanced around. He sniffed, inhaling the musky smell of burning peats. 'I don't see any homes. I see hovels, an' barns unfit tae shelter animals.'

Behind him, his men tittered. Their horses shifted on the frozen ground as if restless to be on their way. But the factor couldn't leave. The removal notices had not been served, again, and it was up to him to make sure they were. Failure wasn't a familiar friend, and he wasn't going to shake hands with it now.

He urged his horse forward a few steps.

The tenants remained where they were.

He urged his horse a few steps closer.

The tenants held fast.

This had never happened before. He had underestimated these natives; hadn't expected them to resist. In the only other farming township he had dealt with, the tenants had accepted their notice to move like meek little lambs. So, why were these blockheads baaing like angry sheep and resisting? It didn't make sense.

He scanned the houses scattered around the township. Granted, the single-roomed cottages, which included space to shelter kye over the winter, were large; most over 80 feet long. But they were built low, lacked windows and were blackened and bleak inside. Dense blue-grey smoke rose through the thatched roofs. The sour stench from the byres mingled with the earthy smell of burning peat, corrupting the crisp air. Why anyone would choose to live in such hovels when they could move to new-built stone cottages was beyond his comprehension.

He turned to Sheriff McKid. Was this any of his doing? He didn't trust the man not to be inciting the natives against him. 'Sort this out!'

Sheriff McKid drew in a deep breath and spoke to the tenants in Gaelic. 'Houses have been built on the coast. There is work there for everyone. Never again will you experience the hunger and hardship you are facing this winter and will face again each time your crops fail.'

'We are not believing the factor,' the elderly woman said. 'The Great Lady would not be wanting us to leave.'

A white-bearded man shook his fists. 'It will be himself wanting our land. For the sheep.'

'Michty, me!' the factor said and let out a sneering laugh. 'Would you have me ask Her Ladyship tae journey here in person tae ask you tae leave? If you are expecting that then you will be sorely disappointed. Tsk. Tsk. What do you think she will have tae say when I tell her you burned her orders?' He smiled and lowered his voice. 'The authority o' the law stands. Are we clear?'

'You are calling our homes hovels,' the white-bearded man said. 'We may not be living in as grand a house as yourself, but we built these homes with our own hands and on our own land, just as our ancestors have for hundreds of years. The Great Lady has no more right to be removing us from our homes than we do to be removing her from her castle.'

The factor shook his head. There was no reasoning with such an ignorant set of savages. 'Enough o' that blather or I'll have you turned out for your insolence. Then there will be nae need for a writ from Her Ladyship.'

The tenants waved their arms and yelled their displeasure.

Smoke drifted from their mouths as their breaths hit the cold air.

A grey-bearded man shouted, 'Ask the Great Lady to be sending us more grain.'

The factor regarded Sheriff McKid, who had already made it clear that a blind eye should be turned on the tenants poaching from the estate. As a strict man of the law, he didn't appreciate McKid, or anyone else, bending the law to suit their own needs. 'Are you in league with these tenants?' he asked him. 'Why haven't you asked for the military tae be brought in?'

McKid squared his shoulders and looked directly at him. 'As sheriff-substitute, I'm not placed to do that. I would need to ask the Sheriff to arrange this.'

'Then dae it!'

'With the shortage of military to guard our coasts against French invasion, I'm reluctant to.'

'If this situation breaks intae a riot, I will personally see you hung.'

The grey-bearded man stepped from the crowd. With tear-filled eyes, he approached the minister. He removed his bonnet and twisted it between his fingers. 'Ask the Great Lady to be sending us more grain. Tell her... Let herself know that we are in most urgent need. For without grain, we cannot be feeding the cattle we need to sell to pay her our rents.' The man put his bonnet back on. He made to turn away but stopped, straightened, and addressed Sheriff McKid. 'And, let her know that if any of us are harmed for our actions today in defending our homes, we will be making sure everyone hears about it. Even if there is only one man left standing amongst us to tell.'

The factor stood in the stirrups and gripped the reins. 'The changes are for your own good. Improvements are everywhere. My grandfaither was a tenant farmer. Removal was the best thing tae happen tae him. As a successful lawyer an' sheep-farmer, I am living proof o' that. My faither—'

A clod of peaty earth smacked into his chest, and he bent over and gasped. He wiped soil from his jacket and flicked away the crumbs lodged behind the silver-coloured buttons. He looked up. 'You are nothing but vermin. You think the theft o' a pheasant here or a rabbit there nae small matter. Be warned, I will have the watch increased.' He smiled, a slow stretching of his lips, and turned to a shepherd. 'Hard labour wouldn't hurt them. If we are lucky, they'll a' be sent tae Botany Bay for poaching, an' good riddance.'

The shepherd's dog snarled and lurched forward. The shepherd held it back.

The factor waved an arm. 'Arrest the ringleaders.' He nodded to a constable who slipped from his horse.

'We stand as one,' a man shouted. The tenants linked arms and joined in his chant. 'We stand as one.'

Despite his need for retribution, the factor hesitated. If news of this abomination reached the other townships, resistance could be formed there too. And, the sheep farmer who was to lease this land would back out. What a mess these savages were causing to his plans. Damn them and their auld ways. There was no reasoning with them. The sooner they were removed to the coast the better. If this situation wasn't resolved, Lord and Lady Stafford would think that he was failing in his duties.

He addressed the justices of the peace, all of them shepherds, who were looking to him for instruction. 'As these barbarians refuse tae tell us who their leaders are, arrest those troublemakers.' He pointed to the men in dresses. 'These three. We'll see what the other prisoners have tae say about their 'bonnie' dresses.'

He turned to Sheriff McKid. 'Have them taken tae the jail in Dornoch tae await trial. Take their statements yourself.'

He whipped his horse into a gallop and made for home. He had no time for such nonsense. Let Sheriff McKid sort this mess out. He had to get back to study the rough map of Strathnaver that Lord Stafford had given to him; he needed to look for areas to lay out as sheep farms. And he wanted to write to Lady Stafford to let her know about Sheriff McKid's ineptitude in dealing with the tenants who were due to be removed from the Strath of Kildonan.

2

DANDELION DREAMS

Strathnaver

Mhàiri leant against the frame of the open cottage door and looked out across the strath. Like the steady beat of a drum, life in Achcoil held its own familiar rhythm. She folded her arms and watched a group of women approach. They came every summer; men or women passing through the inner straths as they made their way between fishing villages on the coast.

'A Mhàiri, seal - Mhàiri, look,' Connor, called as he trailed after the children, who ran alongside the travellers. 'They are here.'

'I see them,' she replied to her young brother's retreating back, while keeping her eyes firmly fixed on the women.

Row after row they passed, walking two astride, carrying with them the scent of seaweed and raw fish. Clickety-clack, clackety-click; their knitting needles echoed the steady rhythm of their stride. With each tug of their hand, coils of wool writhed and jerked inside pouches tied around their waists. Clickety-clack, clackety-click, the women knitted and strode past.

'*Cionnas a tha sibh?* – How are you?' her mother, who had appeared in the doorway behind Mhàiri, called to an older woman who led a pony attached to a cart.

The woman smiled and made her way over. 'I am well, thank you.'

Mhàiri's mother handed the woman a small slab of sheep's cheese, wrapped in a cloth. 'It is not very much but . . . with the failed harvest.'

The woman waved aside her apology. 'We are thankful for whatever you can give.'

'What news?' Mhàiri asked her.

'In the Strath of Kildonan, they are saying that Maister Sellar tried to remove them to the coast.'

Mhàiri's mother's hand shot to her mouth. 'Dear God.'

The woman's eyes sparkled. 'They burned the notices of removal right in front of him and stayed where they were.'

Mhàiri and her mother both laughed.

'Well, that is good news,' Mother said and waved to the woman as she left.

Mhàiri chewed on her bottom lip. Travellers often passed through Achcoil, but something about this group seemed different. She couldn't work out what it was. Then it struck her and she wondered why she hadn't seen it straight away. Without turning her head, she said to her mother, 'Never have I seen so many women passing through before. So many leaving.'

Her mother leant past her and peered out. 'Likely it will be the bad harvest that has caused it. And the latest rise in rents. Where we are meant to be finding the money, I do not know.'

A feeling of dread rose within Mhàiri. What if they couldn't raise the rent money? Would her family be forced from their home? Out of her strath? 'I said I would help, Màthair. I am nearing eighteen, why won't you let me?' She hesitated then made to step outside to ask to join the women. 'A bit of seasonal work will not harm me.'

A firm hand gripped her shoulder. 'Leave it be, Mhàiri. You are more needed here.'

'I could go. The fishing season. It will not last long. I would be back in no time with the money.'

Màthair clacked her tongue and tsked. 'Likely few, if any, of these women will return. We will get by . . . for now.'

Mhàiri turned her head to argue, but Màthair looked her in the eye and said in the tone she used to show the matter was finished with, 'I said, leave it be. With your father away, how am I meant to manage the farm on my own? And keep a watch over Connor? A dreamer you are, Mhàiri nic Niall. I don't know who you get it from. It certainly is not me,' she added as she made her way inside.

Mhàiri bristled. She was the same age as Màthair had been when she had wed. Yet, here she was, unmarried and living in her parent's home. Part of her wanted to go against Màthair's wishes and march off to the coast. It would be an adventure of sorts. But the biggest part of her, the part rooted in the strath, wanted to remain where she was.

She let out a deep breath. Perhaps her family would survive this rent increase, but what then? She shook her head and turned to watch the women leave. Màthair was right. Few would return. Their journey north would be followed by another journey south. Fish or seaweed would become these women's life. And, it wasn't a life Mhàiri wanted. Her mother would have known that.

The miller's second daughter made her way over to the departing travellers. Her older sister, Peigi Ruadh, stood blank-faced, beside her tearful mother, brothers and sisters, and watched her sister leave. After placing a rolled-up blanket, containing her belongings, onto the cart, the departing girl slipped a hand into the pouch around her waist and pulled out her knitting. Clickety-clack, clackety-click, like the beat of a ticking clock the knitting needles fell into the steady rhythm of her stride.

Resigned to remaining behind, Mhàiri waved to her friend. She would rather it had been the older sister who had gone. Mhàiri didn't much like the girl. She was bonnie and knew it. And, she made sure all the men knew it too. But it hadn't been Peigi Ruadh who had left and no amount of wishing would change that. Unable to settle, Mhàiri made her way inside, threw her plaid around her shoulders and picked up a basket. She needed time to think. Needed time on her own.

'I will fetch some dandelions,' she called to her mother. 'Hattie Bantrach's joints are bothering her.'

'Do not be long, Mhàiri. I am all behind with the milking.'

'I will be quick.'

After striding up the brae Mhàiri's footsteps slowed. She gathered dandelions and tried to shake off the unsettled feeling that the arrival of the women had stirred in her. When she reached the top of the hill, she lay down in the long grass, rolled onto her stomach and plucked a seeded dandelion. If she made a wish for the rents to stop going up, perhaps it would come true. She blew out her breath and sent the feathered seeds spiralling upwards. Before she could make her wish, she heard a horse approach.

She shifted onto her elbows and stared down through the floating wishes at a man on a grey horse. The stranger, who sat straight-backed in the saddle, had a sense of purpose about him that made her think he hadn't wandered here by mistake; he wasn't just taking in the view, he was studying it. Although she didn't know what had brought him here, there was one thing she did know for certain— when well-dressed strangers came to Strathnaver it meant only one thing: Trouble.

3

A STRANGER IN STRATHNAVER

Taking care not to be seen, Mhàiri stared down at the stranger who pulled his horse to a halt at the bottom of the hillside. He looked to be in his thirties and wasn't as well-dressed as she had first thought. His riding boots were splattered with mud and he wore a faded, white cloth cravat and a plain, black jacket. It had been the silver-coloured buttons on his jacket that had caught her attention and made her believe that he wasn't from around here. She contemplated going down to ask what he was doing.

When the stranger pulled a spyglass from his satchel, any thoughts Mhàiri had of approaching him disappeared. Holding the instrument to his eyes, the man pointed it towards her township. He seemed to be scanning the view, studying the houses, which included the cottage where she lived.

Mhàiri stretched her neck and tracked the line of his vision. Blue-grey smoke rose from thatched roofs and mingled with the mist which had settled over the valley. Following the line of the houses, the River Naver snaked silently past, heading north towards other townships and the sea. Outside a stone-dyke, partially surrounding the houses and barns, rowan, birch and hazel trees dotted the grazing grounds. All of this was as familiar to Mhàiri as her own reflection, but why was this stranger so interested?

The stranger placed the spyglass back into his satchel and pulled out a scroll. He unfurled it, leant forward over the horse's neck, and glanced from the paper towards the houses and barns of Achcoil and back again to the paper. Mhàiri rolled onto her back and tried to calm her racing thoughts. What should she do? She had already stayed too long. Màthair would be looking for her, but she didn't dare move from her hiding place.

At long last, the sound of horse's hooves thudded across the turf, fading further into the distance. When she was sure the stranger had gone, Mhàiri lifted the wicker basket into the crook of her arm and raced down the brae as if the Devil himself was chasing her. Her coarse, woollen skirt flapped as she careened down the hill and hurtled across the grazing ground. Drops of rain ran down her cheeks, and her long, auburn hair whipped against her face. As she neared home, a weather-beaten woman lay down the basket of peats she'd been carrying. Hattie Bantrach's mouth opened as if to say something, but Mhàiri flew past.

When she arrived at her cottage, Mhàiri pushed open the wooden door and slammed it shut behind her. The peat fire, set on a millstone in the middle of the floor, billowed out pungent grey smoke. Mhàiri leant against the door and let out loud, rasping gasps. She closed her eyes and tried to settle her ragged breaths and racing heart.

'And where have you been, *A Mhàiri nic Niall?* You should have been back long since,' Màthair said, her voice rising in annoyance.

Mhàiri opened her eyes and took a deep breath. Although the stranger's presence in the strath had filled her with a sense of foreboding, she didn't want to distress her mother. Not today, with her father having left this morning to get their summer sheiling ready. Mhàiri laid the basket down, swung the plaid from her shoulders and hung it on a wooden peg on the door. She rubbed her hands down her skirt and took a deep breath. 'I . . . I lost track of time.'

Màthair raised her eyebrows and picked up a pail. 'More likely, you were daydreaming in the high pasture. Again.' She pulled back the blanket covering the gap in the partition dividing the house from the byre. 'Being sorry won't get the cows milked or the meal made. Ach! Never mind. You are here now. Keep an eye on Connor.'

The blanket flapping closed, wafted in a sour smell, like rotting turnips. With a deep sigh, Mhàiri bent down and opened her arms to her five-year-old brother. He hurtled towards her, and she swept him into her arms. 'Ah, Connor, come help Mhàiri put the potatoes on to boil.'

An hour later, after finishing a meal of piping hot potatoes, fried salmon, and griddled oatcakes, Mhàiri stood from the table and threw on her plaid. Still filled with concern about the stranger who'd been spying on the township, she couldn't settle.

She lifted a bowl of food that had been set aside and, after folding it in a cloth, placed it in the basket on top of the dandelions. 'I will take this to Hattie Bantrach,' she said to her mother.

'Let her know that I am sorry I could not spare more.'

Mhàiri nodded. The widow would be grateful for the meal, no matter how meagre. Her husband died fighting in the war against Napoleon, and Hattie, who had followed the drum and gone with him to Spain, had made the long journey back to Achcoil on her own.

As Mhàiri turned to leave, Màthair touched her arm. 'Are you all right? It is not like you to be keeping so quiet. Is it about earlier?'

Mhàiri hesitated. She didn't like keeping things from her mother, but couldn't bring herself to tell her about the stranger she'd seen snooping around. Without turning, she put her hand on the latch and said, 'You were right in what you said. I am just a dreamer.'

She pulled the top of the plaid over her hair and stepped out the door. The drizzle which had started earlier had turned into a steady downpour. She put her head down and kept a fast pace as she splashed through the puddles towards the widow's hut.

A young man stepped into her path. Startled from her thoughts, Mhàiri jumped back. 'Watch where you are going.'

Cameron MacÀidh pushed back his bonnet and stepped around her. Catching a glint of humour in his eyes, Mhàiri felt her face flush and made to move away.

'Mhàiri, hold on.'

She turned, and Cameron lifted the top of her plaid to cover her hair. It had slipped down when they had almost collided and she hadn't noticed.

'There. Now that is better,' he said and walked away laughing.

Mhàiri stared after him and shook her head. He thought himself better than everyone because his father rented the largest stretch of land in Achcoil. Well, maybe Cameron MacÀidh *was* better than her, but that didn't mean she had to fawn over him as the other girls did. She held the hem of her skirt out the puddles and hurried towards Hattie's hovel.

When she stepped through the low door, she was met by a pungent smell of burning peat and damp clothes. The widow sat on a stool beside a smoking fire built against the rock face.

'*A Mhàiri, cionnas a tha thu?* – Mhàiri, how are you?' Hattie Bantrach called to her with pleasure.

'I am well, thank you,' Mhàiri said and looked around. On arriving back with nothing, the townspeople had built this shelter for the widow and given her gifts to furnish the single room.

Mhàiri set the basket down, shook her plaid and laid it by the fire. She lifted the wooden bowl, containing potatoes and fish, from the basket and handed it to Hattie. 'Màthair says she is sorry she couldn't spare more but hopes it will see you through. It is hard for her. But the signs promise a good harvest to come.'

'It will take more than a crop failure to knock your mother down. You are kind, just like her.' She laid the bowl by the fire. 'I will fry that up later. Come. Sit down. What news?'

Mhàiri pointed to the basket. 'I brought you dandelions to boil. Do they help?'

Hattie Bantrach's weather-beaten face crinkled into a smile. 'When your bones ache as much as mine, you will find out.' She stopped smiling and looked thoughtful. 'Were you troubled earlier?'

Mhàiri raised her eyebrows. 'Troubled?'

'You looked as if you were running for your life when you passed me.'

'Ah! I saw . . . Ach, never mind. I was late in returning home.' Mhàiri clasped her hands and placed them on her lap. She felt foolish for racing home. Just because she'd never seen the man with the silver buttons before, it didn't mean he meant trouble.

A hen, roosting in the soot-covered rafters, shook itself out. A flurry of old feathers fluttered down.

'Come on, lass. You can tell me anything. You know that.'

Mhàiri flicked a feather from her skirt, and it floated away. It would be a relief to tell someone. 'Oh, Hattie Bantrach, a stranger was snooping about . . . on the upper pasture. Scared me near to death, he did. I didn't want to upset Màthair.'

'A stranger you say? What made you feared of him?'

'He was watching us.'

'Watching us?'

'Through a spyglass.'

Hattie Bantrach's eyes widened and she gripped Mhàiri's arm. 'What did the man look like?'

Mhàiri told her what she had seen, including details about

the stranger's face and clothes. When she mentioned his beaked nose and the silver-coloured buttons on his jacket, the widow stood.

'Get your plaid, Mhàiri. We need to speak to your mother. I think I know who your stranger might be.'

4

ASHES TO ASHES

Mhàiri's mother stopped stirring the bubbling pot of barley broth and frowned at Mhàiri. 'You should have told me about this straight away.' She turned and shook her head at Hattie Bantrach. 'I am not believing this. Why would they be coming to Achcoil now? Despite the rumours, there has been no word of further removals.'

Hattie Bantrach sighed in exasperation. 'You heard the travelling woman . . . about what happened in the Strath of Kildonan.'

'You know fine well the tenants there refused to leave,' Màthair said. 'Those who were to be removed to make way for the sheep have long since gone.'

'Then who was the stranger, if it wasn't Maister Sellar, Catriona?' Hattie Bantrach sat at the wooden table and tapped Mhàiri on the arm. 'Tell her again what the man you saw looked like.'

'I have never met the man, nor do I want to,' Màthair replied and turned her attention back to the pot. 'And, any further description of the stranger's looks or clothes would be more of a hindrance than a help to me. Apart from what I have heard about that devil, I have never seen him. So, I wouldn't know if he has silver buttons, or not.'

Despite Màthair's claims, Mhàiri saw concern on her face. She looked older than her thirty-seven years. As usual, her dark hair was scraped back into a tight bun at the nape of her neck but, today, it made her thin face look pinched and tired.

No longer sure about what she'd seen, and reluctant to cause further upset, doubts surfaced in Mhàiri's mind. 'Perhaps you are right, Màthair. Likely I am making a fuss about nothing.'

She made her way over to the box-bed built into the back wall. She gently pulled aside the curtain and peered in at her brother. Connor's lips twitched in sleep, and Mhàiri smiled.

'Of course, it is nothing.' Màthair lifted the black, three-legged pot from the hook above the fire and laid it on the hearth. 'I have always dealt with the other factor about the rent and he has always been pleasant enough.' She put the kettle on to boil. 'You will be having some tea, Hattie? Then you can tell me why you are so sure it was that devil, Maister Sellar, that Mhàiri saw. It has been near two years since anyone has been removed. In God's name, why would it start again now?'

At the mention of removals, Mhàiri's belly tightened. Like others in Strathnaver, Màthair lived in fear of being moved to the coast, or worse, having to emigrate. Mhàiri now understood why she hadn't wanted her to take up seasonal work on the coast; she might never have returned. She sat beside the hearth and placed peats on the fire. The whiskers of the dried fuel caught, and blue-grey flames leapt up. Mhàiri recoiled. Like lightning ripping through a darkening sky, memories surfaced of the cold winter morning when her sister, Fionnghal, had clambered from the box-bed and huddled half-awake by the fire. The pleasant dream of Mhàiri's sleep had been broken by screams as the flames licked at her sister's petticoat, devouring the cloth like a starving beast.

Mhàiri looked down at the puckered flesh on the inside of

her forearms, the painful legacy of that day. As the flames engulfed her sister's clothes, Mhàiri had beat at them with her bare arms. It hadn't been enough. By the time Màthair wrapped a blanket around Fionnghal, her legs and body were already burned and blistered. The following day, her sister developed a fever. Six days later she died. Now, though she tried to hide it, Mhàiri felt cold fear at the thought of fire consuming her here on earth as much as she feared being thrust into the burning flames of Hell.

'And my husband has done any fighting duty owed by him to the Great Lady,' Màthair said, bringing Mhàiri back to the moment. 'There should be no argument brooked about that.'

'At the century's turn, when you were a child, Mhàiri, hardly any of the men volunteered to fight in the war.' Hattie Bantrach flapped her hand as if swiping away an annoying fly. 'Hah! But the factors found a way to make them sign up anyway. They collected the names and ages of all the men in the straths and posted a list of the families who had to provide a man to make up a Regiment of Foot. Each family had to decide who to send and who should stay.'

Màthair shook her head slowly from side to side as if reliving the memory. 'When the men mustered in Strathnaver, your father and Hattie's husband marched out with them to fight against Napoleon—'

'And I followed right behind,' Hattie Bantrach said. 'I did not have any children to keep me here and I'd had enough of living apart from my husband. It sounds strange saying it now, but it was as if I knew I wouldn't be seeing him again if I did not go.'

'And thank the Lord, you found your way safely back here,' Màthair said.

Hattie Bantrach nodded. 'What happened was God's will, but when I returned, they told me I was not entitled to a tenancy . . . now that I was a widow.'

Màthair poured out the tea. 'When Niall returned . . .

injured, he agreed to a tenancy term with the factor. We still have a few years left. My husband served his time to earn that right.'

'Now no one can get any more than a year.' Hattie Bantrach's hand shook as she lifted the cup.

Màthair sat beside Hattie at the table. 'Here is me, dragging up memories and complaining about Niall's injuries when your husband never got to come home. Fetch me the papers from my Bible, Mhàiri.'

While Màthair and Hattie Bantrach talked, Mhàiri knelt in front of a wooden chest and lifted the lid. She removed the tartan plaids her parents had worn on their wedding day, folded blankets and various lengths of spun wool. When the chest was empty, Mhàiri prised out a panel from the bottom and laid it aside.

She picked up a circular, metal brooch depicting the MacAoidh crest. Set around the edge were small red stones. She stroked the brooch. It had been passed down through her mother's family, through the generations. Her Mamó and Màthair had both worn it on their wedding day. One day Mhàiri would wear it too. At one time, she had thought Rob Dunn from the next township might have asked her to marry, but he left near two years ago for the war and she hadn't seen or heard from him since. She caught sight of her scarred arms and laid the brooch down. She was a dreamer.

She lifted out the Gaelic Bible. It was forbidden to worship any religion other than the one dictated by the Great Lady and her husband, the established Church of Scotland. Mhàiri stood and removed a folded sheet of paper from between the pages and handed it to Màthair. Although many in her township couldn't read, her father had been taught by a minister, and in turn, he had taught Mhàiri.

Màthair handed the paper back. 'Check the dates, lassie. What does it say?'

Mhàiri sat at the table and smoothed out the paper. She scanned the page. When she found what she was looking for, she stabbed the line with her finger. 'Here it is. The tenancy is agreed until 1817, with the rate of rent to be set by the factor.'

'I am not even a tenant.' Hattie laid her cup down. 'I could be forced out at any time.'

Mhàiri's finger froze on the page. Had the stranger with the spyglass been looking for people like the widow? People who didn't pay rent? She shook her head. 'What good would it do to remove you, Hattie Bantrach?' Mhàiri couldn't fathom why anyone would want the widow's hovel. 'They would need more than your little bit of ground to make any difference.'

'Remember the words of the psalm, The Lord is my Shepherd, I shall not want,' Màthair said. 'The Good Lord led you back here, Hattie. He will look after you now.'

'Hmm! That is all very well and good.' Hattie Bantrach's eyes darkened. 'But also remember what The Great Seer said. On the day ash rains from the sky, a man of great wealth will bring forth the destruction of nature and an age of growth.'

22

5

LANDED LANDLORDS

A carriage clattered along a rutted road, taking Elizabeth ever deeper into her Highland estate. Pulled by four chestnut-coloured horses, it made its way north towards Golspie. Five carriages followed behind, carrying her youngest children, staff and provisions. Thankful to be on the final stage of her long journey, Elizabeth sank back in the seat. Her husband was stretched out on the seat opposite. Snuggled under a blanket, with his head resting on a soft pillow, Lord Stafford's snores were the only thing he offered her in the way of company.

As the well-sprung carriage rolled and swayed towards her Scottish castle, the trundle and clatter of the wheels grew so great that Elizabeth laid her book down. She had long since grown bored— hours had passed since they had left the well-fashioned roads she was accustomed to.

With little else to do, she pulled back the curtain and positioned herself to see out the window. As she passed through flat country with no signs of life her eyes grew heavy. She watched rivers and streams. Further north, rocky cliffs and high grounds stretched for miles along the rugged coast. It was all so different from the bustle of the London and Edinburgh streets she was used to. She grimaced at the irony; she owned all of this. Every gnarled tree. Every berry ripening on over-filled bushes. Every fish swimming in the burns, in the lochs and in the sea. Every mile travelled north took her further from society. Thankfully, the short stay in Inverness, on her journey from Edinburgh, had provided her with a much-needed respite and the chance to catch up with friends.

The carriage clattered to a halt, and she put a hand out to stop herself from falling.

Her husband stirred, blinked and opened his eyes. Sitting upright, he pushed back the blanket. 'Have we arrived?'

Elizabeth handed him his spectacles. 'Not yet. But it is not far now.'

'Thank God for that. I must have slept a good hour.' He put his spectacles on, yawned and stretched his arms. 'Why have we stopped?'

Elizabeth leant forward and peered out the window, trying to see the front of the carriage. 'I can't see anything ahead.'

Lord Stafford picked up his silver-topped cane and rapped on the roof of the carriage.

A moment later, the door swung open and one of the coachmen bowed. 'My Lord, there is an obstruction on the road. We will soon have it removed and be on our way.'

Elizabeth made to stand and step down from the carriage to stretch her legs.

'Ma'am. I would suggest you stay inside,' the coachman said and held a hand to his mouth.

Elizabeth raised her eyebrows. 'Why? What on earth is going on?'

'Tinkers, Ma'am,' the coachman said. 'One of their cows dropped dead on the road and it stinks to high heaven. We cannot go round it because of the deep ditches on either side. They are moving the animal now.'

Elizabeth sank back into her seat. 'Very well, carry on.'

She recalled the first journey she made to her estate, at the age of seventeen. When she first set eyes on her farming tenant's bleak cottages, she had been surprised to see smoke rising from the roofs; believing they housed livestock. She recalled children lying idle on the hillsides— likely dreaming as they let their black cattle graze. Memories of past visits came and went. She smelt heather and fresh honey, tasted the sour tang of crowdie, and salty fish. She heard singing—soft lilting songs sung in Gaelic—about harvests passed and yet to come, of lost loves, and a longing for this land by those who had left and then returned.

Despite her reluctance to make the long journey north, she also felt the tug; a gentle pull that brought her back here, year after year. And, the source of that tug often took her by surprise. It could be a word uttered at an Edinburgh play, the move of a dancer in her London home, the swing of a skirt or lie of a shawl— tricking her into thinking it a kilt or a plaid.

All of this served as reminders of her Highland heritage. Reminders that would increase during her month-long stay here amongst her tenants. Outside the window, one of the tinkers tilted his bonnet, and the woman beside him tipped a curtsey. Blind to the changes that had occurred, these people still regarded her as their clan chief, as they had once regarded her father. Had Papa's heart swelled as he looked over his vast estate? Had this land meant more to him than a heavy millstone grinding his money as it was to her?

The carriage set off again, and Elizabeth continued to watch the miles pass. For years she had ignored this land and its people; had allowed them to lie idle, but not anymore. The tenants in the straths would be moving soon to their summer sheilings— having planted their seeds, they would harvest them in the autumn to feed their families over the winter. But they were at the mercy of the weather for a good harvest, and at her mercy when their crops failed. What impoverished lives her tenants led. She wanted more for them, which was why she would continue with her plans to improve her estate.

There were many changes she wanted to make. Along with her husband, she had been gripped by the industrial improvements sweeping through the country. A few years ago, Lord Stafford had improved his English estate. Now, due to an unexpected inheritance, her already wealthy husband had provided her with the means to conduct an experiment to see if they could implement similar improvements throughout her vast Scottish estate.

The sun reflected off the sea, offering hope on the horizon— of pulling riches out of its uncharted depths. She wiped a hand across her mouth. Her eyes adjusted to a vision of coastal villages blossoming where once there were none. Of people working where once they lay idle. It was a dream, but it was a dream she intended to turn into a reality— with the help of her husband's money, of course.

'The new bridges have made a great difference, Elizabeth. I intend to build more,' he said and settled back against a cushion.

Elizabeth drew her gaze from the window. She wasn't a woman who yearned for small talk from her husband or who expected him to make decisions for her, like many of her friends did. He might snore and provide little to her in the way of stimulating conversation, but he involved her in matters of business on *her* estate.

'While we are here, I will finalise the plans for the new jetty,' he said. 'This is the first time we have made the journey by road, I am sure you will agree it will be our last. It will be much easier in future to travel by boat and dock directly at the castle.' He tilted his head. 'It is a great pity our estate commissioner is not able to join us until August.'

Elizabeth smiled. It had taken much effort on her part to

persuade Mister Loch to travel so far north. 'Our factors do their best, but they are not really up to the task.'

Her husband cupped a hand around his ear. 'Speak up.'

'I said, thankfully, with Mister Loch now overseeing things we can move on to the next phase of improvements.'

Her husband peered over the rim of his spectacles. 'I promised you that your estate would equal anything in the Lowlands for industry and profit.' He pushed his spectacles back from the edge of his nose. 'But—' He pursed his lips and remained silent.

'But?' Elizabeth prompted.

'Our method has not been tried before. For this experiment to work, the farming tenants need to be moved quickly to the coast. It is the only way for the industries there to thrive and to make way for new sheep farms.'

'But . . . it will all take time.' Elizabeth paused. Should they be moving forward with greater speed? She shook her head. There were thousands of tenants living in the straths. 'There is still much to be done. Surely you understand that.' Elizabeth sighed. 'In truth, I find the scale of the improvements overwhelming.'

'Hmm! Yes, it is indeed a much larger acreage than anyone has attempted to improve before.' He leant forward. 'That doesn't mean to say we can't do it. But we will need to progress with greater speed.'

'No. No, I don't think we should. The coastal villages haven't been prepared yet to receive the incoming tenants.' While her husband would see to developing the new industries, the rest would fall to her. She waved a hand, dismissing his argument. 'There is no need for haste. I'm interested to see what Mister Loch has to say. It will be a relief to hand over to someone experienced in these matters. The factors will soon finish surveying the inner straths. For now, we will continue our experiment there.'

The carriage passed a coaching inn and climbed steadily

uphill. The road became surrounded by trees on both sides; many of which leant towards each other, forming a tunnel. Elizabeth watched the afternoon sun flicker through the top leaves. 'How beautiful it is here.'

'And all the better for this new stretch of road. What do you think of it?'

Elizabeth laughed. For many years, her estate had been managed for her. 'If it wasn't for you, I wouldn't be implementing any improvements. If only we had been able to persuade the tenants in the straths to stop farming in the old way, then there would be no need to have them moved to the coast.'

Her husband grimaced. 'And to stop sub-letting our land. We don't even know who pays us rent and who doesn't.'

'Hopefully, Mister Loch will find time to look over the accounts and match them with the details from the surveys.'

The carriage swung right, entered through the castle gates and continued along the driveway.

'Ah, we have arrived at last.' Elizabeth adjusted her shawl. 'We will dine at seven. I have invited the factors. I particularly want to talk with Mister Sellar. He has been invaluable in ensuring that the removals are carried out efficiently.'

6

DONNIE DROVER

The following morning, Mhàiri arose to find her mother standing in the open doorway looking out over the strath. Seeing the concern on her face, she asked, 'Is there any sign of the drover?'

'Nothing yet.'

'I will go up to the pasture. Watch for him from there—'

Màthair looked out the door. 'It would be of more help to me if you . . . Ach! *Seall* - Look.' She pointed. 'Look over there.'

Mhàiri peered out. In the distance, a cloud of dust rose from the ground. 'It is the drover. Thanks be to God, for that.'

Màthair's face brightened. 'I thought he was never coming.'

While they waited for the drover and his lads to arrive, Mhàiri helped her mother pack for the sheilings. They were lifting the spinning wheel onto the cart when a black and white, long-haired, collie scampered around Mhàiri's legs.

The bearded drover gave a shrill whistle and called, '*Sios*! - Down.'

The dog dropped flat on its belly and looked up at the drover, who winked at Mhàiri. 'Like all women, obedient to its master.'

'Ha! Donaidh Dròbhair, you took your time in getting here.' Màthair smiled. 'You will be staying for a cup of tea?'

'Tea!' The drover raised his thick eyebrows. 'Have you not any whisky to help me on my long journey?'

'Now, if I had even a drop of whisky, I wouldn't be standing here talking to you. I would be inside drinking it. Will you be wanting tea, or not?'

The drover laughed and nodded. 'Has your husband taken the animals up to the sheilings yet?'

'He left yesterday with the other men. We are making our way up there later today.'

While her mother brought out the cows, Mhàiri boiled the kettle. She was pouring the steaming liquid into cups when Màthair and the drover came in and sat at the table. She removed four oat bannocks from the griddle and brought them over, along with freshly churned butter and a small bowl of crowdie.

Connor grinned and pointed out the open door. 'Cù.'

'Aye, it's a dog, laddie.' The drover leant forward. 'Trobhad - Come here,' he called, and the collie bounded in. Connor clapped his hands in delight and ran out the door. The collie, after a sign from the drover, followed closely behind him.

'What news?' Màthair asked the drover and bit into a slice of warm buttered bannock.

'A few years back, I was herding over a hundred cows to market. Now, I am lucky to be moving forty. A few more years like this and it won't be worth my time making the journey.'

Mhàiri joined them at the table. 'How will we manage if you don't take the cattle? We wouldn't be able to pay our rent.' She looked around the dark, windowless space. Even with the candles burning and the lit fire, the room remained dismal— grey shadows fought with the orange glow of the fire's embers and the flickering flames of the candles and won. But this was her home, and Mhàiri couldn't imagine living anywhere else.

'It would be difficult, indeed.' Màthair paused and wiped a crumb from the side of her mouth. 'Apart from the bit wool we spin, the money from the cows is often all we earn.'

The drover raked his fingers through his long hair and let out a deep sigh. 'In truth, I fear the drover's days are over. Like many others, I might have to move to Glasgow. Or America.'

Màthair's face paled. 'What do you mean, over?'

'Everything is changing, and there is nothing any of us can do about it. We are lucky to have lasted as long as we have. Near everywhere I go, there are new bridges. Carriages now pass through country where once there were no roads. Our beautiful language has been replaced with the coarse calls of Lowlanders and even of the English. The talk now is of steamships that will carry cattle straight to the market towns. To London even. Can you imagine it? Great big ships, with room on them for a hundred cows or more. Soon, there will be no need of drovers here. It is all new ways now.'

Màthair's eyes widened. 'What is to become of us?'

The drover shook his head. 'It is not just here this is happening. There is nothing any of us can do to stop progress. Indeed, many do not want to.' He pulled a sheet of paper from his money belt. 'Three cows you gave me.' He marked them on his sheet. 'I hope you get a good price for them.'

'A thousand thanks, Donaidh Dròbhair. As long as you keep taking our cattle to market, we should survive. We have weathered the increase for this year, but if this continues, I—'

'You and most others,' the drover said.

'Have you come across Maister Sellar on your travels,' Mhàiri asked him.

'I have, but what makes you ask?'

'We think Mhàiri may have seen the factor around here,' Màthair said.

'That does not sound good,' the drover replied. 'But perhaps Lord Stafford is planning on building a new bridge or a road?'

Màthair stood to see the drover out. 'When we return from the sheilings, I will call on Maighstir MacCoinnich. The minister will know what we should do.'

* * *

While Màthair checked that everything they would need had been placed into the peat cart, Mhàiri attached a horse to the front. She thought about what the drover had said about new roads. Despite her mother's dislike of all things new, proper roads would make their life easier. Perhaps the stranger with the spyglass had been looking for somewhere for Lord Stafford to build a new road or a bridge.

'We best get going, if we are to have any hope of reaching the sheilings before darkness falls.' Màthair pointed to the women and children waiting on the brae. 'The others look as if they are ready.'

Mhàiri waved at Connor to hurry ahead. To keep her skirt from snagging on the gorse, during her trek into the hills, she tucked the bottom into her waistband. As her mother led the horse from the township, Mhàiri looked back over her shoulder at the rowan growing outside their cottage. If what she had been told was true, then the tree would provide their home with protection while they were gone.

7

COUNTY OF CONTRASTS

Maighstir MacCoinnich walked his horse down an incline to the river's edge. The minister pulled to a stop, looked back at the tall man on the grey mount and pointed across the water. 'Is that not the bonniest sight you have seen? I wish I was an artist.'

The sun shone across the hillside, sending spirals of cascading colours down towards the water. Between patches of brown-earth, rich tones of green and yellow grass, mixed with the vibrant blue and purple hues of wild shrubs. The overall effect held the minister in awe. Feeling uplifted, he smiled.

The factor pulled his horse up alongside him. 'The view struck me as soon as I set foot in this shire. It certainly is a county o' contrasts. At times the landscape appears bleak, dismal even, an' at other times, like now, it is transformed intae a sight o' rare beauty.'

'Look! Up yonder on the brae.' The minister pointed to a deer.

They remained silent, watching the deer and walking their horses along the line of the river until a small farming township came into view. When they drew up and the minister dismounted, the silver buttons on his companion's jacket glinted in the sunlight.

'This clachan is all but deserted,' the minister said. 'The women and children left this morning for the summer sheilings . . . to fatten their cattle and keep them from the crops. The men will return tonight, to start readying these houses for winter.'

The factor dismounted and lifted his nose in the air. 'It is nae life these folk lead.'

'It is the only life they know.'

'But that doesn't make it right.' The factor sniffed, indicating his disapproval.

The minister turned in surprise. 'What do you mean?'

'The poverty they live in, an' in houses so filthy I wouldn't shelter animals in them. God's truth, my sheep are fed on better fare than these folk eat. An' what they serve as tea is nae mare than weeds boiled in water. It's not right.'

'Right, or not, they get by well enough.'

'Aye, until their stocks run out and they turn tae Lady Stafford asking for grain tae fill their starving bellies.'

'Poor relief has always been given when the crops fail. It is neither here nor there.' Maighstir MacCoinnich shook his head. 'All the landlords provide it.'

'Not anymore.' The factor leant closer as if confiding a secret. 'As a factor, I hear many things. Few landlords are willing tae put up with the auld ways now. An' why should they? Is it unreasonable tae expect the people living on their land tae work tae pay them rent? These natives *choose* not tae work?' he said, his voice rising. 'Lord an' Lady Stafford cannot be expected to feed these savages indefinitely. It would be different if they paid her a decent rent. Look.' He flicked his hand downwards. 'This soil isn't suitable for farming. When the crops fail, the tenants are left with nothing. They would see their children starve, rather than work?'

'What work? There is no work,' the minister replied, his

manner sharp. 'Two days ago, a young woman left this township to work on the fishing at the coast, but there is no work here.' He should restrain his growing annoyance at Mister Sellar's Lowland ideas, but wanted him to hear this.

'They should a' move tae the coast. There's more than enough work for them there. The sea is filled tae overflowing with cod. An', along with herring an' other fish, they swim about largely untouched. Why?'

'The people from the straths are of the land, not the sea. They are farmers, not fishermen.'

The factor scoffed and walked closer to the water's edge. 'Farmers, you call them. Look there.' He pointed up the strath. 'They plant their potato crops so near tae the river's edge that most are destroyed by mildew. Yet, time an' again they dae this.'

The minister lifted a handful of stone-filled soil. 'Only because they have no other choice. They use whatever soil they can find. Even then they have to clear it of stones.' He held the soil out on his open palm. 'They farm this land as best they can, as their ancestors did for hundreds of years before them.'

'That's the point I'm trying tae make. This ground isn't suitable for farming. It is only suitable for pasture. Yet, the kye are thin for want o' grass, an' when the ground is frozen over, they are sheltered inside the hovels these folk call home.'

The minister let the soil filter through his fingers. He threw the stones into the river and mounted his horse. 'So, what do you suggest?'

'These people are your flock.' The factor stepped into the saddle. 'You are their shepherd. Guide them.'

'Guide them, how?' the minister asked and set off towards the manse. Was the factor suggesting that he should influence his 'flock' into leaving? 'What are you saying?'

'There is work tae be had on the coast. Not just bringing in the fish, but harvesting seaweed for soap, gathering salt an' preparing limestone. New houses, roads an' bridges need tae be built. Aye, there is work aplenty for those who are willing.'

'These tenants are simple in their needs. They don't want money for fancy clothes and fine things.' He laughed at the notion. 'They are content with what they have.' He almost added that they had no desire to adorn themselves with silver buttons, like the factor did, but held back.

'Only because they know nothing other than this life.' The factor sniffed, showing his displeasure. 'But you . . . We know different. We've travelled on proper roads. We live in clean houses, with chimneys, an' windows built into stone walls.'

'True enough. By all means, give them the option to move to the coast, but what about those who don't want to go?'

'Guide them into making the right decision. As minister here it is expected o' you. Remember who pays your wages.'

The implied threat wasn't lost on Maighstir MacCoinnich and he tilted his head to hide his annoyance.

'You only need visit a cottage in the new coastal villages tae see the difference in the way your flock would live,' the factor continued, ignoring his lack of response. 'If you saw inside a fisherman's house . . . the family with their bellies full. Would you rather see your flock starve for want of good guidance? And there will be a new manse an' church for you. All you need tae do is get your flock tae the coast with you.'

A proper church appealed to the minister. Although he lived in a decent enough house, he worked from a crumbling mission hall. He lifted his head. 'A manse, you say, and a church?'

'Aye. Imagine a church filled with a willing congregation. A place where you can preach a proper service, no' the weekly catechisms you rely on others tae carry out for you here. Mind you, if Lord Selkirk has his way, you'll have nae parishioners left tae preach tae.'

'Lord Selkirk. Of the Red River Settlement?'

'You will have seen his posters offering low prices tae any Highlander wanting tae emigrate.'

The minister had seen them. 'My parishioners have been complaining about the steep increase in their rents. They don't know how they will find the extra money. Many will take up the offer to leave.'

'Her Ladyship doesn't want her tenants emigrating. That is why she's building houses for them on the coast . . . an' providing them with work so they *can* pay her a decent rent.'

They neared the mission, and the familiar, comforting sound of water splashing down from the hill, flooded Maighstir MacCoinnich with a sense of sadness. It was as if the land wept with him; gushing great tears of sorrow for Strathnaver. He turned and faced the factor. 'Let me consider this. Give me time to think about what you are asking.' With a heavy heart, he slipped from his horse and waved in acknowledgement of the factor's departure.

Deep in thought, he led his horse into the barn. What should he do? His shoulders drooped. There was some truth to what the factor said. It was hard to watch such hunger and poverty as raged around the strath in the winter. But this was home to these people. The land belonged to them as much as it did to Lord and Lady Stafford. But, a proper church with a manse, and stone-built cottages for his parishioners. And, winter would be upon them again soon.

He entered the manse and made straight for the parlour.

When he stepped through the door, his wife looked up from reading. She placed the book on the arm of the chair and stood. 'David, what is it?'

'Ach! Who would have the duties of the Kirk or a Chieftain?'

She poured a good measure of whisky into a glass and handed it to him. 'You aren't making any sense. What are you talking about?'

The minister took the glass and slumped onto a chair. He

sipped the drink. The pungent, peaty taste tantalised his palate, and warmth spread through him, soothing his racing thoughts. He looked around. The fire had been set, awaiting a taper. The tenants in the inner straths rarely let their fires go out; they considered it bad luck. But their fires were set in the middle of earthen floors, in houses that were no more than hovels.

His wife sat on the chair beside him. 'David, speak to me. Has something happened?'

He uncrossed his legs and sat forward. 'All of this will have to go.'

'All of what?'

'The manse. The mission.' He waved his hands. 'All of it has to go. It is God's will.'

8

SUMMER SHEILINGS

Six weeks after arriving at the sheilings, Mhàiri sat on a three-legged stool in the dairy. She leant her head against a cow's side and grasped a teat in each hand. The warmth of hide against her face soothed her and she settled into the task. With a thumb and forefinger clamping the top of the teat, she alternately squeezed her hands. Soon the clatter into the pail settled to a steady splash, and the sour smell of the dairy became mixed with the sweet smell of warm milk.

Lulled by her rhythmic movements, Mhàiri's eyes grew heavy. Behind her, her mother and a woman from their township washed pails. Mhàiri listened to them talking as they worked.

'I cannot stand it,' Mòrag Mòr said. 'No word have I had about my son. So many left to fight in the war yet few have returned. You have been lucky, Catriona, your husband came home to you.'

'He came home right enough, though a different man to the one who left.'

'The war, it does that,' Mòrag Mòr said. 'My husband, he

would not talk about it. What he saw. The things that happened. It is the shock.'

'Neither does Niall. He hardly sleeps and when he does, he screams out in the night.'

Mhàiri recalled hearing her father wake from the nightmares of the battles he had fought. She recalled evenings when he sat beside the fire sipping whisky and becoming more maudlin until a drunken argument broke out between him and Màthair. There were too many nights like that.

Her thoughts turned to a blurred image of young Rob Dunn waving goodbye as he left for the war. She tried to recall his face and failed. They had been so close, people asked if they were courting. Two years had passed since then. Would Rob Dunn return? If he did, would he be tormented like her father? She shuddered at the thought. But there was no point thinking about Rob; he was nothing to her now but a distant memory.

'Your husband might have lost two fingers and the full use of one leg, but it was a small price to be paying to keep his life,' Mòrag Mòr said. 'Thanks be to God, I still have Iain to help me. If only I could hear news of my other son. Two years now, and not one word have I heard from Micheal. I cannot help but think he is already dead . . . like his father.'

The women's voices faded as they headed out the dairy, and Mhàiri couldn't make out anything else they said. The darkness increased as the two figures blocked the light from the open door. Then they were gone.

Mhàiri's thoughts returned to her father. She'd been a young girl when he'd first left for the war and almost twelve when he'd returned for good. She couldn't imagine what it had been like for her mother, to have looked after her children, her home, and tend to the land. Yet, even when the crops failed, they had never gone without. Mhàiri recalled travelling with her around the townships, begging seeds to plant in the spring. Without a doubt, she didn't have her mother's strength and endurance.

Even now, her parents were apart. When they'd arrived at the sheilings, her father had shared a meal of bread and crowdie with them before returning home to tend to the crops and ready their house for winter. When Mhàiri married she wanted her husband beside her, always. A vision of Cameron MacÀidh flashed before her eyes. He had stayed away from her on the walk up to the sheilings and had done his best to avoid her since. She shook her head. There was no point in wishing; it wouldn't change anything. Whatever happened was God's will.

Mhàiri lifted the full pail and set it beside the others. There would be enough top-milk now for another batch of butter. She stretched her arms and raked her hands through her hair. There was to be a musical ceilidh outside the meeting-house tonight. She had time to wash her hair before then.

After retrieving a slab of soap and fresh clothes from the chest at the bottom of her bed, Mhàiri made her way to the stream. She filled the pail then sat beside the gurgling water, listening to the birds chirping their songs of summer. On the hill, deer grazed with their young. Mhàiri looked away. The life she imagined for herself was nothing but a dream. Who was she fooling? Rob Dunn had been taken from her by the war, and Cameron had never shown any interest. She held her arms out and looked at the puckered flesh. Nor would anyone. Ever.

With a resigned sigh, she lifted the pail and made her way back. Most of the huts were built into the ground with only a slight rise of thatch showing. They looked like large versions of the mushrooms she gathered in the wood. Others, like her own, had been built in a circle, rising to a point at the roof. A few, like Cameron's and the meeting-house, were built of stone and roofed with timber and thatch.

Once inside, Mhàiri stripped to her shift, wet her hair and lathered it with soap. She poured water over her head, rinsing again and again until the water ran clear. Her auburn hair hung down the length of her back and after combing it through, she dressed and sat on a pile of turf outside to help it dry. The warmth of the sun felt pleasant on her face and arms, which had already turned a deep shade of brown.

She closed her eyes and tilted her face upwards. Beside her, her Màthair spun wool at the wheel, talking Mhàiri through her actions. 'One day, *A Mhàiri nic Niall*, you will need to spin for a family of your own. It will be poor children you will have if you have no wool to make their trousers.'

Mhàiri laughed and opened her eyes. 'I will soon learn, for I have watched you often enough.'

Cameron MacÀidh arrived carrying bunches of heather. After a nod from Màthair, he entered the hut to pack the heather into the bed-frames. As he made to leave, merriment appeared in his eyes. He bowed. 'Fresh bedding has been provided for the ladies. Sleep well tonight. I hope your dreams are most pleasant.'

Màthair laughed. 'Pah! Away with you, Cameron MacÀidh. You should practice your blather on the cows before spouting it here, for surely even they would not be taken with that.'

He burst into laughter.

Mhàiri tried to join in but her laugh came out more like a throaty whimper.

That evening, Mhàiri made her way to the meeting-house with Màthair and Connor. They joined the tenants sitting around the fire outside, sharing their news.

A woman laid a large pot of rabbit stew at the edge of the fire— amidst calls for the Lord's protection, from the factor's wrath, for whoever had stolen the rabbits. Griddles were set on the fire, and bowls of oats mixed with water for bannocks were placed on the ground.

Beside Mhàiri, the fiddler tuned his fiddle, stopping now

and then to savour a sip of whisky or to puff on his pipe. At seventy-three, he was the oldest in Mhàiri's township. The other men were preparing his cottage for the winter; allowing him to stay at the sheilings with his wife.

Jugs of ale were passed around, and Mhàiri lifted cooked bannocks from one of the griddles. She buttered the bannocks and handed the dripping slabs out to waiting hands.

When everything was set for the feast, and the throng grew impatient with waiting, the fiddler lifted his fiddle. He placed the end under his chin and raised a merry jig. The tune made Mhàiri's feet twitch and then tap. She clapped her hands to the beat.

The first dancers took to the turf, and Mhàiri's mother and her sister, Úna, joined them. Before long, most of the women and the young men were dancing. They swirled and twirled and stamped their feet and some whistled and yelled encouragement.

When the fiddler set up a popular jig, Mhàiri picked up Connor and settled him onto her hip. Her brother giggled in delight. Mhàiri swayed in time to the music and watched Cameron dancing with Peigi Ruadh. The girl's red hair glowed in the light of the fire, and a bright smile lit up her pale, freckled face. When Màthair and Aunt Úna kicked their long legs in the air, Mhàiri pulled her gaze towards them and joined in the laughter.

Big-bellied with child, Mhàiri's friend, Anna, danced by her side. Mhàiri turned and smiled at her. Last year at the sheilings her friend had fallen for Fearghas MacUilleam. They had married soon after returning home. Mhàiri's eyes strayed back to Cameron. Did he have his eyes set on Peigi Ruadh? It had been the same with Rob Dunn. Peigi Ruadh always seemed to be fawning over him. It had been the cause of much of the present dislike between them. Unable to watch the couple dancing together, Mhàiri looked away.

The fiddler's wife swayed beside her husband and clapped her hands. The fiddler nodded to his wife for his pipe. She filled it with tobacco and puffed it to make sure it was well lit before holding it between his blackened teeth. Mhàiri heart swelled to see the closeness between them.

Connor grew heavy in her arms and her legs felt as if they would give way beneath her. She set Connor down and took a swig of ale from a jug. Around her, hands clapped, bodies swayed and feet stomped. Cameron danced past and held out an arm. Mhàiri linked into it and was pulled into the dancing throng. As she birled and swirled and leapt together with Cameron, she felt herself relaxing.

When the fiddler took up a lament, Cameron swept her into his arms and leant towards her. His face was so close she felt the warmth of his breath and smelt the sweet scent of ale. Their eyes met, and Mhàiri flushed. She made to pull away, but Cameron pulled her back.

He put his arm firmly around her waist, locking her against his body. 'At last, I have you all to myself.' Cameron leant closer. 'There is something I have been meaning to tell you.'

Unsure how to respond, Mhàiri held his gaze. What trick was he playing on her now? Trying to spare herself the embarrassment that was sure to follow, she tried to wriggle free.

Cameron's arm tightened around her waist and he bent his head so that his mouth was close to her ear. 'A Mhàiri nic Niall, you are the girl I am going to marry.'

Certain now that he would fall into a fit of laughter if she showed any sign of believing him, she said, 'And the snow will fall green as we do.' She only had to amuse him until this tune finished. Then she could make her escape, and he could move on to the next girl.

'I am not fooling. A Mhàiri, tha gaol agam ort – Mhàiri, I have love for you,' he said. 'I have wanted to tell you for some time now. Most often I cannot speak to you for fear you will turn me away. But I knew if I didn't say anything tonight, before we left the sheilings, then likely I would never get up the courage.'

Mhàiri laughed— a soft tinkling sound. Something about the way Cameron looked at her told her that he was serious. 'That will be the ale talking then?'

'Likely it is, and thankful I am for it too. Do you want to sit by the fire?'

Still unsure of his intentions, she nodded.

'When I saw you earlier . . . drying your hair in the sun, I thought you had never looked bonnier.' Cameron moved closer. 'I decided there and then to tell you tonight how I felt.' She remained silent, and Cameron grinned, 'Likely that is what made me take a little bit too much ale tonight.'

For the first time in years, Mhàiri was enjoying Cameron's company. 'You have had a few. I will admit, that is not like you. I have never seen you under the drink like I have some of the other men.'

'Well, if I hadn't spoken out tonight then I might not have got another chance . . . before someone else claimed you for their wife.'

Mhàiri laughed and looked around. 'The drink must be making you imagine things. I cannot see anyone waiting in line to ask me.'

'What about Rob Dunn? You are not betrothed to him, are you?'

She shook her head. 'What made you think that?'

'You seemed close before he left for the war.'

'We were, but not like that. And, there never any promise made between us that there ever would be.' Was there? It had been such a long time ago. She struggled to remember what had been said between them. She had barely turned sixteen at the time. 'Rob Dunn always dreamt of being a soldier. It was what he wanted.'

'That is true,' Cameron said. 'He was always a bit of a rebel. If he had not signed up for the war, likely he would have emigrated.'

Soon, it was as if there was nothing they couldn't say to each other. Time passed in a flash. The sky darkened, and a chill crept in. Cameron shuffled closer, and Mhàiri felt the warmth of his thigh against her own.

The fiddler stopped playing. A woman sang a song, and Mhàiri grew silent and listened.

When the woman sat down, Mhàiri's mother stood and sang.

'I met my darling, wandering free,
  He said to me, come away with me,
  He asked me to dance, the dance of life with him,
  His mother she was a Mackay, and soon so was I.
  Our firstborn son had his father's name,
  He grew and met a bonnie lass or three,
  But said none of them are meant for me.
  I will look for a lass by the name of Mackay,
  And she will dance the dance of life with me.'

Mhàiri clapped along with the others. The words brought tears to her eyes. Her mother had looked happy as she sang; the years falling from her like feathers dropping from a chicken being plucked.

A woman brought bowls of food over, and Mhàiri accepted a generous dish of the succulent rabbit stew. As she ate, she remained beside Cameron and listened to the conversation around them. Talk turned to the removals and how the Great Lady would stop the factors. Talk moved to the Kirk and how the minister would help them. Some tenants, who hadn't paid rent or were behind in their rent, had already been removed.

A woman, who was known to have the sight, said, 'All the signs show that the rents will continue to rise.'

Around the fire, people agreed, and Mhàiri voiced her concern along with the others. How would her family manage another rent increase? How would any of the tenant farmers?

9

DARKNESS DAWNS

T he night grew dark, and the air chilled. Anna built the fire higher. As she threw the peats on, ashes spiralled into the night sky. Mhàiri relished the warmth of Cameron at her side. He leant closer, and the skin on her arm tingled.

The older children scared each other with talk of wolves prowling the woods. Mhàiri laughed, recalling telling similar sheiling tales only a few years earlier.

'Ach, there are no wolves around here,' Mòrag Mòr said.

The fiddler chuckled. 'Mind you, there was, and not so long ago.' He clapped his hands and lifted his fiddle. 'Now let us be having you for the last dance tonight.'

Cameron stood and held out his hand. Mhàiri smiled and took it. As the dancers swirled around them, Cameron held her close. He stopped dancing and clasped his hands one on each side of her face. She stared into his deep-blue eyes. Concealed amidst the moving throng of bodies, he bent forward and kissed her lips. The taste of butter mixed with ale was pleasant, but his kiss took Mhàiri by surprise and she tilted her head back.

Keeping his eyes fixed on hers, Cameron pulled her face back towards him and kissed her again, this time with a depth that she wouldn't have thought possible had she fallen into the deepest part of the sea and sank to the ocean bed. When his lips separated from hers, Mhàiri remained open-mouthed. It felt as if he had taken something from her and she ached for his lips to return it to her again. Her cheeks burned, but she couldn't look away.

The music stopped, and Mhàiri set off alone to get her plaid. As she picked it up, she heard Cameron's mother, deep in conversation with the fiddler's wife. On hearing Cameron's name, she stopped and listened.

'So, you are serious about emigrating?' the fiddler's wife asked.

'I am more than serious,' Cameron's mother replied. 'Who is to say that Cameron will not be sent to fight in the war? Every time we think it is about to end it doesn't. I have already lost one son to that war. I won't risk losing another.'

'If it is to be God's will then what can you do?' the fiddler's wife said. 'But I agree. So many slaughtered and not even laid to rest in their own ground. It is not right.'

'And now, with all this talk of more removals, well . . . there will be nothing left here for my children. It is not just Cameron I have to think about. It is Eilidh and Marta too. Lord Selkirk has offered passages to his settlement for a fair price, and we have applied to go.'

'And you will be given a bit of land to farm when you get there?'

'A decent bit of land it will be too. And with the low cost of the fares, there will be plenty left over for us to set up a decent life there. With Cameron helping his father, we will have a new farmstead built in no time.'

Mhàiri stifled a sob and moved away. 'I will get Connor to bed,' she said to Màthair and swept her sleeping brother into her arms and strode off. She opened her mouth to call to Cameron but closed it. Why had he declared his affection for her when all the time he had planned on emigrating? She couldn't bring herself to bid him goodnight.

As she marched towards her hut, Cameron caught up with her.

He touched her arm. 'Mhàiri, what is it?'

Unable to find the words to explain, she kept walking.

'Mhàiri, have I done something to upset you?'

The confusion in his voice made her stop. She turned towards him. The pained expression on his face mirrored the confusion in his voice, and the anger and sense of betrayal she felt evaporated to be replaced by a deep sense of sadness.

'Why did you not tell me you were to be leaving?'

'Leaving,' he repeated as if he hadn't understood what she meant.

'I heard your mother talking . . . about a passage to The Red River Valley.'

'Ah, that.' Cameron rubbed his hands over his mouth. 'I was planning on staying here, with you.'

'Your parents are counting on you to help them build a farmstead when they get there.'

'So they have been telling me.'

That night, sleep failed to come, and Mhàiri cried silent tears. She wept for another loss from Strathnaver. And even more tears for her loss. Cameron's mother was right; he should move to North America with them. His family needed his help. And, if he stayed here, he could be called to fight against Napoleon. Either way, stay or leave, Cameron MacÀidh was lost to her, just as Rob Dunn had been, and she had better get used to the idea. She would rather Cameron emigrate than stay here for her sake and then die fighting in the war like his brother. She would tell him that.

* * *

A few weeks later, Mhàiri woke to the sweet smell of heather. She blinked and opened her eyes. It took her a moment to realise what day it was. As she stepped from the bed and pulled on her overdress, she smiled. Summer had turned to autumn, and it was time to return to the township. The cold winds had started early, and there had been talk between the older tenants of a bad winter to come.

Mhàiri helped her mother store their butter, cheese and curds into barrels. When they finished, they placed the wool they'd spun for weaving over the winter into the peat cart, along with two flasks of ale and a jug of whisky Màthair had procured in exchange for some cheeses.

While they waited for the women to finish packing, the young men played out a game of shinty. Mhàiri made her way over to watch them. As Cameron raced around the brae-side wielding a stick, she followed his movements. When he turned his face towards her and smiled, Mhàiri's chest tightened. She smiled back and made to leave. As she stepped away, Peigi Ruadh raised her arm and waved at Cameron, trying to attract his attention. Mhàiri swallowed her regret, but she wouldn't be the one to hold Cameron back from going to a safer life.

* * *

An autumn haze settled over the valley, and people drifted away in small groups; heading for home. Before going on her way, Aunt Úna hugged Mhàiri and promised to visit soon. Mhairi looked around. The people from her township had gathered together and were moving off. It was time for her to depart the sheilings— time for her to leave another summer behind.

Cameron walked at the front of the group, with his mother and sisters. When they descended the final brae towards home, he turned his head and looked back at Mhàiri with a puzzled look. Although it tore at her heart, she looked away.

Soon, her cottage came into clear view. Her father was tying a line of stones, woven into nets, around the edge of the thatch on the roof to keep it in place. '*Athair*! Father!' she called and waved when he turned.

He climbed down the wooden stepladder and limped towards them.

'*Mo chèile* - my husband' Màthair called to him and waved. 'I have missed you,'

Mhàiri ran to him, and he swung her in his arms. After putting her down, he lifted Connor and hugged him. He stroked his wife's face, and the two missing fingers on his left hand served as a stark reminder to Mhàiri of the wounds he had received in the war. His inner scars ran deeper, and for the most remained hidden. Her stomach knotted at the thought of Cameron gaining such injuries or even worse; of him dying in battle like his brother and Hattie Bantrach's husband.

'You made it,' he said to her mother. 'Donaidh Dròbhair? Has he—'

'I got word from the drover. All three of our cows sold and the rent money has been paid into the commissioner's office, so there is no need to be worrying.' Màthair's face brightened. 'There was enough to pay our rent and a little more besides.'

He touched Màthair's arm. 'Unfortunately, my news is not as good as your own.'

10

WINTER WINDS

Mhàiri's mother sang as she worked the loom, weaving blankets. Mhàiri sat beside her, close to the fire, listening to her mother's songs and winding the wool they'd spun at the sheilings. Connor sat crossed-legged on the floor, spinning a small wooden top.

Winter had come early to Strathnaver. First, the dark nights crept in and the days had shortened. Cold winds followed. Then, a hard frost gripped the earth with its icy fingers and refused to let go. It made its presence known in the strath and left everyone in no doubt that it would be staying for some time.

The cold added a chilling foreboding to the stories Mhàiri's father had told about the removals in the Strath of Kildonan and how Clan Gunn had been evicted from their land. Despite their refusals, soldiers had been brought in and they'd been forced out in the end.

With the animals sheltered in the byre, the harvest gathered and the peats cut and stacked, her father worked outside, while Mhàiri spent most of her time indoors with Màthair and Connor. She edged closer to the fire. Snug in the warmth of her home, and with her hands absorbed in the repetitive task of winding wool her thoughts turned to Cameron. Had it only been a few months since she'd danced with him at the sheilings? It felt like such a long time ago. Feeling stifled in the smoke-filled room, Mhàiri stood and pulled her warmest woollen plaid from a chest.

'The water in the barrel has frozen,' she said and picked up the pail. 'I will fetch some before it gets dark.'

Màthair looked up from her weaving and nodded.

When Mhàiri stepped out the door, a gust of wind whipped the empty pail, almost pulling it from her grip. She held her plaid tight against her neck with one hand and the pail against her body with the other.

'Mhàiri!'

She turned.

Cameron held up a pail. 'Can I walk with you?'

Mhàiri nodded, and they made their way down to the river.

'They didn't get them,' he said, raising his voice to be heard above the howling wind.

'Get what?' She bent and dipped the pail into the water. How did Cameron expect her to know what he was talking about?

'The passages. To the Red River Settlement. My family. They did not get them.'

She stopped filling the pail and looked up. Below a woollen bonnet, Cameron's dark-blonde hair flapped in the wind, and his face creased into a concerned frown.

'I am sorry,' she said and meant it. 'It would have been a new life for you . . . For your family.'

'Over five hundred applied. There were only passages for a hundred.'

'There will be other chances.' Her belly churned. She wanted to beg him not to apply again but understood his reason.

'We have heard that another ship will be leaving in the spring. Mother is determined to get us a place on it.' He looked towards the ground and shuffled his feet. 'You could come. We could go together.'

Mhàiri tilted her head to the side. Had she heard correctly? She stood and hoisted the handle of the pail into the crook of her arm. 'Me, emigrate?'

'Why not? The new life you talk about for me could belong to both of us.'

'How would I find the money?' She gave a hollow laugh. 'What would I need? Ten pounds, or more?'

He nodded and dipped the pail into the water. 'It is not impossible. I could save. I . . . I could ask my parents to help. The minister might give you something. Between us, we could find a way.'

Mhàiri touched his arm. 'It is but a dream. I could never find the money. We both know that.'

'We could— '

'Cameron, my parents have no desire to leave the strath, and even if I could find the money to emigrate, I would never leave them behind. Or my strath.' Even as she spoke the words, she knew they were not true. Being with Cameron MacÀidh was all that she could ever want and more. Why did life have to be so difficult?

Mhàiri shook her head. 'Surely you can see that what you are asking of me is impossible. With another rent increase, my family need every penny they have just to get by. And they are not the only ones. There is no extra to be had.'

She couldn't exist on dreams alone. Nothing had changed. Cameron's family would keep applying to emigrate until they succeeded. Then where would she be?

Mhàiri turned and pulled her plaid around her head. 'We best get back.'

'Say you will think about it, Mhàiri.' When she didn't reply, he took the pail from her. 'At least let me carry this for you.'

* * *

The next morning, the door of the cottage flew open, and Mhàiri looked up from the wool she was winding.

Her father hurried into the room. A lock from his slicked back, dark hair clung to his forehead. 'It is Maighstir MacCoinnich. He is on his way, and he has got someone with him. A stranger.' His voice rose. 'Come quick, Catriona.'

Mhàiri raced out the door behind her parents. Dark clouds had formed, threatening rain and casting dismal shadows across the valley. At the sight of the approaching stranger, Mhàiri's pace slowed. With heavy-leaden steps, she continued forward. Beside Maighstir MacCoinnich was the tall man on the grey mount she had seen watching the township through a spyglass. She couldn't pull her eyes from the silver-coloured buttons on his black jacket.

The townspeople poured from their homes and gathered outside, watching the two figures draw closer. Mhàiri stopped beside her friend, Anna, who clutched her tightly wrapped baby daughter to her. Fearghas placed his arm protectively around his wife's shoulder. The fiddler and his wife stood beside Mòrag Mòr and her son, Iain. Cameron and his family hurried up the brae and huddled beside the miller and his wife and children. Peigi Ruadh shuffled closer to Cameron. Hattie Bantrach, who wasn't a tenant, stood in the shadow of her hovel and waited with the others to find out why the minister had brought a well-dressed stranger to their township.

The man on the grey mount pulled to a halt and fixed his gaze above the sea of concerned faces. Maighstir MacCoinnich drew up his horse and pointed to the man with the silver-coloured buttons. 'Mister Sellar speaks no Gaelic. As most of you do not understand English, I have accompanied him to make sure you hear what he has to say.'

The factor's horse snorted and stepped forward. It swished

its tail as if urging its master to hurry. Mister Sellar tilted his large nose in the air. He spoke, and the warmth from his breath clouded in the icy air above him.

The minister translated the factor's words. 'In some of the townships within Strathnaver, it has been decided not to call rents for this coming year.'

A cry of protest erupted from the crowd, and Mhàiri stifled a sob. She glanced around and placed a hand over her mouth. What was Maighstir MacCoinnich saying? How could he be telling them this? She leant against her father, who had one arm draped around Màthair's shoulder.

She looked at Cameron. His mother would push harder now to emigrate. Perhaps Peigi Ruadh would go with them. The miller's daughter seemed eager enough. Mhàiri shook her head as the reality of the situation hit her— they would all be leaving. Tears stung her eyes, and she brushed them away.

'Silence,' Maighstir MacCoinnich called. He lowered his voice. 'I have arranged a special service to be held at the mission tomorrow. You are, of course, aware of the trouble Clan Gunn caused in the Strath of Kildonan when they refused to move to their new homes on the coast. Soldiers had to be brought in. Mister Sellar wishes to avoid such an abhorrence happening again. He can be no fairer than that. A service will be held at two o'clock tomorrow. I will talk to you then and provide you with the information you need.'

11

POWER OF THE PULPIT

The following day, Mhàiri trudged towards the mission. The chill seeped into her bones, and she shivered. Connor ambled along beside her, slowing her steps. Despite holding his gloved hand and trying to hurry him along, she soon fell behind the other tenants from the township. Her parents walked ahead, neither of them talking, as they waited to learn their fate. Like them, Mhàiri believed that the minister would help them and that the Great Lady intended them no harm.

Cameron turned back and scooped Connor onto his shoulders. Her brother whooped and giggled as Cameron raced to catch up with the others. The sound of her brother's laughter pierced the solemn mood surrounding Mhàiri and, running along behind Cameron, her steps lightened. When they caught up, Mhàiri was still smiling.

'You should have seen him,' Anna's husband, Fearghas pointed to Cameron. 'That chicken took the rise out of him without a doubt.'

Cameron shook his head. 'The whole of Strathnaver will know about it before you are finished stretching the telling of the tale. And now is not the time to be telling it.'

Mhàiri looked at Cameron. 'What happened?'

'Nothing.' Cameron tilted his bonnet back and glared at Fearghas. 'He just likes spinning a yarn.'

'It is no yarn. Hattie Bantrach's chicken hadn't moved from the same spot in the rafters for over two days. She was convinced it had died. She asked Cameron to climb up and bring down her dead chicken so she could put it in the pot. Well — ' Unable to continue talking for his growing laughter, Fearghas slapped his thigh and snorted.

Mhàiri tilted her head to one side. 'And?'

'And,' Fearghas said. 'When Cameron picked up the dead chicken and tried to put it under his arm to climb down, it flapped its wings and flurried off, leaving him swinging from the rafters convinced he had witnessed a miracle.'

'What? Cameron MacÀidh witnessed a resurrection.' Iain said. He adopted a serious expression and raised his arms to the sky. 'And, behold, the dead chicken rose again from the rafters .. . resurrected.'

Mhàiri relished the short respite from the dark mood of the day and joined in the laughter. A woman from another township glared at them, and another woman urged them to be quiet. Suitably chastised, the group carried on in silence. While Cameron continued to carry Connor on his shoulders, Mhàiri walked beside him. She caught his eye and smiled her thanks. They settled into a steady stride, and a comfortable silence developed between them.

At the mission, Mhàiri made her way with Connor and her parents to visit Fionnghal's grave. After saying a prayer for her dead sister, her family returned to the front of the mission and listened to the catechist explain the meaning of the Bible reading for the service. When he finished, Mhàiri entered with her family. Maister Sellar was already there, sitting in a pew at the front.

At two o'clock, the bells pealed out the hour and Maighstir

MacCoinnich strode to the pulpit. He looked down on the congregation and raised his hands. 'Let us pray.'

For the next hour, Mhàiri listened in shocked silence to the minister's words.

'— You must follow the orders of those whom God has placed above you. An eternal life of hell and damnation waits for anyone who disobeys the order to leave their home when it comes. To question such an order would be to question the will of God, and damnation and all the wrath of Hell will be wreaked upon those who refuse to obey His word.' He banged the pulpit with his hand.

Mhàiri sat straight-backed as she listened to the minister's threats, and her eyes remained focussed upon him. His words swam around her head like a dark storm swirling around the mountains. A few words joined together to make some sort of sense, but others floated around in a chaotic stream that made no sense at all. Why would God punish them if they didn't leave their homes? It didn't seem right. But who was she to question Maighstir MacCoinnich's words? Surely, he knew best. He spoke on God's behalf.

After concluding the service, the minister held up a hand for the congregation to remain seated. 'A meeting has been arranged for nine days' time, outside the inn at Golspie. Bids for the lease of a large stretch of Strathnaver will be auctioned off then. As most of your townships are included, I will travel with you, to ensure you understand what is said. Later, you will be informed which townships will not have their rents called for the coming year. His Lordship and Her Ladyship want to do what is in your best interest and have no wish for trouble. They cannot do fairer than that. Remember, it is God's will that these moves take place. Consider this as just punishment for your sins and an opportunity for sinners to repent.'

Mhàiri made her way from the mission hall. While her father walked ahead with Connor, Mhàiri gripped onto

Màthair's arm. Despite the minister's warnings of reprisal, some tenants expressed their enraged indignation at what the minister had said. Others, like Mhàiri and her mother, left with their shoulders hunched in despair and their mouths firmly closed.

Outside, a crowd had gathered and Mhàiri made her way over with her family.

A bearded man shook his fist. 'We have to do something.'

'What can we do?' A white-haired woman pushed her way to the front. 'You heard the minister. All the wrath of Hell will be sent on us if we disobey.'

'The wrath of Hell is already being wreaked upon us, woman,' the man replied. 'We have to fight back.'

The woman glared at him. 'Pah! Look what happened in Kildonan when Clan Gunn resisted. Soldiers were marched in. Those who refused to leave were forced out anyway. Then arrested.'

Cameron held up his hands. 'Wait. The minister said that the lease for the townships is to be auctioned off at Golspie? Surely between us all, we could place a decent bid.'

As she absorbed what Cameron had said, Mhàiri held her breath.

Amidst the clamour of raised voices, Fearghas called, 'With what we are paying in rent. I for one will join in.'

Mhàiri's father called out, 'Even if we are allowed to remain the rents will keep going up. We have nothing to lose by placing a bid for the lease.'

Mhàiri let out a deep breath. There were more ways to fight than with swords or raised fists.

GOING TO GOLSPIE

An icy wind stung Mhàiri's face and whistled in her ears. She gripped onto her plaid and tried to keep out the biting onslaught. With her head down, she placed one frozen foot in front of the other and tried to keep pace with her father. Why had she insisted on going to Golspie? It had been agreed that her parents would go. Then, Connor had taken the Whooping Cough and Mhàiri had persuaded Màthair to let her go in her place.

The wind lashed at her, and she willed herself to keep walking. Frozen leaves crunched under her boots, and the bare branches on the twisted trees glistened with frost. She recalled the stories from the sheilings about wolves and glanced around. Were there still wolves roaming in the woods? No longer certain, she remained watchful. Her footsteps slowed and she lagged behind. She couldn't let the others down. Either she kept moving or she would have to return home, alone. Something stirred behind a tree. Mhàiri glanced over her shoulder and quickened her pace.

Twenty-seven tenants were making their way to Golspie to meet with representatives from the estate. If they didn't get the lease, surely they would be enough of a force to persuade whoever did win the bid not to evict them. They had travelled all day yesterday and sheltered overnight in a barn. This morning, they had set off at first light and had walked for about three hours. If they didn't make the meeting, her family could be thrust out of their home. She had to keep moving, they all did.

She ran and caught up with her father. 'I am sorry. I don't know what is wrong with me.'

'The cold is getting to everyone, lassie. We just need to keep up a steady pace.'

Ahead, Cameron walked beside his sisters, Eilidh and Marta. As Mhàiri watched his confident strides, her stomach twisted. She wished she could walk beside him. Wished she had his resolve. Even his mother seemed to be faring better than she was. At the front of the walking group, Maighstir MacCoinnich bent over his horse's neck and led them forward. Strapped to his saddle were their supplies of oatcakes, cheese and dried fruit. Apart from asking the tenants to join in an occasional prayer, the minister remained silent. Mhàiri was grateful for that; it was too cold to talk. Flakes of snow drifted onto her cheek. She brushed them off and looked up. The grey sky from this morning had been transformed into a mass of thick white clouds. Minutes later, a light fluttering of snow fell, and Mhàiri shivered.

By mid-day, the snow fell in earnest and Mhàiri found it difficult to keep her footing on the slippery path. Ahead of her, the tenant's steps slowed. With backs hunched and heads bent against the biting wind, a line of snow-covered plaids trudged wearily forward. The shuffle of their steps and the clunk of the hooves of the minister's horse alternated with the rise and dips of the whistling wind. Thick snow swirled around Mhàiri. She bent her head and battled onwards. When it seemed as if she couldn't take another step, a gloved hand slipped into hers. She turned and gazed into Cameron's concerned eyes. Snow settled and melted onto his lashes, and she smiled. Warmth spread through her and she gripped his hand.

Cameron leant towards her. 'Do you think your father would mind if I put an arm around you? Just to warm you a bit.'

'Laddie, if you can get her to Golspie, you can keep your arm around her.' Her father winked at her. 'That would be if Mhàiri does not mind.'

Her flushed face must have been answer enough, because he left them alone and strode ahead to walk beside Mòrag Mòr' and her son, Iain. Anna and Fearghas walked with Cameron's parents and the miller and his wife. Aunt Úna was linked into her husband's arm.

'It is not far now.' Cameron raised his voice against the biting wind. 'When we get to the inn, we will find shelter. You will soon be warm.'

By the time they arrived, Mhàiri felt chilled to the bone and she wasn't alone. Mòrag Mòr was shivering so hard, Mhàiri thought the woman might collapse. Outside the inn, the minister dismounted and the townspeople gathered round. The wind whipped at his woollen cloak, swirling it behind him.

'We are early. Find some shelter,' the minister called and hastened towards the door. 'I will meet you back here in one hour.'

Mhàiri followed the others to the back of the inn. Rows of stables lined a cobbled courtyard. They found an empty stable and took shelter inside. Mòrag Mòr's son helped his mother to sit down on a bundle of straw. Iain bent over her and rubbed her hands, trying to bring life back into them. Mhàiri dusted the snow from her clothes and sat beside her father.

He slipped his hand into his jacket pocket and pulled out a purse. 'I brought some coin. There should be enough for a bowl of broth and perhaps even one for Mòrag Mòr.' He rose to his feet. 'I will go see what is what.'

Her father arrived back, hefting a black, steaming three-legged pot. Iain came in behind him with an armful of bowls. Cameron followed, carrying a basket of bread. The sight of bread and broth had never been more appealing to Mhàiri. The nourishing smell made her faint with hunger and she salivated in anticipation of the warming meal. The men had pooled their coins and bought the remains of the soup pot from the innkeeper.

Cameron's mother filled bowls, and Mhàiri took one over to Mòrag Mòr. 'Here, sup this. It will bring warmth back to you.' She handed the steaming bowl to the shivering woman.

Mhàiri obtained a bowl of broth for herself and sat on the straw beside Rob Dunn's mother. 'You will have had news of Rob Dunn? It has been nigh on two years since he left.'

'Ah, Mhàiri, it is good to see you. We are living in hope of Rob being returned to us soon.'

Mhàiri nodded and bent her head. The woman had looked at her with such fondness in her eyes, but Rob was a stranger to her now. Mhàiri didn't know what to say in reply. She dipped bread into the bowl and savoured the first warming mouthful. She licked her lips and spoke above the clamour of people trying to find a place to sit and sup. 'There were times during the journey when I thought I wouldn't be able to keep going.'

'We had no choice.' Rob Dunn's mother looked at her with tears in her eyes. 'If we do not get the lease, we have to put our case forward. We need to persuade the factor not to remove us. And, I could have been punished if I did not get here. It was that thought that kept my feet moving.'

'You are right. We could at that,' Mhàiri replied. Although she couldn't fathom why they would be punished for not attending the meeting, her family also hadn't wanted to risk finding out.

* * *

Outside the front door of the inn, Mhàiri stamped her feet to keep warm. The snow had stopped, but it remained bitterly cold. The tenants' representative at the bid and another man came out and stood together, deep in discussion. The tenants had bid £250. Mhàiri prayed it had been enough to secure the lease.

A stranger came out the door and hurried down the steps. Maighstir MacCoinnich and Maister Sellar followed close behind. Wrapped against the cold, in a long woollen coat and a scarf wound around his neck and lower face, the stranger marched over and stood in front of the tenants. The factor and minister took up places on either side of him, and the tenants grew silent. From behind his scarf, the stranger spoke in English.

Mhàiri listened as Maighstir MacCoinnich translated his muffled words. 'Let us get this business over with as quickly as possible.' He pointed to the stranger. 'This is the landlord's agent.'

On the other side of the inn, the landlord's castle snuggled behind the trees in the distance. Mhàiri looked towards it. Would the Great Lady be at home? If she was, would she be looking out a window towards the inn? Or, sitting around a warm fire, perhaps?

Maighstir MacCoinnich continued, 'On the first point of business, as Mister Sellar placed the highest bid in the auction for the large section of land on the eastern side of the River Naver, the lease for this goes to him.'

Mhàiri looked around in disbelief. The tenants had not won the bid. Her family were now sub-tenants of Maister Sellar. Mhàiri struggled to take this in. Cameron rushed to her side and gripped her arm. She placed a hand over his and continued to stare towards the castle.

The stranger spoke again. 'Notice is hereby given to the tenants of Strathnaver whose farms are to be set at Golspie on this day, the fifteenth of December. Each person of good character will be accommodated and provided with a new home. By Whitsunday next, in the year of our Lord, 1814, you will leave your houses and move to the coast, where your landlord, in concern for your welfare has provided you with new plots.'

Mhàiri's legs felt as if they would give way beneath her. The pain she had felt on the journey here, as she battled against the biting cold, paled into insignificance in the wake of the agony she now felt. It was as if a bitter storm of words battered her very being, dragging her to the ground. She fell forward onto her knees, and a keening sound rose in her throat and grew to a wail which, when given vent, joined forces with the loud laments around her.

Cameron dropped to his knees and placed an arm around her shoulder. Mhàiri looked up to see the stranger's retreating back and Maighstir MacCoinnich and Maister Sellar hurrying into the inn behind him. Her wails settled into racking sobs and she let her tears fall. They fell for her parents and Connor, for Anna and her new baby, for Hattie Bantrach and Mòrag Mòr.

She turned and looked into Cameron's tear-filled eyes. Her own tears continued to fall for the life that she could have lived in the strath and for the children she might have raised there, who now never could, but who, if they had been able to, would have ran free through the open pastures, and blown wishes on dandelions, and gone to the sheilings, and pulled fish from the river, and scared each other with stories about wolves in the woods. And her tears fell for Strathnaver's loss— of the tender touch from those who had loved and would have continued to love even its most barren soil and its hardest winters and its ever-changing views. She wept for the loss of waking from a bed of heather at the sheilings to see the hillsides and the streams. And she wept for the loss of her youth, which she would now leave behind her in Golspie.

13

LILIES AND LAUDANUM

Elizabeth lay on a daybed in the drawing-room of her Scottish castle. Her youngest son leant over and said in a concerned voice, 'Are you ill, Mama?'

Elizabeth smiled. 'Mama has toothache. That is all. Now you see why I tell you to clean your teeth. If you don't, they will grow soft and fall out just as Mama's are.'

'But even without all your teeth, you are still the most beautiful lady in the land.'

Despite the agonising ache ripping through her jaw, Elizabeth laughed and pulled her thirteen-year-old into an embrace. 'You are such a sweetheart. No mother could wish for a more loving son.'

The boy was such a gentle, caring soul, but she couldn't abide talking right now. 'Sit quietly for a moment while I try to walk off this pain.'

She paced over to the window and looked out at the snow-covered ground. In the far distance, the sky looked bleak. Her intention had been to return to Edinburgh tomorrow, but the weather had changed trapping her here. And now she had an infernal toothache, the likes of which she had never experienced. She would have to have the tooth extracted. She gave a hollow laugh— but not here. Where would she find a decent surgeon?

A thought occurred to her and she turned from the window. Entrapped in pain, she had almost forgotten what day it was. This evening, their estate commissioner was coming to dine. She never spent time at her Highland castle over the winter but, with the improvements happening throughout her Scottish estate, there were many pressing concerns for her to attend to. There would be much to talk about tonight. But how would she manage to eat? She could barely sit still for the pain. There was nothing else for it; her husband would have to meet their estate commissioner without her.

Elizabeth picked up a silver handbell from a low table and rang it. She had to get rid of this pain. The turmeric that she had packed around the tooth and gum half an hour earlier had brought no relief. She needed something stronger.

Her maid hurried in and curtsied. 'Ma'am.'

'Ah, you are here. I have such toothache, and cannot abide the pain any longer. I need to lie down on my bed, and please . . . please bring me my medicine. The strong one.'

The maid curtsied. 'Of course, Ma'am. Let me get you to your room and then I will bring your elixir.'

An ache ripped through Elizabeth's jaw, and she yelled. 'I have never suffered such agony.' She held a hand to the side of her swollen face. 'Bring my medicine and I will make my way upstairs.' She bent her other arm. 'My son will escort me.'

Like a knight saving a damsel in distress, her son linked into her arm. He lifted his head with the importance of the task and led her up the winding staircase. He stopped outside her bedroom door. 'Will Mama be all right now?'

'Mama will be just fine, once she has rested. Hurry off, now. Perhaps Papa can arrange for you to sledge in the snow.'

His face broke into a grin. 'And you will be all right while I am gone?'

'Mama will be just fine.' She smiled, bringing on another bout of pain. Where was her elixir?

Minutes after swallowing the draught, the laudanum took effect and the pain was replaced by a pleasant sensation of drifting. Mellowed, Elizabeth floated through a range of warm and vibrant colours; of red and orange. The warmth of the colours flooded through her and, as she folded into its embrace, she drifted back through time. Although it was only snatches of her life that she watched in the visions that came to her, it was as if she were watching someone else. Soon she was lost to any world but her visions.

She had been a baby when *it* happened; the event that had changed and shaped her life. An unfortunate accident everyone had called it. Everyone that is, except her father, who blamed himself. He couldn't forgive himself. Wouldn't forgive himself.

On the day Elizabeth was born, her sister, Catherine, had been exactly one year old. Her young father now had two daughters and he doted on them both. He would swing them into his arms. Play with them, and rub his rough whiskers into their necks, making them giggle. They both adored him back.

It happened on New Year's Day. Papa had taken a few extra glasses of wine with his meal. Later, when the nurse brought the girls through to the parlour, Papa picked Catherine up. As usual, he swung her into the air, but this time she stopped giggling. Her sister had stopped doing anything because she was dead. Catherine died the moment her soft head hit the hard floor when she tumbled from his outstretched arms.

Her parents left her with Grandmama in Edinburgh while they went to Bath to give Papa time to recover from the shock. But he couldn't get over the guilt. While they were there, he developed a fever. Mama stayed with him, amongst the smell of lilies, and sponged his fevered brow. Mama caught the fever too and was placed into the bed beside Papa. Servants mopped both of their brows until her parent's faces had turned as white as alabaster. Mama and Papa never returned to collect her from Grandmama's house. They were buried together with the lilies, deep in guilt.

Elizabeth had no real memory of these events, but having heard the stories from Grandmama often enough, she had no problem visualising them as if she had been there. And she had been, even if she had been too young to form any real memories of her own.

The halo of bright colour surrounding her vision faded to grey and then disappeared. She tried and failed to visualise again the loving parents she had lost and the sister she never got to know. Tears fell for the hole their deaths left in her life and for the incompleteness that remained in its place.

At one year old, she inherited her father's Highland estate. She didn't know the land and its people the way her grandpapa had known them. Like Papa, she had never learned to speak in the Gaelic, her tenant's language. Tears fell for the weight of the guilt her father had found too heavy to carry and had taken her parents from her. She cried for the young girl who had been left alone with Grandmama and her new husband and his daughters. And now, that young girl was growing old and losing her teeth, and she needed to return to Edinburgh, and soon.

14

HOME AND HEARTH

Darkness descended. Frozen, and almost asleep on her feet, Mhàiri gripped onto her father's arm and battled to take the final steps home. In the distance, smoke curled from their cottage roof, as if rising in welcome. The walk from Golspie had been more difficult than the journey there, and the tenants had trekked through biting winds and falling snow. If it hadn't been for the long stretches of His Lordship's new roads, it would have taken them even longer than two days. Close to tears and with tiredness threatening to overwhelm her, Mhàiri pushed open the cottage door and stumbled inside.

Màthair rose from the chair and hurried towards them; her face filled with concern. When they made to speak, she held up a hand. 'Get changed out of these sodden clothes. Then we can talk.'

Mhàiri's father held his hands out to the fire and nodded his agreement. 'How is Connor?'

'He took some broth earlier and his fever has settled,' Màthair replied and kissed his stubbled cheek.

Mhàiri removed her plaid and hung it over a stool by the fire. 'I can hardly feel my feet, they are so cold.'

'Your clothes are soaking, lassie, you best get out of them.' Màthair patted her husband's arm. 'You too Niall, your news can wait. There is some kale broth heating. I will dish it up while you both get changed and then you can tell me all that was said.'

With frozen fingers, Mhàiri removed her wet clothes and dragged on a thick nightdress. The sensation returned to her hands, and she wrapped a warm, woollen shawl around her shoulders. On the way back from Golspie she'd started to think the journey would never end. Mòrag Mòr had been unable to keep pace, and Maighstir MacCoinnich had insisted that she take his horse, while he walked. There had been no prayers and little conversation during their bleak journey home. Even the minister had thought better of it. There had been no discussion with the factors either, outside the inn. Mhàiri sat on a stool beside the fire.

'Come to the table, Mhàiri. You will be getting chilblains if you sit so close to the fire,' Màthair said and laid bowls of soup down. 'Here, sup this. The two of you can tell me what happened. From the look on your faces, it is not good news.'

Mhàiri and her father both looked at her with pained expressions.

'Well?' Màthair said and sat at the table. 'You best get it over with.'

After he had told her what the landlord's agent had said about rents not being called in some of the townships around Strathnaver and that these tenants would have to move to the coast, Màthair reached out and gripped her husband's hand. 'Our rents are not up for renewal, so none of this affects us. Does it?'

'It shouldn't.' His face furrowed into a frown. 'But, the factor . . . Maister Sellar, he won the auction for the lease— '

'Which includes our township,' Mhàiri added.

Màthair's face paled. 'So, now we are sub-tenants to Maister Sellar. What will this mean for us, Niall?'

'I am not sure.' He raised his eyebrows. 'But I am sure we will be finding out soon enough.'

'Likely, we will.' Màthair stood and rubbed her hands down her skirt. 'Was the journey very bad, lassie? You look all but done in. You best get to bed. We can talk more about this in the morning.'

'The journey was hard.' Her father looked at Mhàiri. 'But Cameron MacÀidh helped whenever you faltered. Didn't he?'

What was he bringing that up for? Mhàiri felt her face redden, and stood.

'Ach, sit down, Mhàiri.' Màthair placed the kettle on the fire and looked over her shoulder. 'It wasn't as if I hadn't noticed how attentive he was to you at the sheilings.'

Father's spoon paused halfway to his mouth. 'You have known since then? Why did you not say anything, Catriona?'

'Because, since we got back nothing has developed between them.' Màthair touched Mhàiri's shoulder. 'What happened, lassie?'

Grateful for the chance to talk, Mhàiri told them about Cameron's family applying to emigrate.

'Ah, well,' Màthair said. 'That does make things difficult.'

The following morning, Màthair poured hot milk into a cup and filled a bowl with cooked oats and handed them to Mhàiri. 'Mòrag Mòr has come down with a fever. Take this over to her, lassie.'

When Mhàiri entered the woman's cottage smoke from the peat fire billowed up and stung her eyes. She coughed and looked around. The black, soot-ridden rafters looked as if they had not been attended to in years. Beside the fire, Iain sat on a stool with his head bent into his cupped hands.

He looked up at her with red-rimmed eyes. 'I should have stopped Mother from going to Golspie. I don't know what I would do if she wasn't here. She is the only family I have left. The war has taken my father and likely my brother. I cannot lose Màthair too.'

Mhàiri nodded and held out the cup and bowl. 'I have brought some boiled oats.'

He pointed his thumb towards the box-bed on the back wall.

Sweat poured from Mòrag Mòr's reddened face, and Mhàiri placed a hand on the woman's fevered brow. 'Bring me a cloth and a bowl of warm water, Iain.'

After bathing Mòrag Mòr and changing the soaking gown, Mhàiri fed her the milk and oats. 'There you go, you will soon feel better,' she said, not really believing her words. She lifted a blanket out of a box and placed it on top of the bed covers and turned to Iain. 'Your mother needs to break this fever, keep her warm.'

Iain stood and nodded. 'Maighstir MacCoinnich called to see how Mother was. He told me to let everyone know that there will be a service at the mission on Sunday and that Maister Sellar will be in attendance. We have all to be there.' He snorted. 'How I am to get Mother there, I don't know.'

Mhàiri reeled. Things were moving too fast.

* * *

By Sunday the snow had stopped falling, but the ground remained covered in a thick blanket of white. Mhàiri trudged to the mission beside her friend Anna, who carried her daughter wrapped in a warm, woollen blanket. Although all the tenants from the strath had been instructed to attend, Mòrag Mòr had not recovered her strength and remained in bed. To avoid the deep marshes and peat bogs, the tenants followed the drover path.

After visiting her sister's grave, Mhàiri entered the rapidly filling mission hall with her family. They found seats near the back beside Aunt Úna and her husband. When the minister finished the opening prayer, the catechist stood.

'Faith,' the catechist roared, and the word reverberated around the room. 'You need to retain your faith in God. Not just while you are reaping His rewards and enjoying the fruits of your triumphs but also when He is testing you, as He will. When you are faced with trials, you need to keep faith in Him. When you are struggling, that is when it is most important to keep your faith in Him. Without faith, it is impossible to please God. Just as the Israelite's failure to believe His word kept them from entering the Promised Land, so too will you be left to wander in the wilderness of your own sin if you refuse to obey His word.'

When the service ended the factor spoke. 'Some tenants currently occupying parts of Strathnaver and other areas will be required to leave their homes by this coming Whit Sunday. Surveying will start soon to allocate these people with lots on the coast.

'I also give formal notice to some of the tenants on my land. I have been given right of entry for the twenty-sixth of May. Removals will begin as soon as possible after that date. Other tenants will be asked to leave later. Once tenants are removed it will be considered a breach of tenancy to provide them with shelter. Anyone harbouring a removed person will be considered in breach of their tenancy agreement and will forfeit their right to remain in their home.'

As he called the names of the first families whose rents would not be renewed and who would receive a visit from him to serve a notice of removal, a cold draught crept along the floor and circled Mhàiri's legs. When he called out the names of Aunt Úna's and Rob Dunn's families a feeling of sheer horror flooded through her. All the talk she had heard about removals, and now it was happening.

Aunt Úna was to move to the coast along with over twenty other families. Before Mhàiri could heave a sigh of relief that her family had been spared, the factor said, 'Be assured, within a few years all of Strathnaver will be under sheep.'

15

BURNING BROOM

By the middle of March, the last of the snow had melted, and Mhàiri led one of last year's calves out to graze on the heath. A gentle morning breeze blew Mhàiri's hair and tugged at her long brown skirt. Buds formed on the bushes creating a promise of spring. Earlier, Cameron's father had arrived at their byre with his bull, to breed with the calf's mother, and Mhàiri had the task of keeping the heifer out of the way.

Plumes of white smoke rose in the distance, and Mhàiri became aware of the smell of burning heather. As she rounded the brow of the brae, she saw a line of men carrying flaming torches and setting the heath around the next township alight. Behind the men, for as far as she could see, smoke curled upwards and formed a thick mist. She stared at the men. Why were they burning so much of the heath? Unable to comprehend what she was seeing, she stumbled down the brae towards home.

When she arrived at the township, the tenants were gathered outside the meeting-house. She raced towards them and called, 'The whole of the heath upriver is aflame.' She looked over her shoulder and pointed to the brae. 'They are torching the heath.' Her chest burned from the exertion of running while pulling the calf behind her. She handed the rope to Mòrag Mòr's son, Iain, and bent forward and placed her hands on her knees.

Cameron's father, who had been addressing the tenants about the volume of smoke in the distance, stopped talking and faced her. 'What did you see, Mhàiri?'

She took a deep breath. 'At least four men. With torches. Setting the heath alight. Upriver.'

Her father held up a hand and gazed around the townspeople as if looking for affirmation of what he was about to say. 'It is usual to burn out some of the heath, but the smoke yonder seemed too great for muirburn.'

'How much of the heath were they burning, Mhàiri?' Cameron touched her arm. 'How much?'

'It looked like all of it.' She leant against him. 'What is happening?'

'We don't know but we are going to find out.' Cameron's father signalled to her father who nodded and mounted his horse. 'We were about to head off.'

'I am going with them,' Cameron said to her. 'I will be back soon.'

After the men departed, the townspeople gathered in the meeting-house to wait for their return. The din from raised voices grew as people drifted in and huddled together in concerned groups. Peigi Ruadh was linked into her father's arm, deep in conversation. Amidst the uproar, Iain lit a fire and the fiddler's wife put the kettle on and made tea. Mòrag Mòr remained at home, bed-ridden and wracked with a cough. Hattie Bantrach busied herself frothing milk in small wooden bowls and passing them out to the children.

'I have never heard the likes of this before,' the fiddler's wife said as she sat beside Mhàiri and her mother.

Unable to settle, Mhàiri left the two women talking and

went in search of Anna. As she made her way across the room, she felt a tug on her sleeve. She turned.

Cameron's mother stared into her eyes. 'We need to talk.'

Mhàiri nodded.

'Without other ears listening,' the woman added and strode to the door.

Mhàiri followed her.

As soon as they were outside, Cameron's mother leant towards her and pointed her index finger. 'Stay away from my son, *A Mhàiri nic Niall.* Don't think I haven't noticed what you're doing?'

'What do you mean?'

'You know fine well what I mean. I saw you earlier with Cameron. I also saw what you did to him at the sheilings.' She screwed up her face. 'Kissing him. You should be ashamed of yourself.'

Mhàiri held a hand to her cheek and made to move away.

Cameron's mother gripped her arm. 'Stay where you are, I haven't finished with you yet, you sinner.'

Mhàiri paused. 'What do you want?'

'I want you to stay away from my son. Leave Cameron be. I saw how you fawned over him on the journey to Golspie. Laughable it was, the way you hung onto him. Pretending to be too cold to walk. Humph! Fine well, you could walk. You were just trying to get his attention, and it worked.'

Anger flared in Mhàiri's chest, and she swallowed. A burning sensation built up within her and she wanted to give vent to it. She wanted to scream at Cameron's mother to leave her be. Instead, she took a deep breath and shook her head. 'Why could you not have been happy for us? Why did you have to tie him down? Has Cameron no say in the matter?'

Cameron's mother pushed her face closer and screwed up her eyes until they were narrow strips. The fine lines around them crinkled. 'He has a say. And he has chosen to emigrate—

with his family. You may as well know, we heard today that we have places on a ship. We are sailing in a few months.' She shook Mhàiri's arm. 'So! Leave my son alone.'

Tears stung Mhàiri's eyes, and she turned and shook herself free from the woman's tight grip. As she broke away, she hurtled straight into Cameron.

He placed his arms around her and glared at his mother. 'What is going on?'

'I was telling Mhàiri that we have passages to the Red River Valley.' His mother turned to go back into the meeting-house.

'Wait!' Cameron called. 'I heard what you said. As did Father and Mhàiri's father too.'

His mother stopped and turned.

Cameron's father shook his head at his wife. 'We will talk about this later, once we have sorted out this business with the grazing grounds.'

'There is nothing to sort out.' Cameron looked at Mhàiri. 'We are getting wed.'

His mother's hand shot to her open mouth. 'But . . . you are coming with us.'

'No, I am not, Màthair. Why will you not listen? Either I wed Mhàiri or I sign up to fight in the war.' He turned Mhàiri to face him. 'That is if you will have me?'

Stunned by Cameron's announcement, Mhàiri tried to take it in. He had asked her to marry him. Her heart raced. She glanced over his shoulder. Anger flared on his mother's face and burned there like the torches the men had used to set the heath alight. Did his sisters feel the same way? How could she join a family that did not want her? Her face fell. Would Cameron always blame her for making him choose between her and his family?

'Mhàiri?' Cameron touched her arm. 'Well? Are we to wed?'

She gazed into his eyes. The love reflected there dimmed the impact of his mother's anger. With a flash of understanding, she realised that no one else's opinion mattered but theirs. She couldn't imagine life without Cameron MacÀidh. Warmth surged through her and she smiled. 'We will be wed.'

Cameron lifted her and twirled her around.

His mother placed her hands on her face and sobbed. His father put an arm around her shoulder. 'I think you have said enough, wife. Go home.' He looked at Mhàiri. 'Cameron and Mhàiri can always join us once we are settled abroad. We can speak more about it later. But for now, I need to let the townspeople know what we learned.'

Still linked into Cameron's arm, Mhàiri turned to her father. 'What did you find out?'

'It is not good. The grazing grounds up river have been set alight. Maister Sellar ordered the heath burned to make the shrubs better for his incoming sheep, but he's left nothing for these township's cattle to graze on.'

The elation Mhàiri felt a moment earlier turned to deep concern. Without grazing ground, the cattle the tenants depended on to pay their rents wouldn't survive.

16

PROMISES AND PRAYERS

Mhàiri sat on the hillside and snuggled into Cameron. He held her close and stroked her hair. 'We could wed at the end of next month.'

Mhàiri tilted her head and looked up at him. 'That is only a few weeks away. The minister said not to get our hopes up. And, anyway, Lord Stafford is not approving marriages in the townships that are to be cleared.'

'But that shouldn't apply to us. Be damned. If he says no, I will go speak to him myself, even if it means travelling all the way to London to do so. There is no point in us delaying, Mhàiri. We should wed before my family leave.' Cameron grinned. 'My sisters would never forgive us if they missed the wedding. Eilidh and Marta will want to be there.'

'That may be so, but what about your mother?'

'Having realised that she couldn't persuade or force me to emigrate, she has come round to the idea of me staying.'

Mhàiri remained unconvinced but smiled. She wouldn't let Cameron's mother spoil her happiness. And, though a week had passed since the heath in the neighbouring townships had been burned out, there had been no further burnings. Mhàiri started to believe that the removals might not happen. She snuggled back into Cameron, relishing his distinctive smell; like ripe brambles mingled with smoky peat.

Around them, signs of spring blossomed. Shoots sprang from the ground, and buds formed on the bushes. The green leaves bursting out on the branches of the trees reminded Mhàiri of one of Màthair's sayings; "After every winter, there comes a spring." The winter had been hard on them all, in more ways than the weather, but a new season beckoned.

'My family's tenancy is secured for the next three years.' Cameron grinned. 'Father is having it transferred over to me. We can live there. My family cannot take their furniture with them, so we will have everything we need.'

Mhàiri's head jerked up. 'Tell me I won't have to sleep in your parent's bed.' Even saying the words felt strange and she screwed up her face.

Cameron laughed and made to kiss her.

She tilted her face away. 'I mean it. It is not that I'm ungrateful for what they are leaving. It is just that . . . well, I couldn't bring myself to sleep in *their* bed.'

'So, what can we do?'

'There's nothing else for it, you will have to build another one.' She blushed at having to talk about sleeping beside him at night. She knew what would be expected of her once they married, and she was determined it wouldn't be happening in his parents' bed. Her thoughts raced ahead. What if Cameron found her scars ugly?

'If that is what you want then we will have a new bed.'

Mhàiri remained silent, and Cameron's face filled with concern. 'Have I said something wrong?'

She pulled back her sleeves, exposing her arms. She held them out, palms upward. 'You may as well see this and have the matter done with. Now, why would you want to marry me?'

Cameron bent and kissed one arm and then the other, looking at her scars as he did so. 'A Mhàiri, mo ghràidh – Mhàiri, my love,' he said. 'I know what happened to Fionnghal. I also know that you tried to save your sister. Why wouldn't I want to marry you because you carry the scars from that day?'

Mhàiri stared at him through narrowed eyes; trying to work out if he was telling the truth. He hadn't flinched as he had looked at her puckered flesh. 'Do you really not mind?'

'There is none of us perfect, Mhàiri. Do you think your mother loves your father any less because he doesn't have all his fingers? What if the same happened to me? Would you stop loving me?'

'Of course, I wouldn't.' She shook her head at the thought of not loving him because of some scar or imperfection.

'Then let the matter be.' He stood and held out his hand. 'Will we plan to wed soon? I still haven't had your answer.'

She gripped his outstretched hand and pulled herself up. 'If Lord Stafford says we can. In the meantime, we may as well start planning. There's no time to waste.'

Cameron wriggled his eyebrows. 'Ah, so this is how it is to be between us when we are married; you, ordering me around.'

Letting go of his hand, Mhàiri broke into a run and called back over her shoulder. 'Of course, and remember that bed you have to build.'

* * *

Despite a wracking cough, brought on when she walked, Mòrag Mòr was now able to be lifted onto a chair. Mhàiri made her way over to see her with Anna. She carried her mother's wedding plaid in her arms, and in her hand, she clutched the MacAoidh crest brooch which had been handed down to Màthair, from her mother, Mamó MacAoidh. Anna carried the skirt and corset she had worn at her own wedding in one arm and her baby daughter in the other.

Mhàiri smiled. 'Aw, she is a bonnie one, Anna.'

'You will be having plenty of your own, now that you are to be married.'

Mhàiri frowned. 'The weeks are passing and we still haven't heard from the minister.'

'I am sure you will be hearing something soon. It all takes time. You both have years left on your leases. There is no reason for Lord Stafford not to allow you and Cameron to wed.'

Mhàiri looked at her with hope. 'Do you think so?'

'Of course.'

When they entered Mòrag Mòr's cottage, the woman greeted them with a smile.

'Ah, you brought them. Good. Good. We may as well get started,' Mòrag Mòr said and wagged a finger for Mhàiri to change into Anna's skirt and corset.

Mhàiri stood by the chair while Mòrag Mòr positioned the plaid onto the dress.

'Mhàiri still hasn't heard back from the minster,' Anna said.

Mòrag Mòr shook her head and clicked her tongue. 'You just have to bide your time.'

'But what if Lord Stafford says no? What if we are not allowed to wed? Cameron might emigrate with his family.'

'He wouldn't go to all the trouble of asking you to marry him, just for him to leave,' the older woman said. 'Now stop fidgeting.'

'You could still live with him as his wife,' Anna said. 'It wouldn't be a sin if you are not allowed to marry. Would it Mòrag Mòr?'

'I am sure it will not come to that.' Mòrag Mòr said as she pinned the brooch with the red stones onto the plaid to hold the two front pieces together. 'Now let me look at you. What do you think, Anna?'

'Aw, *A Mhàiri nic Niall*, you do look bonnie,' Anna said and wiped a tear from her eye.

'It *is* perfect.' Mhàiri said and beamed. 'No amount of gold could buy a bonnier dress.' Positioned around her shoulder, part of the tartan plaid fell down her arms, like sleeves. The remainder was belted around her waist and gathered to leave the front open, revealing Anna's dark blue skirt which glittered in the firelight. Mhàiri thought the overall effect beautiful and couldn't wait to wear the dress at her wedding.

If only they would hear back from the minister.

* * *

Another week passed without any word, and Mhàiri feared the worst. With her back stooped and aching, she pulled weeds from the earth. Strong shoots sprung from the peaty soil, promising a good crop of potatoes to come.

Connor worked beside her, gathering the weeds into a basket for the horses to chew on later. 'It is Cameron,' he called and pointed across the field.

Mhàiri stood and rubbed her hands together. Wiping away the last of the moist soil on the cloth tucked into her waistband, she watched Cameron approach. Sensing the urgency in his steps, she hurried towards him. 'What now?'

With his mouth turned down, Cameron shook his head.

Mhàiri bit on her bottom lip and nodded. Life was but a dream. Of course, she wouldn't be allowed to marry Cameron. Why had she let herself think otherwise? As she made to return to the weeding, Cameron lifted her up and beamed.

'What? Has Lord Stafford said yes?'

'He did,' Cameron said, still smiling. 'And the minister has agreed to marry us.'

Connor whooped and ran around them.

In that instant, Mhàiri knew without a doubt that if His

Lordship had refused, she would still have lived with Cameron as his wife. As Anna had said, it would not have been a proper sin if they had been refused permission to marry.

'Well,' she said to Cameron. 'What are you waiting for? You best go tell your mother.'

SOLDIER'S SURPRISE

Mhàiri and her mother made their way to Aunt Úna's township, to let her know about the latest turn of events.

When they arrived, Aunt Úna hurried from the field to greet them. She wiped her hands on a cloth tucked into the waistband of her skirt. 'What news?'

Mhàiri smiled and tilted her head. 'I am to be married. In two weeks.'

Linking into each other's arms, Màthair and Aunt Úna laughed together as they made their way inside; no doubt already planning what needed to be done. Mhàiri followed them in.

As she poured milk into a pot, Aunt Úna said, 'The men have taken the cows to look for pasture. With the heath burned out, the animals keep wandering off.'

Màthair shook her head. 'I don't know how you manage.'

'It is a struggle. We cannot—'

The sound of raised voices had the women hurrying out the door.

Mhàiri's mouth opened in surprise. Three dust-covered

soldiers marched into the township. They looked worn out. Mhàiri's thoughts turned to Mòrag Mòr's son and, as the men drew near she scanned their faces searching for Micheal. As she did so, she fixed on a heavily whiskered face that looked familiar. She swallowed and then let out a deep breath. It had taken her a few moments to recognise who it was. The differences in his features and manner had confused her.

When he saw Mhàiri, Rob Dunn dropped his bag and ran towards her. He gazed into her face and lifted her into a birl.

She tried to conceal her revulsion for this stranger who had replaced the young man she had once thought she loved. His breath smelled of whisky and tobacco. From underneath bloody bandages, his body gave off the sour smell of rotting flesh. She recoiled from his touch and pulled back from his whiskered face.

He laughed and pulled her closer until she thought she might choke.

'Put the lassie down,' Mhàiri's mother said in a stern tone, 'she is to be married.'

Rob Dunn's eyes showed his confusion. 'All the time I was away. All the times I thought I would surely die. The only thing that kept me going was the thought of returning here to you, *A Mhàiri nic Niall*. And you— you couldn't even wait for my return.'

Mhàiri stepped back. 'I am so sorry Rob Dunn. It has been near two years and so much has changed.'

He spat on the ground. 'I know how long I have been away fighting. I don't need you to be telling me. But it looks like I was mistaken in expecting any kind of welcome from you. Who is he?'

Rob Dunn's mother tugged his arm. 'Come away son, let it be. Let me get you inside and fed.'

Mhàiri didn't want to leave things as they were but was reluctant to show Rob Dunn any sign that he could misunderstand. She was promised to Cameron, and Rob Dunn's touch felt like a betrayal. He was nothing like the fresh-faced seventeen-year-old she remembered marching off to war. This version of Rob Dunn scared her. He looked hardened and angry. And, she felt sure that his anger wasn't just from hearing that she was to be wed.

Dear God, what if she had married him before he had left, she wouldn't have had any say in the matter now. She felt sick at the thought. She recalled her father screaming out in the night and the comfort Màthair gave him. But she also saw how it had nearly shattered her mother's heart and soul to have a stranger return from war in the place of the man she had married. But her mother had learned to love her husband again. Mhàiri didn't have her resolve. What she'd felt for Rob Dunn had been no more than a young girl's dream, but her love for Cameron felt real.

Rob Dunn stepped away from his mother. He gripped Mhàiri's arm and turned her to face him. 'Now I have returned, this changes things, don't you think?'

Mhàiri realised how heavily he had been drinking. His words were slurred and his anger plain. She wasn't his wife. In truth, even if he had remained in the strath, she doubted she ever would have been. But now wasn't the time to be telling him this. 'Perhaps when you have sobered Rob Dunn, we can talk as friends.' She pulled back and planted her fists on her hips. 'Have any of you heard word of Micheal? Mòrag Mòr is filled with concern for her son.'

Rob Dunn shook his head as if trying to focus his thoughts. 'Not long before we left, Micheal was reported missing.'

One of the other soldiers nodded. 'He wasn't amongst the dead. No one knows if he escaped or was taken prisoner.'

Rob Dunn rubbed a hand down the length of his face. 'I will visit Mòrag Mòr tomorrow. Let her know.'

Mhàiri saw a trace of the old Rob in his manner and she

91

clasped his hand in hers. 'She will like that.' She made to step away but turned back to face him. 'I am to be married in two weeks to Cameron MacÀidh. You are welcome to attend with your family. She lowered her voice. 'But, if you plan on causing trouble, stay away.'

18

PIPERS AND PLAIDS

On the morning of her wedding, Mhàiri sat on a bench outside her parent's cottage and watched for her guests arriving. Her freshly washed hair blew in the gentle breeze. The sun, appearing in the blue sky, whispered promises of a warm day to come.

Aunt Úna and her husband were the first to arrive, each carrying a basket and leading a cow. Her husband attached the ropes tied around the cows' necks onto stakes in the ground so that they could feed on the grass.

They made their way over to Mhàiri. 'With no heath, the cows have been wandering off,' Aunt Úna said. 'They're so thin I am not sure how much longer they'll survive without grazing.' She immediately set to, helping Mhàiri's mother bake bannocks and organise the food to be taken over to the meeting-house.

Her uncle joined Mhàiri's father who was setting out benches and tables, both inside and outside the meeting-house. Mhàiri looked over at the thin cows foraging in the ground for blades of grass. Bones protruded through the wrinkled skin on their backs. Tomorrow her uncle would take them up to the higher pasture, but without regular feeding, Mhàiri doubted they would last until the winter.

Hearing her name called, she turned. Cameron and his father had wheeled barrels of ale up the brae and were setting them outside. Mhàiri skipped over to Cameron.

After ushering them aside, his father handed Mhàiri the ten pounds that would have been used for Cameron's fare. 'Be sure to keep that safe. Don't spend it.' He tapped her hand. 'Do you hear? No matter how hard things get, and they will at times, keep that money safe. If you do decide to join us, this will help with your fares.'

Mhàiri nodded.

His face grave, Cameron's father touched his son's arm. 'Work hard to save for Mhàiri's fare. Join us as soon as you can? God forbid that you delay. The thought of you joining us is the only thing stopping your mother from staying. I know neither of you want to emigrate but things could change.'

Hattie Bantrach approached, halting further discussion. She handed Cameron a small basket containing four eggs. 'They are from your resurrected chicken.' She set off again, guffawing with laughter.

'Don't ask,' Cameron said to his father and frowned at Hattie's retreating back.

His father raised his eyebrows. 'Perhaps after a few whiskies, you will tell me the story.'

The piper appeared rolling a barrel of ale. Mhàiri placed the ten pounds into her pocket and left the men talking. Over eighty guests had now arrived from around Strathnaver and the Strath of Kildonan, all of them bearing gifts, mostly towards the wedding feast. Iain and Fearghas carried Mòrag Mòr into the meeting-house in her chair and set it down near to the door so that she could watch the women set up the tables. Mòrag Mòr had woven two blankets. She handed them to Mhàiri as she passed, and Mhàiri thanked her. Excitement pumped through Mhàiri's very being.

She laid the blankets down and pulled Connor into her arms as he tried to race past her following a squad of squealing children. 'Calm down Connor or you will be too tired to see the day through.' He wriggled and tried to break free from her grip. 'Let me go.'

'Do you hear me, Connor? Calm down.'

With his lips pursed, he nodded, and she opened her arms. He raced off and glanced over his shoulder. Mhàiri wagged a finger, and he slowed to a walk. Still smiling, she noticed Anna talking to the fiddler's wife. She picked up Mòrag Mòr's blankets and made her way over.

Anna linked into Mhàiri's arm. 'There are enough here helping set up. You are just getting in their way. It is time to get you ready.'

Mhàiri caught sight of her father and turned to look over her shoulder. 'He has started on the whisky already.'

'He will be fine, Mhàiri. Let him celebrate.'

She nodded. 'I just hope he doesn't become argumentative later, with Màthair. I don't know how she puts up with him when he is in one of his maudlin moods. She has little enough sleep without him keeping her up half the night; singing songs or shouting about her faults.'

'He is not the only man to do that, Mhàiri. It is the war that changes them.'

'After tonight, I won't be there to help settle him when his anger becomes too much for him to bear.'

'Your mother will manage. Now, let me get you ready.'

Mhàiri changed into her wedding clothes. Anna positioned the sections of plaid, just as Mòrag Mòr had shown her. She pulled a strand from the front of each side of Mhàiri's hair and tied them together at the back of the head with a blue ribbon.

Above the ribbon, she wound small blue and white flowers into the hair. Anna had dried some summer blooms and gave them to her to carry. She hugged Mhàiri. 'It is time to go.'

Mhàiri's mouth dried and her heart beat faster. She touched the MacÀidh brooch on her plaid for good luck and took a deep breath. As she headed out the door, she made sure she put her right foot out first.

A loud cheer erupted.

Cameron smiled and stepped towards her— dressed in a kilt, his dark-blonde hair swept back from his face, his blue eyes shining. He had never looked more handsome, and Mhàiri linked into his arm.

The piper played a lively tune and they set off behind him and the minister to make the walk to the meeting-house; taking a long route around the township. The wedding party cheered again and set into step behind them. When they stopped outside the meeting-house the guests gathered around Mhàiri and Cameron. The piper stopped playing and the minister took up a position at the front.

He held up his hand. 'We are gathered for the marriage between Mhàiri nic Niall and Cameron MacÀidh. In joining together in the eyes of God, do you promise to keep each other only unto yourselves and make life's journey together through hardship and ill-health and through good times and bad?'

Mhàiri looked into Cameron's eyes. 'I take you to my hand, my heart, and my spirit to be my chosen one. To desire and be desired by you, to possess you, and be possessed by you, without sin or shame, for nothing can exist in the purity of my love for you. I promise to love you wholly and completely without restraint, in sickness and in health, in plenty and in poverty, in life and beyond, where we shall meet, remember, and love again.'

When the minister had completed the ceremony, he smiled.

'In the eyes of God, you are now husband and wife. What, there-
fore, God has joined together, let no man put asunder.'

Cameron lifted Mhàiri into his arms. Her face flushed as his
lips met hers. A loud cheer erupted followed by a chant of,
'Feast. Feast. We are famished.'

In total agreement with the sentiments of the wedding party,
Mhàiri linked into Cameron's arm and led the party in to the
wedding feast.

On the edge of the crowd, Mhàiri noticed Rob Dunn glow-
ering at Cameron. Her step faltered, but she forced herself to
keep smiling.

19

CRADLE AND CAKE

The ale and the whisky flowed, and the wedding feast was consumed amidst loud banter. Rob Dunn had remained beside his parents and, so far, hadn't approached either Mhàiri or Cameron. That was fine by Mhàiri. She had other concerns on her mind. When she felt filled to the full, she stood. She caught Cameron's mother's attention and signalled that she wanted to talk. The woman rose and followed Mhàiri out of the meeting-house.

They remained silent as they walked together past the full tables outside. When they were out of everyone's hearing, Mhàiri turned to face her mother-in-law. She rubbed at her wedding band. 'I will take good care of him.'

'You had better, or you will have me to answer to.'

Mhàiri stared at her, and her mother-in-law smiled. 'You will try to join us abroad, Mhàiri? That way I won't feel as if I have lost another son, but have gained another daughter.'

Mhàiri nodded. 'Perhaps we might one day. Mind you, I am not promising. The removals look set to continue. Had that not been the case, I wouldn't consider leaving the strath.'

Tears sprung up in the older woman's eyes and she brushed

them away with her hand. 'I never wanted to leave either. But circumstances are such that I need to secure the best life for my children. That is why I was set against you marrying Cameron. Holding him here where the hard life we know is set to become harder. Of that, I am certain.'

Mhàiri nodded. 'It wouldn't be easy for me to leave my family behind. They will never leave Strathnaver.'

'You and Cameron will soon have a family of your own. Seeing my grandchildren grow. Helping to keep them safe is all I ask.'

'I understand and will think about it.'

'You know in your heart that Cameron would have been better coming with us. It is only you holding him here.'

Mhàiri opened her mouth to protest but closed it again. For the moment, she'd made some sort of peace with Cameron's mother. She remained silent as they walked back to the meeting-house. When they entered, Mhàiri's mother stood.

Mhàiri listened enthralled as Màthair sang the song she had sung at the sheilings.

'I met my darling, wandering free,
    He said to me, come away with me,
    He asked me to dance, the dance of life with him,
    His mother she was a MacÀidh, and soon so was I.
    Our firstborn son had his father's name,
    He grew and met a bonnie lass or three,
    But said none of them are meant for me.
    I will look for a lass by the name of MacÀidh,
    And she will dance the dance of life with me.'

An arm linked into Mhàiri's. She turned to see her mother-in-law's tear-filled eyes. 'It is true right enough, *A Mhàiri.*' She let out a deep breath. 'Cameron has made his choice, and the sooner I accept that, the better.'

Hopefully, Rob Dunn had too, Mhàiri thought as she spotted his face in the crowd. She turned her attention back to her mother-in-law. 'We will be living together, now. We just need to get on with it.'

'It won't be for long. We will be leaving soon. I can now go content, knowing you are both wed and no longer thinking about being together in sin.' Cameron's mother looked around. Spotting her husband, she set off in his direction.

Mhàiri watched her leave. How did Cameron's mother always manage to have the last word?

Rob Dunn tapped Mhàiri's arm. 'Can we talk?'

She glanced around. 'Not now, Rob Dunn. Not here. Not in front of everyone.'

'I am not going to cause any trouble. It was just the shock of seeing you . . . and hearing that you were to be wed. In truth, the drink had got the better of me.'

She wanted to walk away but Rob Dunn appeared to be sober. 'It had, indeed.'

'I wanted to let you know that I am leaving. Today. Now.'

'Leaving Strathnaver?'

He swallowed and held his head down. 'I won't lie. There is a great anger raging through me.'

'Well, I noticed that.'

'My anger can be put to better use. I cannot stand idly by and watch the straths destroyed. I am going into the hills to join the Kildonan men. They need all the help they can get.'

'Take care, Rob Dunn,' she said and meant it.

He grinned. 'Mind you, if it had been anyone other than Cameron MacÀidh you were marrying, I wouldn't have let you go without a fight. Cameron is a good man.'

She recalled the way Rob Dunn had always made a joke out

of his troubles and grinned back. For a moment, she had seen a glimpse of the Rob she had known and remembered. 'The Lord be with you. The tenants will be grateful for what you are doing.'

Mhàiri remained watching as Rob Dunn strode from the township. He too was a good man. When she could no longer see him, she made her way back into the meeting-house. The tables had been cleared and pushed back towards the walls. The room barely held all the guests and the piper had set up outside for dancing, leaving the fiddler inside.

Peigi Ruadh pushed back her red hair and smiled at Mòrag Mòr's son, Iain. He asked her to dance. Cameron pulled Mhàiri outside behind them.

As she settled into Cameron's arms, all thought of Peigi Ruadh, Rob Dunn and her mother-in-law disappeared.

'Are you happy, *A Mhàiri, mo ghràidh*— Mhàiri, my love,' he whispered in her ear.

His warm breath hit her cool skin, and she shivered. Snuggling closer, she closed her eyes.

* * *

The evening wore on and the sun set. The sky darkened. Fires and lamps were lit, setting up moving shadows. People drifted off into chattering groups, many with eyes heavy with drink. The children grew tired and, as they dozed off, were placed on top of the straw and covered with a blanket.

Cameron helped Iain lift Mòrag Mòr's chair; to take her home. The piper stood and waved at him. 'Take care there, laddie. Don't you be doing yourself' an injury, you will be needed tonight.'

The guests around them roared with laughter, and Mhàiri joined in.

A red flush crept up Cameron's neck. He turned to the piper.

'Very amusing, but as you are so concerned you can help us carry the chair.'

When Cameron returned with Iain and the piper, the young men surged forward and lifted him into the air. On seeing this, the women gathered around Mhàiri and followed the men over to Mhàiri's cottage. Peigi Ruadh stood back and watched with a smile on her face. As the cottage was too small to hold them all, Iain and Fearghas carried Cameron in and dumped him onto a bed of straw that had been made up on the floor. Anna and Aunt Úna followed behind with Mhàiri and set her down beside Cameron.

The fiddler's wife came in, carrying a slice of the bride's cake; baked by Mhàiri's mother. She crumbled the cake between her fingers and scattered the broken pieces over Mhàiri and Cameron's heads. As the crumbs dropped, everyone cheered. The omens were good that the marriage would be fruitful.

Mhàiri wiped crumbs from Cameron's hair and laughed. Fearghas and Iain who had disappeared during the cake scattering returned carrying a cradle bedecked with white ribbons. They set the cradle down beside the bed. Amidst calls that Mhàiri and Cameron were to make sure to fill the cradle soon and to keep it filled, the guests departed.

Alone with Cameron, shyness overcame Mhàiri. Her parents and Connor would sleep in the meeting-house tonight along with some of the tenants from the other townships. Mhàiri looked at the cradle and its significance was not lost on her. She reached behind her head to remove the flowers from her hair.

'Let me do that,' Cameron said. After removing the flowers, he untied the blue ribbon and her hair fell around her face. He combed his fingers through her auburn locks. When he kissed the side of her face, tracing a line of soft kisses to her mouth, Mhàiri's shyness melted like butter on a hot day and she returned his kiss with a passion she had until now not known she possessed.

20

HIGH HOPES

In the study at his sheep farm, the factor signed a letter he'd penned. He sat back in the desk chair, placed his hands together as if in prayer and carefully read through his words. Since the day he'd caught the Sheriff-Substitute poaching, McKid had harboured a personal and ongoing gripe with him. In his letter, he wanted to inform Lady Stafford about McKid's latest act of vindictiveness towards him. Satisfied that he'd made his point, he sprinkled a dusting of sand over the ink, sealed the paper and rang the hand-bell on his desk.

His housekeeper entered and tilted her head to the side, waiting on his instructions.

He handed her the letter. 'Ah! Miss Lowrie. Make sure this gets tae Her Ladyship the day.'

'I'll give it to my young lad. He can ride over with it.' She placed the letter into her apron pocket.

'Now, what is for luncheon? I need you tae serve early. I am leaving soon for Strathnaver.'

'I've a tasty mutton and vegetable stew simmering. It is ready to serve whenever you are.' Miss Lowrie opened the door to leave but turned. 'If you don't mind me saying, Mister Sellar, you work too hard. You've been busier than ever these last few weeks.'

He waved a hand. 'Nae more than most others. Now that I have the new lease in Strathnaver an' Strath o' Kildonan, I have tae get my new sheep farms organised there as well as doing my work here. An', I still need tae carry out my duties as factor. Money doesn't make itself.'

'That is as may be, but you don't need to be wearing yourself out in the process.' She laughed. 'As my mother always said, "there are no pockets in a shroud".'

'My faither would agree wholeheartedly with her on that.' Touched by her comment, he smiled. 'I appreciate your concern but you are worrying needlessly about me. A spot o' hard work never harmed anyone. I'll rest when the task at hand is done.'

Once the housekeeper closed the door behind her, he rose from the chair. He looked out the window at his sheep farm. In truth, he did feel tired. He was trying to set up his new sheep farms, but everything seemed to be working against him. He'd been interviewing shepherds for weeks and hadn't found anyone suitable. More importantly, Whitsunday had come and gone without any tenants being moved from his land. As long as they remained, he couldn't shift his large stock of sheep from here. And, this posed a problem. Every day, more of his sheep died for want of free grazing. The longer the land he'd leased went unused the more money he lost.

After finishing his meal, he strapped his luggage onto his saddle and set out to meet a shepherd who wanted to take on a tenancy for a sheep farm. John Riddell came from the border country, somewhere in the Ettrick Valley. Unlike most others he'd interviewed, this man seemed to have the experience he was looking for, but he had to be sure.

He'd arranged to stay overnight with a justice of the peace, near the mission where he would meet the shepherd the following morning. He made the journey there with enough time left to enjoy a light supper and a whisky with his host before retiring. By the time he climbed into bed, and despite his earlier uncertainties, he harboured high hopes that John Riddell would prove a suitable applicant.

In good spirits the following morning, he set out for the mission. The ride proved pleasant, and he relaxed for the first time in weeks. After a long, hard winter the spring had proved mellow and the weather now held a hint of summer.

When he arrived, the minister waved in acknowledgement. He guessed that the man with him was the shepherd, and he cast an appraising eye over him. Though not in any way grand, the man was dressed well enough in a twill jacket and dark trousers. The man raised his bonnet. And well-mannered, he thought.

As soon as he dismounted the shepherd shook his hand. 'John Riddell.'

The man had a firm grip. Sellar liked that. His first impression proved favourable and he returned the greeting. 'We can set off straight away an' I will show you the land I have in mind. I have high hopes that it will prove most profitable as a sheep-farm.'

The minister nodded his agreement. 'There will be a meal waiting for you both when you get back. I'll catch up on your news then.'

As they rode towards the area he planned to clear next, the factor tried to find out about the sheep farmer. 'The area I am taking you tae see is one o' the largest. I'm looking for someone experienced tae manage a sheep-farm there. I have had the heath burned out. There should be abundant shrubs for the incoming sheep. If it is tae big, just say. I've a couple o' smaller holdings.'

The shepherd smiled. 'The Cheviot sheep are hardy beggars.

They can survive anywhere. For ma needs, the larger the fairm the better. And, you've no need to doubt me, I've experience in abundance.'

'Is it Cheviot sheep you manage?'

'Aye.'

'It is Cheviots I bought. There's great enthusiasm for trying the breed up north. Few breeds survive the harsh winters here. With the war ending cattle is nae longer in demand.'

The shepherd nodded. 'The profit now is to be made frae mutton an' wool. Any guid shepherd would be mair than able to set up Cheviots here. Have the people no desire to fairm sheep?'

'None at all. They've nae knowledge o' such matters.'

'Truth be telt, I'm more feared o' the natives than ony winter, harsh, or no'. The ones I've seen were savages. Coming frae the border o' the English-speaking Lowlands, I find their language . . . strange.' The shepherd scoffed and added. 'How dae you understand what ony o' them say?'

'I don't. If these natives would only rouse themselves tae learn English it would make it easier for everyone. But, as in most things aimed at progress, they've proved reluctant. They talk in their strange tongue an' remain uninvolved in the improvements. Instead, they cling tae the auld ways. There's none o' them suited tae sheep farming or any other kind o' farming.'

They reached the bottom of a hill, and the factor pulled his horse to a halt. He dismounted and signalled for the shepherd to follow. They climbed to the top.

The factor pointed. 'There is the sheep-farm I have in mind for you.'

'How much land is included?'

The factor waved his hands 'The farm below an' a' the heath stretching frae it. A' the way tae the next farm, there in the distance, an' east and westward the pastures for as far as you can see.'

'There's smoke rising frae thon cottages below. Do folk still live in them?'

'Aye, that township still has tae be cleared.'

'Turnips will grow in abundance here for the sheep.'

'You are a man o' my ain heart. This farm is yours if you want it.'

The shepherd turned and shook his hand. 'How soon are we talking?'

'Well, I was due tae start clearing the tenants out at Whitsunday, but I've fallen behind schedule. I plan on starting next month, whether their coastal houses are ready, or not. All going well, I will have this land ready for you by early autumn. It pleases me that my largest farm will be managed by someone like yourself.'

Excitement coursed through his belly for the changes he had in mind. He visualised how it would be. People would talk about his success for years to come. There was money to be made from sheep farming and he knew exactly how to do it. If only the tenants would move to the coast and McKid would leave him alone.

Elizabeth hurried through the corridors of her Scottish castle. She entered her husband's study and held up a letter. 'I have received another complaint from Mister Sellar. That man is continually annoying me now with trifles. I'm losing my patience and changing my good opinion of him.' She collapsed into a chair beside the unlit fire and dabbed her forehead with a handkerchief.

Her husband stood from his desk and ambled over. He took the letter and adjusted his spectacles. After reading it through, he frowned. 'Sellar is always convinced he is in the right and takes pleasure in condemning those who disagree with him.'

'Only last week he tried to cause ill-blood between us and one of the other factors.' Elizabeth considered this for a moment. 'I think he's envious of their successes.'

'So, what has McKid done to annoy him now? Has Sellar caught him poaching again?'

'No doubt we will find out. I wish Mister Sellar would settle to the job at hand.'

'Yes, dear. So do I.' Her husband shuffled back to his desk and pointed to a drawing. 'I'm glad you have arrived. I need you to look over the plan for the new fishing village. Our agents advise reducing the size of the lots. . . to accommodate more removed tenants.'

'Smaller lots?'

'Their reasoning seems sound enough. If we provide too much ground, they believe the tenants will try to farm it and live off their own produce.'

Elizabeth made her way over and looked down at the drawing. She tapped a finger against her top lip. 'So, in effect, if we allocate large lots nothing will have changed.'

'There is no question about it. The tenants need to take up employment. With the drop in cattle prices, it is the only way they'll be able to pay us their rents. And, if they can't pay, they may well turn to the likes of Lord Selkirk.'

Elizabeth frowned. 'I cannot fathom why Lord Selkirk got involved in one of these colonisation schemes. It doesn't make sense. Why would he waste his inheritance on such a cause?'

'His talk is full of social reform. He claims such ideas are sweeping through Scotland.'

'Humph!' Elizabeth replied and shook her head. 'He believes the poor and displaced should be helped to emigrate. Humph! To North America! It is odd. He didn't strike me as a liberal thinker when we met in Paris during the revolution.'

Elizabeth sat beside her husband. 'Selkirk is fond of attaching himself to 'good' causes. But if this estate is to be brought into the 19th century, then emigration needs to be stopped. The poor *don't* need to emigrate, they need to work. And, there is much work here. Yes. Less ground will encourage the tenants to take up the coastal employments. Reply to our agents. Tell them to make the lots smaller.'

21

TINKERS AND TEARS

Mhàiri arrived at the dock with Cameron, to see his family off. They made their way to the harbour, where his mother, father and sisters would board a ship bound for Stromness in the far north of Scotland. Once there, they would wait on the Hudson Bay ship that would take them over to the Red River Settlement.

Cameron was quiet. It was as if he had something he wanted to say but couldn't. Mhàiri understood; unless he emigrated, it might be the last time he saw his family. She chewed on her bottom lip. If she emigrated, she would have to leave *her* family. Why did life have to be so difficult?

Dressed in their best travelling clothes, Cameron's sisters, Eilidh and Marta, strolled one on each side of Mhàiri. At the front, his parents each led a horse, carrying their belongings. Cameron walked beside his mother. Mhàiri left him to it.

Time and again, Mhàiri's head turned first one way and then the other, as she tried to take in her surroundings. Never had she witnessed anything like it. Everywhere she looked, people milled about. Somewhere in the distance, bagpipes sounded out a haunting lament, adding to the sense of confusion. She recalled the journey she'd made to Golspie in the bitter cold and shivered. But, unlike that December day, the present June morning proved pleasant. Dressed in a long skirt and a summer shawl, she relished the sea breeze.

Her thoughts turned to the Red River Valley. What would it be like? Would a warm breeze be blowing? She had heard tales of snow lying so deep in winter that grown men sank into the deep drifts to be lost without a trace until the snow thawed in the spring. Though the winters were harsh in Strathnaver, she couldn't imagine surviving such conditions.

Eilidh gripped Mhàiri's arm and pointed. '*Seall*. Look.'

A white-haired man stood on the back of a cart and called out to them as they passed, 'The Lord said, 'repent'.'

Eilidh leant closer and whispered to Mhàiri, 'Look away.'

'But he could get into trouble for preaching there.'

'That's as maybe, but do not draw his attention.'

'And there, look.' Marta giggled as she pointed to a kilted man dancing on his own.

'Drunk?' Mhàiri said, and Eilidh and Marta nodded and hurried on.

The closer they got to the harbour, the thicker the crowds grew. A family huddled under a makeshift shelter of branches with blankets tied to the top caught Mhàiri's attention. Her step slowed. They didn't seem like travellers. The children looked thin and unwashed.

Marta gripped Mhàiri's arm and hurried her on. 'They have likely been removed from their home. Don't stare. They won't be the only tinkers you'll see. The docks are a draw to those left to wander.'

'Tinkers,' Mhàiri said and turned to look back at the family.

'Most likely they paid no rent, so they wouldn't be given a house on the coast. They live off the fish waste here. And— ' Marta pointed to a crate of coal on the dockside. 'Any spillage they can gather. They sell what they can't eat. Maighstir MacCoinnich warned us we might see this.'

'But that is no life they lead.'

Eilidh snorted. 'Likely that is what the factor said when he turned them out. I am sure they would rather live that life than this. We are fortunate. We had the option to emigrate.'

Mhàiri quickened her pace. There was some truth to what Eilidh said. What would happen if her family was removed and had nowhere to go? They too would be forced to wander the countryside, homeless and referred to as tinkers. Like a blanket removed to reveal a bright light, Mhàiri now understood why Cameron's family had decided to emigrate. Had she been wrong to refuse to go with them?

'Mhàiri,' Cameron called and pointed to a large open-fronted hut.

She nodded and made her way over with Eilidh and Marta. Outside the hut, filled with barrels, a white-whiskered cooper talked, while a young lad beside him demonstrated the many uses for their barrels. The family positioned themselves beside the small group who had gathered to watch.

'Are ye' bound fir' the New Land?' the white-whiskered man asked, and Cameron's father nodded.

'Then you'll need some o' these here barrels. A couple o' shilling each, but worth every penny. You'll find a hundred uses for them when ye' get there.' The cooper tapped the top of one. 'Ye' can use them for a table, stools or a meal store. But, more importantly, this here barrel will keep yer' belongings safe and dry on yer' journey. Aye, they've been treated with tar to keep oot the water . . . or––' The cooper paused for effect, and the young man picked up a pail. 'Tae' keep the water in,' he said, and the lad poured the water into a barrel. 'When ye' get tae' where yer' going ye' can use them tae' gather rainwater. And . . .' He pointed to Cameron's mother. 'Cut in half ye' can soak yer' clothes in ane side while washing yerself in the other.'

The crowd laughed, and Mhàiri joined in.

Impressed with the size and quality of the barrels, and declaring their need for them, Cameron's father bought two. On arriving in the New Land, the family would be taken upriver on a boat. There would be none of the new steamships Mhàiri had heard about for them.

In a small clearing, Mhàiri helped sort the blankets, clothes and food Cameron's family would need for the long journey ahead. The rest of their belongings were stored in the barrels. They packed two butter pats, a cheesemaker, thread, needles, wool, dishes and their kettle and pot into one. In the other, they packed blankets, clothes, a gun, an axe, and small sacks of grain and potatoes that would be used for planting when they got there. They divided up the remainder of the clothes and food and wrapped them in four blankets; one for each traveller. Cameron's family each hoisted a bundle onto their shoulders and they made towards a building where they could stable the horses for a few pennies. Mhàiri and Cameron would ride the mounts home.

After a hurried meal of water, cheese and dried fruit, they made their way to the dockside. The smell of raw fish and tar grew stronger. Bile rose from Mhàiri's belly. She held a hand to her mouth and said to Cameron, 'I hope their journey fares better than last year.'

He shook his head. 'Hopefully they won't get the fever that struck then. I'm glad they didn't get passages on that ship.'

While Cameron's father arranged for a porter to take their barrels on board, Mhàiri and the others joined the queue waiting to board the large ship laying to anchor in the harbour. A tall man with stooped shoulders shouted names from a book. He called them in alphabetical order. Those whose names started with A to D had already boarded. E to H had already been called and now formed into a line. Next, he would call for names beginning with I to L, then it would be time for

Cameron's family to board. A lump formed in Mhàiri's throat and she swallowed. Despite her initial dislike of Cameron's mother, the woman had taken her to live in her home and an understanding of sorts had developed between them; they now accepted that they each had Cameron's best interests at heart.

As Mhàiri waited for MacÀidh to be called, she watched a group of women gutting fish. Dressed in small tartan shawls tied around their heads and larger ones around their waists, the women stood behind a line of tables outside a large hut. They worked quickly, tossing the fish into barrels and letting the head and innards fall into baskets on the ground. This is the life the Great Lady wanted for her. Mhàiri shuddered and turned away. The work looked hard, and the women's bandaged hands red raw. Eilidh and Marta had escaped, but would such a fate await her? And what fate awaited Cameron? Looking out across the wide expanse of sea, she rubbed her churning belly.

At last, the white-whiskered clerk called, 'M to O step forward and form an orderly queue. Get in line. Hurry up. We don't have a' day.'

Cameron's mother clung to him and wept. After pulling herself away, she hugged Mhàiri and between sobs said, 'Remember what I said. Think about following us out. Anyone can see that Cameron wants to go. The only thing holding him back is you. I have had my say, now it is up to you. I will write when we know where we're staying. Write back. I'll send my letters to Maighstir MacCoinnich . . . in case you're moved.'

Although she felt uncomfortable at her mother-in-law's words and closeness, Mhàiri returned her embrace. 'Yes, write.' Reaching a decision she added, 'I will talk to Cameron. See if we can raise the money. So we can go, *if* the need arises.'

Cameron's mother stopped sobbing. 'Did you say you will consider emigrating?' She whispered in Mhàiri's ear. 'I cannot wait to see that child you are carrying. My first grandchild.'

'What?' Mhàiri stared at her, puzzled.

'Feeling queasy?'

She shook her head. But she had been feeling a bit . . . queasy. Could her mother-in-law be right? Counting out the days on her fingers since her last bleed, realisation dawned and she beamed. If the woman was right, she would know soon enough. Still feeling dazed, she turned and hugged Marta and then Eilidh.

She remained on the dock with Cameron and waved his family off. When the ship moved away, Cameron leant towards her. 'What did Màthair whisper?' His voice sounded heavy as if it would break with sorrow.

Though she wanted to tell him, caution took over; it was better to wait until she was certain. 'She said to talk to you about following them out. That you still wanted to emigrate. Do you?'

When Cameron didn't answer, Mhàiri linked into his arm and they set off for home.

22

COCKEREL CROWS

M hàiri awoke to the sound of a cockerel crowing. The noise seemed louder than usual. In her half-asleep state, she tried to figure out why. She opened her eyes and scanned the bedroom. Everything appeared unfamiliar: the glass window, the whitewashed walls and the smell of fresh wood.

The night before slowly came back to her— Returning home late. Cameron carrying her through to his parent's bedroom and laying her down on the bed amidst much laughter. The new bed he had promised her when they had sat together on the hillside deciding when to marry. He had remembered his promise and had arranged for Iain and Fearghas to build the bed while they'd been away seeing his family off. And, he'd kept the secret so well she hadn't suspected a thing.

She lifted herself up onto one elbow, swept her long, auburn hair back from her face and gazed down at her sleeping husband. Since they had wed, she'd felt pleasure at waking beside him. The early morning light shone through the uncovered window, illuminating his face. She could get used to having a window in her bedroom. The thought made her smile.

Sensing Cameron's grief, she had wanted to tell him last night that she would emigrate, but the words would have been false; joining his family would mean leaving her own behind and she wasn't ready to do that.

She pulled the blankets back and stepped from the bed. Not wanting to wake Cameron, she tiptoed around as she picked up her skirt, blouse and boots and carried them through to the main room. After she had washed and dressed, she blew on the embers and added more peat to the fire. The fire took, and she put a pot of milk on to heat. She drank the warm milk and explored the living area in a way that she hadn't been able to when her in-laws had been around. She trailed a hand along the large dresser and relished the feel of the smooth wood and the sight of three blue patterned cups; which Cameron's father had brought back from a working trip to the Lowlands. Pottery bowls lined one shelf. Mhàiri lifted two down and laid them onto the wooden table.

Unlike her parent's home, where a blanket covered the space between the house and the byre, a wooden door separated these two areas. Mhàiri liked that. She also liked the way the small window brightened the room. She hummed as she retrieved the dried flowers Anna had given her to carry on her wedding day and placed them into a dish on the dresser. When she stepped back to admire the display, an arm snaked around her waist.

Mhàiri smiled and tilted her face upwards to receive Cameron's kiss. 'I cannot believe we have our own home.'

'For how long? I am thinking it might have been best if we had emigrated too.'

She turned and searched his face. Was he was telling her that they were to leave? Now they were married was Cameron already telling her what to do? If he was, then she would have no choice but to go with him. She licked her lips. 'But— I thought we had agreed.'

'I am not saying I am going back on my word. I am just

saying that we need to keep our options open. Maybe even find out how much it would cost for our passages. See when ships would be leaving.'

'My family are here. I want to stay in the strath. You know that. This is all the factor's doing. The Great Lady and the Good Lord will look after us.'

He kissed the top of her head and stepped away. 'You put too much faith in the Great Lady. And the Lord. But, yes, we can leave it for now. We will talk more about this later. I best get on. With Father gone, there is much for me to do.'

Mhàiri picked up a pail and made her way through to the byre. As she milked the first of their cows, doubts circled in her mind. Cameron was her family now. Her first loyalty should be to him. But how could she push all thoughts of her parents aside? It was too soon. Doubts continued to plague her. The time she had most feared and prayed for in equal measures had arrived. Would she be able to run this house by herself? What was she thinking? Of course, she could. Màthair had taught her well.

Her thoughts turned to what Cameron had said about leaving. She would talk to him about emigrating. Let him know that as his wife, if he wanted her to, she would board a ship bound for North America. She would miss her family and her strath, but Cameron's doubts and the memory of the tinkers on the quayside disturbed her. Sheltered here, she hadn't realised the extent of what was happening. In truth, she had preferred to think it wouldn't happen. She couldn't stand idly by, to be thrust out of her home and left to wander the countryside. No doubt, Cameron had already realised this. With no land to farm, how would they survive? And, if Cameron's mother was right, they now had a child to think about.

Mhàiri made her way through to the main room and placed a pot of water on the fire. She stirred in a few handfuls of oats and added a sprinkling of salt. Would her cooking be as good as

Cameron's mother? She laid the spurtle down and paced over and stared out the window. What was wrong with her? It wasn't as if she hadn't cooked before. She had everything she could want, and more. Why was she thinking this way?

She made to turn away, but stopped when she saw her mother racing up the brae; her eyes wide with terror. Dear God, what has happened? By the time she had flung open the door, her mother was already standing outside clutching the latch.

Filled with fear, Mhàiri gripped her mother's arm. 'What has happened? Is something wrong with Connor . . . Father?'

Màthair shook her head and slumped forward.

Mhàiri took the woman's arm, helped her inside and sat her on a chair. 'Màthair, you are frightening me. What is wrong?'

Màthair drew in a deep breath then let it out slowly. 'My sister. Úna has been told to leave. She must remove everything. Now.'

'What? Leave her home? Today?' Though she had tried not to think about them, she couldn't push the removals away any longer. Mhàiri hunkered down onto one knee and looked Màthair in the eye. 'Evicted?'

'Úna had another visit from the factor . . . this morning. The devil gave the tenants two hours to get their belongings out and leave. They have to move to the coast.'

'Two hours.' Mhàiri couldn't take it in. How could her aunt make ready to leave in that short time? 'But—'

'We need to hurry if we are to help.' Màthair stood. 'The poor lad who came to tell us rode as fast as he could. Dear God, Úna's been given no choice but to leave.'

Mhàiri lifted the pot off the fire. Her thoughts swirled. She would have to find Cameron. He would know what to do. 'Where is Connor? Father?'

'Hattie Bantrach has Connor. Your father's ridden ahead with the men. Cameron's gone with them,' Màthair said as she made her way out the door.

Mhàiri grabbed a shawl and followed her outside. 'We can go over the brae. It will be faster.'

Màthair stopped in her tracks and gripped Mhàiri's arm. 'If I am not mistaken, you have got a baby to think about. Maybe you should stay here.'

A flush crept up Mhàiri's cheek. Of course, Màthair would have known. What had made her think otherwise? 'I am coming with you. I cannot stay here when I could be helping. We best get moving.'

Màthair hesitated and then nodded.

When they reached the top of the brae, Mhàiri's steps slowed. In the distance, grey smoke darkened the summer sky. Just beyond Aunt Úna's township, red and orange flames leapt up and filled the air with an acrid smell. With a groan, Mhàiri quickened her pace. With each step she took, the smell of burning grew stronger.

23

MAYHEM AND MEMORIES

M hàiri and her mother hurried towards Aunt Úna's township. When they arrived, her aunt raced towards them. Choking back tears, she called, 'It has started. We were given no choice. We have to leave. The factor came earlier—' She broke into sobs. 'I never thought this would happen. I thought the Great Lady would stop him. It is why I stayed put, why we all did.'

On hearing her aunt utter the same words she had said to Cameron that morning, *"The Great Lady will stop the removals,"* Mhàiri groaned. She looked around and tried to take in what was happening. Around the township, people hurtled belongings from their homes and barns and thrust them onto peat carts or bundled them at the gable ends of their cottages. In the distance, from the direction of the smoke-filled sky, a line of horses approached.

Màthair made to enter the cottage but stopped at the door. 'We best get moving if we're to get this cleared before they get here.'

Mhàiri looked around, her heart racing. 'Where is Cameron?'

With panic on her face, Aunt Úna pointed to a hill beyond the high pasture. 'He has gone with your father to find the men. They had already set off to bring back the cows. The poor beasts are half-starved. Every day they wander away.'

'If Cameron and Niall have gone to get them, the men will be back soon.' Màthair wiped her hands down her skirt. 'Until then, we need to get what we can out. Mhàiri, you fetch the blankets.'

Mhàiri's hands trembled as she crammed all the clothes and blankets she could fit into a large chest. With Màthair's help, she dragged it outside. Aunt Úna and Màthair hauled the spinning wheel to the gable end, beside pillows, pots and bowls, while Mhàiri returned inside and threw small items into a basket.

A sob caught in her throat. This was her aunt's life she was packing away. Is this what they had been reduced to— throwing a lifetime of memories into a basket? Anger welled up. It wasn't right. And why had the minister said that this was punishment for their sins? What sins had her aunt committed? What sins had any of them committed that the factor and his like hadn't?

A series of screams had Mhàiri rushing to the door. Maister Sellar and a group of at least fifteen men rode into the township, setting up clouds of dust. Mhàiri's belly turned, sending bile to her throat. The townspeople stopped what they were doing and watched the men approach. High pitched moans mingled with children crying and dogs barking.

Mhàiri gripped the open door and whispered, 'Lord in Heaven, help us. It has started.'

At the front of the large group, the factor tugged on the reins, and his horse came to an abrupt halt. He stood up in the stirrups and glanced around. Beneath the brim of his hat, his face turned white and then crimson. 'Why are you all still here? Did I, or did I not, issue you with notices to leave?'

No one moved or stepped forward.

Mhàiri gripped the door tighter. She stared at the man who

translated the factor's words as if transfixed by what he was saying.

'Well? I am waiting.' The factor glanced around. He pointed to a cottage with its roof timbers and thatch already removed. 'At least someone heeded me and moved out. But as for the rest of you . . . apart from three houses, for which the leases are not up, everyone else was ordered to go. Were you not?'

Four law officers slid from their mounts and stood two to each side of the factor's horse.

A child cried. Everyone else remained silent.

The factor dipped his chin onto his chest and boomed, 'Do you expect to live here rent-free?' He laughed as if amused at his own wit and tilted his beaked nose in the air. 'As you've left no time to remove your roof timbers, leave them be. You'll each be paid three shillings for them.'

A white-haired woman stepped out her doorway and dropped the basket she'd been carrying. She threw herself to the ground, wailing and scrabbling at the soil; the contents of the basket lying scattered at her side.

The factor sat down on the saddle and shouted orders to four law officers. 'This one first.' He pointed to the cottage belonging to the woman lying on the ground. 'That crone shouldn't be here. She moved in from another township and pays no rent.'

At least eight of the factor's men had dismounted and they now stood in front of him, their axes in clear view.

The white-haired woman lying prostrate on the ground screamed, and a dog barked.

In the distance, Cameron and the other men rode towards the township. Mhàiri staggered out the door to meet them. Màthair and Aunt Úna followed behind.

Cameron slid from his mount, and Mhàiri threw her arms around him and sobbed. 'Dear Lord, look what is happening?' His arms encircled her and she slumped against him.

Mhàiri's uncle made straight for his house and dragged the meal-box out. When her father placed a ladder against the cottage and climbed up to remove the roof timbers, a law officer stepped forward and roared, 'Leave them be.'

'We are not to be taking the timbers.' Aunt Úna said, her voice rising in fear.

Mhàiri's father stepped off the ladder and held up his hands, 'What? Are you saying that you are not to take your roof timbers? That is unheard of.'

Aunt Úna laid an axe into a box and closed the lid. 'We are to be paid for them.'

'And how are you meant to find good timber on the coast?' he asked.

Mhàiri couldn't make sense of it. 'Why are they doing this?'

Aunt Úna's shook her head. 'To prevent us from rebuilding our houses and returning to live in them, that is why.'

One of the lawmen set the trusses of the white-haired woman's cottage alight. The woman lay wailing on the ground. Two neighbours dragged her away from the door.

Cameron stepped forward and raised his fists.

'There is nothing any of us can do to stop this carnage,' Mhàiri's father said and grabbed hold of Cameron's arm. 'If you fight back, soldiers will be brought in and you will be arrested.'

A law officer entered Mhàiri's aunt's cottage, while the factor remained astride his horse outside. As if in a daze, Mhàiri followed the man inside. The officer flicked a hand at her. 'This house belongs to Mister Sellar now. You had best leave. There is nothing for you here anymore.'

Mhàiri's legs trembled, but she did as he asked. Unable to do anything to stop them, she watched, helpless as three men removed the thatch and timbers from the roof of her aunt's house and piled them up outside. One of the men torched the bundle, setting it alight.

The sound of the thatch catching and crackling sent shivers

of fear through Mhàiri. She groaned and sank to her knees. The smell made her retch.

Cameron knelt beside her and placed an arm around her shoulder. As she watched the flames leap and flare, Mhàiri's thoughts returned to the day her sister's clothes had caught fire. She felt the searing flames and flailed her arms. A sharp pain ripped through her belly and she slumped to the ground. Arms pulled her up, but her head flopped forward and she couldn't right herself. Her legs scrabbled beneath her as she tried to get leverage, but she couldn't get on to her feet. Warm liquid trickled down the inside of her legs.

* * *

Mhàiri awoke from a dark dream. She opened her eyes. Bright sunlight spilt through her bedroom window, blinding her with reality. She closed her eyes again. The dream had seemed so real. But now, the bits she could remember seemed . . . daft.

Daft or not, the fear she had felt remained. In the dream, she had been standing on a hillside looking down at her cottage when a strong wind started to blow. The walls of her home turned to dust, and the wind blew on the walls sending the dust spiralling upwards. The thatched roof crumbled inwards and caught fire; where it landed on the hearth. Orange and yellow flames plumed upwards, and the thatch crackled as it caught and spread.

Mhàiri groaned and opened her eyes, and the memories disappeared. Although the visions had only been snippets from her dream, she shuddered as she recalled the blazing timbers of her aunt's cottage. What if the dream had been a bad omen; a warning of things yet to come?

Unable to remain still, Mhàiri threw back the covers and sat on the edge of the bed. How long had she slept? An hour? Two, perhaps? She dropped her feet to the floor and made to stand.

'And where do you think you are going?' Màthair's voice called and her head appeared around the door.

Mhàiri caught her mother's eye and lowered her gaze. She wasn't in any mood to argue. 'What are you doing here, Màthair? Where's Cameron?'

'Get back into that bed. You have had a fright, lass.'

The events of the morning flashed before Mhàiri's eyes as if she were watching them again. 'No more than everyone else and less so than those who were removed.' Brooking no argument, she pulled a fresh petticoat and skirt from the dresser and stepped into them.

When Màthair shook her head, Mhàiri tilted her chin. 'Since when did you start proposing lying in bed as a remedy for a fright? I'm not lying here while there is work to be done.'

Having made her point, she stood and unsteadily made for the door. As she passed, Màthair reached out and held her. Enfolded in her mother's arms, Mhàiri sobbed. She could no longer push back the pain she felt and she let her tears fall.

She felt a tug on her skirt and looked down at her brother.

'Why are you crying, Mhàiri?'

Màthair pointed a finger at the door. 'Away you go, Connor. Leave Mhàiri be. Don't be pestering her with questions.'

Mhàiri pulled Connor into her arms and nuzzled into his neck. He was almost eight years old and too heavy to lift, but holding him comforted her. 'Mhàiri's fine. I am just tired,' she said and carried on into the main room. As she entered, her step faltered and she said to him, 'Be a good laddie and feed the hens for Mhàiri. Leave a bit back and take it up for Hattie Bantrach's hens.'

Connor nodded and hurried out the door.

Five minutes later, Mhàiri sat with her mother beside the fire, clutching a cup of nettle tea. 'I lost the baby, didn't I?'

'If it is God's will then you will have more.'

Mhàiri turned her gaze to the fire. There was no point

dwelling on what might have been. Regardless of the searing pain she felt for the loss of her baby, this was her lot and she had to accept it. Just as her mother had, many times before. It was God's will.

She lifted her head and ran her fingers through her hair. 'Would you emigrate, Màthair? If I have to go abroad with Cameron, would you come with us?'

Màthair looked up at the rafters and sighed. After a few minutes, she turned her gaze to Mhàiri. 'I have thought for a while that you might emigrate. Cameron has family to go to. And, let's face it, with the ever-increasing rents and talk of removals, there is nothing to keep you both here. But, your father and I . . . Well, it is different for us. I have my sister here. No doubt I will join her on the coast soon enough. Truth be told, your father has done all the travelling he intends to do. It wasn't easy for him, you know. Near ten years in total, he spent fighting in the wars. When he was abroad, he missed his home, more than he'll ever miss the fingers he lost there.'

Understanding dawned on Mhàiri and she nodded. 'Where is Cameron?'

'Out with your father. They should be back soon.'

'I cannot believe Aunt Úna has been moved. It will be us next—'

'Unless we do something.'

Mhàiri stared at her and saw a pink flush rise on her mother's cheeks. Moving her glance upward, she noticed flecks of grey hair. Her mother was growing old, just as she soon would. For the first time, Mhàiri realised that her family were at the mercy of those who held power over them. 'What can *we* do that will make any difference?'

24

PLOTS AND PLANS

It darkened outside, and the moon rose and lit the sky.
Mhàiri sat on a stool by the dying embers of the fire. She
knew she should bring in some peats but couldn't rouse herself
to action. Her belly knotted and she leant forward and groaned.
Over an hour had passed since Màthair had left and Cameron
still hadn't returned. Fear continued to build inside her that her
township would be next for eviction. Although she hadn't
received notice to leave, it was just a matter of time until she
did. Should she emigrate? She had the ten pounds for
Cameron's passage safely stowed away, but with the price of
cattle still dropping, how could they raise the ten pounds for
her passage?

She placed her hands on her belly. She hadn't told Cameron
about the baby, but the pain showing on his face when he had
found out about the loss told her that he was as devastated
about it as she was. The anger in his eyes had frightened her.
She had never seen him so enraged, and hoped that he wasn't
out there doing something daft. She rose from the stool and
looked out the window— to near darkness. After lighting the
candles, she placed a few peats on the fire. Her thoughts raced,

and she paced the room. Should they sell the animals they had left and try to get low-cost passages? What would her mother and father do? What about Connor? How would they manage?

The door opened and Cameron entered. Mhàiri threw herself into his arms and sobbed. In all her days, she had never been so relieved to see someone. Once she had satisfied herself of his safety, her crying ceased. She looked over his shoulder. Anna and Fearghas entered, followed by Mòrag Mòr's son, Iain. Then, Mhàiri's mother and father, the fiddler and his wife and other tenants from the township came in. They all seemed to be talking at once.

Why were people coming into her cottage? Mhàiri took a step back and looked up at Cameron. 'What is going on?'

He placed his mouth close to her ear, to be heard over the din. 'After what happened, we are not going to just sit by and do nothing. Are we? You will hear soon enough where I have been, but first I need to bring this hubbub to order.'

She followed Cameron through the growing crowd and stopped beside her mother. Her mother spoke, but Mhàiri couldn't make out what she said. She shook her head and pointed to the wall. They made their way there and jostled forward until they found a space near the front. Filled with so many bodies, the room felt stifling. Mhàiri dabbed at her forehead with her hand. Her mother stood beside her with her arm around Mhàiri's waist.

Cameron raised his hand. 'Silence. If you want to hear why you have been called here then you need to remain quiet.'

Once the chatter dwindled and died, Cameron spoke. 'What the factors and Lord and Lady Stafford call "removals", we call "evictions". What they call "improvements", we call "clearings". Have no doubt, these evictions will not stop until every last one of us has been cleared from our homes. To make way for sheep.'

Behind Mhàiri, Anna sobbed and Fearghas comforted her.

Mhàiri's father stepped forward. 'Brutally cleared. After we left today, we . . .' He pointed to Cameron. 'We met with some of our neighbours who experienced eviction in the Strath of Kildonan. We have been in discussion with them. And they agree, Maister Sellar's actions today cannot go unpunished.'

'The factor went too far this time,' Cameron said. 'Many people were injured. Two seriously.'

A collective gasp went up from the crowd, and people started talking amongst themselves.

'Silence!' Cameron shouted and the chatter settled to a hum and then stopped. 'We need to take action and everyone can help.'

'We can try. But they brought soldiers into Kildonan. They will not hesitate to do the same if we resist,' the fiddler said.

'That is as maybe,' Mhàiri's father said, 'but there are many ways to fight a battle. Hear first what Cameron has to say about what happened today and then judge for yourself if you will join us, or not.'

Mhàiri gazed around and followed the words as they floated around the room.

'A cotter's house was set ablaze while his mother-in-law was still abed, unable to leave,' Cameron said. 'When the woman was dragged out on her bedding, the blankets were smouldering.'

Cameron's account of the day went on, and Mhàiri swayed.

'The sick are lying in barns with no roofs. Two already near death.'

'The corn houses were destroyed.'

'The heaths have been burned out leaving nowhere for the animals to graze.'

'We cannot allow the factor's cruelty to go unchallenged. He has to be brought to account for his actions.'

Mhàiri focussed on the words, "brought to account". How could they do that? The thought of the cotter's house being set alight with his mother-in-law in it horrified her. She rubbed her belly. And, she had lost her baby. She rose up on her toes and said, 'How can *we* bring Maister Sellar to account?'

The fiddler's wife called, 'It is not possible?'

'The Kildonan men will support us,' Cameron said. 'They say we should send a petition to Lord and Lady Stafford. Make them aware of what happened today . . . of the injuries that resulted from the factor's orders. And, we should ask for Maister Sellar to be brought to account for destroying the corn houses and burning the heath.'

'All of this will cost,' Mhàiri's mother said. 'With the increased rents, we cannot afford to be fighting the factor. Even if the Great Lady and the Sheriff agreed that we could take him to trial.'

Cameron nodded, acknowledging her points. He rubbed a hand across the back of his neck. 'Some Kildonan men are hiding out in the hills. They have contacts in Edinburgh and in London. They will raise such a fuss in the newspapers and bring Maister Sellar's actions to the attention of as many leading figures as they can. As to the cost of bringing that devil to trial, they also had a suggestion about how we can raise the money.'

Mhàiri called, 'What? What do we have to do?'

'It will soon be time for the men to take the animals up to the sheilings,' Cameron replied.

'We cannot be going to the sheilings and leave our homes unattended,' the fiddler shouted. 'Are you daft? Our houses could be burned down while we are gone.'

Cameron held up a hand and waited for the noise to die down. 'The men will set up a distillery there. A large one.'

Mhàiri grasped the significance of what Cameron had said. Distilling whisky made sense. With the limits on how much whisky could legally be distilled and the high taxes on whisky, illegal stills could raise the money they needed.

Anna said, 'If we are caught, we will be imprisoned.'

'Then we need to make sure we are not caught,' Cameron

replied. 'By the time the men return home, the women will have arrived at the sheilings and will have a good few months to distil the whisky. Our contacts in Kildonan will make sure we have enough malted barley and will sell the raw whisky on. If we all go to the sheilings as normal and keep to our usual timings, no one will suspect a thing. We never start distilling until after the harvest has been gathered. The factor and his men will not be looking for stills until then.'

'And the profits we make will be used to fight the factor?' The fiddler pointed to his face. 'As you can tell from my ruddy cheeks, my wife is the best whisky distiller in these parts.' He coughed. 'I will be needing her to bring a bit back for me from the sheilings.' He coughed again. 'Just enough to see me through the winter.'

Mhàiri joined in the growing laughter. Most of the towns-people had small stills for their own use. Distilling whisky was second nature to them. She liked the idea. Perhaps they could stop the factor after all. Hope surged within her and she smiled at Cameron.

'Are we agreed then?' her father asked. 'The men will gather in the stills and take them up to the sheilings. We will have a few days at most to set them up before the women arrive. To avoid arousing suspicion, the men will return here as normal, to ready our homes for winter. The women will keep the stills going throughout the summer. A Petition of Complaint will also be drawn up and signed by everyone, including the tenants who were evicted. The petition will be sent to Lord and Lady Stafford. And, we will ask for Maister Sellar to be brought to account for his actions.'

PAINT AND PETITIONS

Elizabeth's Highland Castle

E lizabeth sat straight-backed on a stool in her garden. She dipped a paintbrush into a dish of clean water and then into the blend of blue, brown and yellow paint on her palette. Earlier, when she'd taken her morning stroll, a tree's unusual shape had caught her attention and her fingers had itched to paint it. She studied the hues of the bowed apple tree. Satisfied that she had selected the right colour to start, she bent towards the easel and dabbed the brush onto the paper.

Lost in the task of capturing the essence of the tree in water-colour, Elizabeth startled when her butler said, 'Excuse me, Ma'am.' She hadn't heard him arriving and fought to conceal her annoyance. The staff knew not to disturb her when she was at her easel. She dipped her brush into the water and picked up a rag and wiped the bristles. 'Speak. What is it?'

The butler bowed. 'I'm sorry to disturb you while you are painting, Ma'am, but Lord Stafford said I should inform you that Mister Loch has called. He wishes to talk to you both, most urgently. He is waiting for you in Lord Stafford's study.'

Elizabeth gave a curt nod and beckoned for her lady's maid to gather up the paints. They set off towards the front entrance, and the butler followed, carrying the brushes, palette and easel.

Elizabeth made her way alone up the main staircase. She smiled as she passed the full-sized portrait of her father in his kilt. When she reached the top, she glanced at the clock. It was only 11 am. What had brought her estate commissioner here, and at this early hour? Had it been her long absence?

For some time now, her husband had not been keeping well, and the journey north taxed him. He had become slower in his movements. And of late, he had taken to spending a few hours working in his study in the morning and napping in the afternoon. In truth, he offered her little in the way of stimulating conversation; something she thrived on. For the first time, she found some truth to what her friends had said when she had announced her intention to marry him; "Lord Stafford *is* dull company".

The thought of a visitor brightened Elizabeth's mood and she quickened her steps. It would be good to talk with her estate commissioner and catch up with him on what was happening in Edinburgh and London. And, of course, hearing about the plans he had for the improvements.

She entered her husband's study and tipped her head to her guest, who was rising from his chair. 'Ah! Mister Loch. This is unexpected. I trust all bodes well with you.' She patted her husband's arm and adjusted the blanket over his knees, before making her way to a chair.

Her estate commissioner bowed his head and waited until she was seated before sitting down.

'The last time you made an unexpected call it was to inform me that the houses on the coast hadn't been made ready for the incoming tenants.' Elizabeth smoothed out the skirt of her dress and settled into her seat. 'You said something about the land surveyor having to return home because of family illness. Has the surveyor not resumed his work on the lots?'

Mister Loch rubbed his hands together. 'My calling today has nothing to do with the new coastal lots. It's related to the latest phase of the evictions Sellar supervised.'

'Ah, yes, Elizabeth,' her husband said. 'We seem to have a problem on our hands. And we need to sort it out.'

Elizabeth leant back in her chair. Less than fifteen minutes earlier, she'd been relaxing in her garden, painting a bowed and misshapen tree; her thoughts smooth and calm. Now, it was as if a tight band encircled her head, pulling ever tighter. To ward off the headache that threatened, she rubbed her forehead. 'Let me ring for some refreshments, and then you can tell us what has happened, Mister Loch. I am sure you are parched after your long journey.'

Two maids arrived with the tea and set it out, Elizabeth lifted her cup and sipped at the hot brew. There was no point in delaying the inevitable. Bad news or not, she had to hear it at some point and it was as well to get it over with. The moment the door was firmly closed behind the retreating servants, she laid her cup down. 'So, what is Mister Sellar saying now?'

'It's not so much what he is saying this time, but more what he has done,' Mister Loch held out papers he had retrieved from his satchel.

Elizabeth took them. 'What are these documents?' She carried them over and stood beside her husband. So that they could look through them together, she laid the papers out on his desk. 'Well, what is this?' she repeated. 'What are all these signatures for?'

Mister Loch let out a deep sigh. 'It is a petition from the tenants who were removed from the straths last month. It is a complaint about Sellar's erm . . . actions, during these removals. It is signed by many who claim to have witnessed this.'

Elizabeth sucked in her breath and tried to control her rising anger. 'And why are Lord Stafford and I only hearing about this now? On Monday, I made myself available in the castle grounds as I always do when I am here. The tenants should have presented their petition to me then.'

Mister Loch nodded his agreement. 'It was sent by Reverend MacKenzie, who, knowing I was in Edinburgh, posted it on to me. I received this petition a few days ago and have brought it straight to your attention.'

Elizabeth scanned the first two pages and looked up. 'Is there any truth to these complaints?'

Mister Loch coughed then said, 'There is some substance to the accusations. Sellar did burn out the grazing grounds before the land was legally his, and some corn houses and mills were destroyed during the removals— '

'God's truth,' Lord Stafford said. 'What was Sellar thinking? He knows very well that the tenants have the right to return to lift their crops after they have been resettled. And, he shouldn't have destroyed their mills or removed the heath until after this time either. This could cause great problems for us, Elizabeth. It could hinder our progress.'

Elizabeth nodded her agreement. 'And bring further criticisms to our plans. We've already had our share of wrath for what we are doing. You are a man of the Law, Mister Loch. Could the complaints against Mister Sellar result in any legal action being taken against him? Or, dear God, against the estate?'

'Most of the accusations contained in the petition are exaggerations of the truth. But, if grazing grounds were burned before the land was legally his, and if corn houses or mills were destroyed during the removals, then Sellar may indeed have exceeded the law.'

'The last thing we need is to have a legal action brought against the estate.' Elizabeth turned to her husband. 'We will have to inform our lawyer. He will advise us further on what we should do. Is there anything else, Mister Loch?'

Her visitor shuffled forward in his seat and reached into his satchel. He pulled out a single sheet of newspaper and held it towards her. 'The press has already reported on Sellar's supposed actions during these evictions. This is a page from the Military Register.'

Elizabeth waved the page away. 'I cannot bear to read this, but I am sure there will be many with grievances against Lord Stafford and myself who will relish the content.' Reaching a decision, she added, 'Haste a reply in response to this petition. If any of my tenants have cause to seek legal redress, let them know I won't stand in their way. And, have Mister Sellar conduct an enquiry into the points raised against him. Have him send his findings directly to me.' She stood. 'Will you be staying to dine, Mister Loch?'

26

BARLEY AND BABIES

Mhàiri heaved the last bag of barley from the long cart and dragged it into the meeting-house. After dropping the sack beside the others, she placed her hands on her hips and yawned. It had been another long day at the sheilings, and it wasn't over yet.

'I will be back in a couple of hours,' she said to Anna. 'I am going to get some sleep. You should head home too. Your daughter can barely have seen you today.'

Anna turned from the still. 'Ah, I intend to. I am struggling to keep my eyes open, and this baby is lying heavy in my belly. I will be back before the Kildonan women arrive tonight.'

'Mind that you do get some rest,' Mhàiri said and made her way out the door with her mother.

Mhàiri removed the cloth from her head and raked her hands through her hair. 'Although I desperately need to sleep, Màthair, I also need to be free for a while from the cloying smell of whisky. It is turning my belly. I am going to walk for a bit. Do you want to come?'

Màthair nodded. 'Likely it will do us good.'

They remained silent as they wandered down to the stream.

Eight weeks had passed since Aunt Una had been cleared from her home, but the events of that day still lingered in Mhàiri's thoughts. For now, she pushed them aside. The late afternoon sun shone on the pasture, heightening the colour of the heather and bracken. Mhàiri slowed her step and breathed in the familiar smells. On reaching the stream, she knelt down and cupped her hands into the cool water. After drinking a few mouthfuls, she leant forward and splashed some onto her face. Refreshed, she lay down and stared up at the cloudless sky.

Màthair stretched out beside her.

Birds chirped their songs of summer, and water gurgled along the stream. Lulled by nature's lullaby, Mhàiri's breathing slowed. Her eyes grew heavy and she closed them. 'It is hard to believe that only a year has passed since we were last at the sheilings.'

'So much has happened since then.'

Mhàiri yawned. 'The girl I was then is nothing but a distant memory. I was filled with despair when I heard that Cameron was planning to emigrate.' She gave a hollow laugh. 'How naïve I was then, thinking that when I married, I could refuse to spend time apart from my husband.'

'It is just the way it is here. When your father was called to fight, I just had to get on with it. It was hard not knowing if he was going to come back.'

'At least I've been spared that,' Mhàiri said and thought about how close she had come to it with Rob Dunn. But, just as her parents and every generation had done in the strath, she had to spend time apart from her husband. Having been forced to face the truth of the matter, she now accepted it— her life was set out, and she couldn't change it by wishes alone. She hadn't been married a year, and here she was at the sheilings while Cameron slept alone at their cottage; just as other husbands in the clachan had done every summer for hundreds of years before him.

Mhàiri stroked her belly. She had been coming to the sheilings all her life, but this was the first time she had been here as a married woman. The girl she'd once been had departed a long time ago. She'd left before Mhàiri had wed and lost her baby. Mhàiri had said goodbye to that girl outside the inn at Golspie.

She opened her eyes and sat up. 'Cameron is right. We have to fight back. Despite the minister's threats of hell and damnation to those who don't comply with the factor's orders, hell and damnation is more likely to be wreaked upon those who *do*. That is why tonight, I will make the trek with the Kildonan women, to smuggle our whisky to the coaching inns.' Mhàiri stood and dusted down her skirt. 'But first, I need to put my head down and get some sleep.'

* * *

A few hours later, having returned to the meeting-house, Mhàiri stripped off her dress and held up her arms.

'Hold still, Mhàiri. Stop fidgeting.' Anna struggled to tie a belt with two tins of whisky attached to it around Mhàiri's waist. 'There. I have got it. How does that feel?'

Mhàiri looked down at the padded cans nestling against her hips. 'They feel fine. But I don't know how I will feel carrying that.' She pointed to a hollow, tin breastplate filled with whisky.

Ciorstag, a young, red-haired Kildonan woman, adjusted the straps on her own breastplate. 'You soon get used to it. It is not much different from carrying the milk to feed your baby.' She nodded to Anna, who looked at Mhàiri and winced.

Ignoring the reference to babies, Mhàiri tutted and flapped her hands. 'Hurry up and put it on me then.'

A dark-haired Kildonan woman pulled the straps of the contraption over Mhàiri's shoulders, wound them around her waist and then tied them in place at the back. 'We know you have been working all hours getting the whisky ready, and we are sorry we had to ask you to come with us tonight, but we are three women down.'

'Ah well,' Ciorstag added. 'Beatrice and Seònaid left over a week ago to take an order to Tain and they have not returned.'

Mhàiri turned around. 'I hope they are safe.' Filled with concern for the women, her thoughts raced. 'Do you think they have been arrested?'

'Arrested.' Ciorstag snorted. 'Beatrice and Seònaid know how to look after themselves.'

The dark-haired woman nodded. 'Pah! Even if they *have* been caught, the Justice of the Peace will let them go soon enough. He gets his share of the whisky, and besides, he knows fine well most rents there are paid out of the profits from illegally distilled whisky. He turns a blind eye to our comings and goings. The most they would get would be a fine.'

'It is true enough about whisky paying the rents,' Mhàiri said. 'But Lord and Lady Stafford won't turn a blind eye. Nor will Maister Sellar.' She pulled a large dress over her head and tugged at it until it settled around her.

'Oh my,' Màthair exclaimed, as she entered and saw Mhàiri. 'You look . . . huge.' She held a hand to her mouth to stifle her laughter. 'I barely recognised you.' She wrapped a plaid around Mhàiri's shoulders and her face took on a concerned look. 'You take care. And do everything these Kildonan women tell you. You understand the risk you are taking, so I will not say any more about it. You do know that I would have gone?'

'I do, Màthair.' Mhàiri tilted her head towards her and smiled. 'There is no need for us to go through this again. Connor needs you. And, there's milking to be done. If you were caught and taken to the jail, who amongst us would make as good a crowdie as you do?'

Màthair shook her head and hugged Mhàiri, who laughed as the tins swayed beneath her dress.

'We need to get going, if we are to be back before dark tomorrow,' Ciorstag said.

Mhàiri picked up a small bag, containing oatcakes and cheese, and waved goodbye to Anna. As she made to leave a thought struck her and she stopped in her tracks. She gripped Ciorstag by the arm. She turned the woman around and looked her in the eye. 'Earlier, you said you were three women down. You said that Beatrice and Seònaid had gone to Tain. Where is the third woman?'

Ciorstag grimaced. 'Locked up in the jail at Dornoch.'

Mhàiri let go of Ciorstag's arm and hurried out the door. She strode ahead of the Kildonan women, making for the horses. What had she got herself into?

* * *

Mhàiri rode beside Ciorstag and the dark-haired Kildonan woman. For the past hour, they had journeyed together in comfortable silence. Her companions had smuggled whisky many times before, and Mhàiri was happy to follow their lead. Although in truth, Ciorstag seemed to be the one in charge.

The sky had already started to darken, but there was enough light for Mhàiri to clearly make out the path in front of her. As they passed through an empty township, she pushed the horse forward and tried to keep her eyes down. The pain of seeing the skeleton's that had once been homes to families like her own seared through her heart.

'Psst! Mhàiri,' a voice called in no more than a whisper.

Mhàiri looked up to see Ciorstag pointing east. She shrugged her shoulders and brought her mount closer to the two women who had already stopped. 'What? What is it?'

Ciorstag continued to point. 'If we go through that sheep farm, we will cut a fair bit off our journey.'

The dark-haired woman shook her head from side to side. 'I

am not sure if it would be safe, Ciorstag. I have never gone that way before.'

'For most of the time we will be staying near the edge of the farm,' Ciorstag said. 'Anyway, the shepherd will be fast asleep by now. As long as we are quiet, we will be fine.'

Mhàiri shrugged and looked at the dark-haired woman, who shrugged back. She turned her mount east and followed the women.

A sheep bleated, and Mhàiri startled. The weight of the whisky containers grew heavier along with her fear that they would be caught. Why hadn't Ciorstag stuck to the planned route? A sudden urge to urinate, gripped Mhàiri and she tried to hold it back. Of all the times, why had this happened now? She gritted her teeth and kept going.

Unable to continue she called, 'I need to stop.'

The women pulled to a halt, and Mhàiri slipped from the horse and hurried towards a bush. She realised that she couldn't manage without help and let out a frustrated squeal. She waved her arms, and Ciorstag hurried to her side.

'There is a knack to it Mhàiri. You just need to learn it.' She adjusted Mhàiri's skirt for her.

By the time she had finished, Mhàiri was desperately holding back a desire to giggle. 'Dear God, I thought I would never make it on time.' The tins at her side swayed as she pulled herself back onto her mount.

They continued in silence and Mhàiri's light mood was replaced by dark thoughts. She kept her eyes fixed ahead and remained watchful. As they moved further into the heart of the sheep farm, a dog barked. Bile rose in Mhàiri's throat. The sound was soon followed by another bark. Mhàiri leant forward and urged her horse forward. Beside her, the two Kildonan women pushed their mounts into action. Mhàiri raced along beside them. The weight of the breastplate and the cans rattling at her side nearly had her toppling off, she righted herself and steadied her pace.

The thump of hooves appeared behind them. Mhàiri turned her head to see a man with his fist raised, careening towards them on a large horse. Realising that they wouldn't be able to outrace him, she called, 'Go right. Turn right.' She turned her horse and raced ahead.

The women pushed their horses forward and followed her towards the edge of the sheep farm. Sweat poured down Mhàiri's back and her heart raced. She drew in a deep breath and willed the horse on. Once she realised that the man was no longer following them, now that they had left the sheep farm, she slowed to a walk. 'How do you manage to keep doing this?'

Ciorstag shook her head. 'It is a case of having to,' she said keeping her voice low. 'The thought of that devil, Sellar, behind bars is what keeps us going. I have been married a year, but what future is there for me and Alasdair? Most of the townships around us have been cleared, but my heart is set on remaining in the Strath of Kildonan. I won't give that up without a fight.'

'Ciorstag has never been caught so far,' the dark-haired woman said with a note of pride in her voice.

As they rode in silence, Mhàiri couldn't wait to return home and see Cameron again. She counted out the weeks until she would leave the sheilings.

27

WANDERING THE WILDERNESS

Mhàiri stopped pacing and turned towards Cameron. 'I am coming with you.'

'That is not possible.' Cameron rubbed the whiskers on his face. 'You were worn out when you got back from the sheilings. You need to rest.'

She placed her hands on her hips and glowered at him. 'If you do not take me with you, I will follow you. One thing is for certain, I am not staying here doing nothing.'

'I am meeting with Dòmhnall Beag and Lachlann. They are living in the hills with some other Kildonan men. It would be far too dangerous for you to come with me. There could be trouble.'

'All the more reason then why I *should* go with you.' She dropped her arms. 'Please, Cameron, I wouldn't settle while you were gone.'

Cameron stood from the table, where he'd been counting the money they had made from selling their whisky. 'Fifty-two pounds we made, and more to come when we sell what is hidden in the peat-stacks.' He pointed to the table. 'But, I need to get this money to the Kildonan men. And, I have to leave today. This money will go a long way towards helping in our fight against the factor.'

Mhàiri went over to him. He folded her into his arms and held her close. 'Do not be worrying about me, Mhàiri. Dòmhnall Beag and Lachlann are good men, and your father will be with me.' He kissed the top of her head. 'A Mhàiri, mo ghràidh – Mhàiri, my love,' he said. 'It pains me too for us to be apart again so soon, but it is our baby we need to think about.'

* * *

An hour later, Mhàiri stood at the exit of the byre waving goodbye to her husband. As he receded into the distance, she rubbed her belly. Cameron was right; they had a baby to think about now. This time, Mhàiri hadn't needed her mother-in-law to tell her, she knew the moment she boiled her first pot of cabbage at the sheilings. She grimaced as she recalled the way her belly had turned at the smell. And, she hadn't waited to tell Cameron about the baby either. On returning home, it was the first thing she'd said after banging the front door open and racing into his outstretched arms.

Now, with her arms folded across her chest, she stared in the direction of her mother's cottage, contemplating whether to brave the downpour or leave it until later to call. She shivered. All morning, the rain had poured down, forceful and relentless. The weather had started to turn, and a chill had crept into the air. But fortune had been shining down upon them. She had returned from the sheilings in time to gather in the crops before the weather changed.

She should call on her friend too. Anna had birthed a bonny boy. Mhàiri placed her hands on her belly. Strange as it was, she had thought right from the start that this one was a girl. She studied a spider's web on the stone wall inside the exit. Covered in dew, the web glistened in the weak rays of the low-lying sun. Winter would be upon them soon. Just like the spider, her home was ready and stocked with food to see her through the cold months ahead. And, just like the spider, her home could be torn from her at any moment.

Mhàiri swiped her hand through the web. She felt a pang of guilt but quickly extinguished it with the thought that the spider could build another home elsewhere. She paused, with her hand in mid-air. Is this what Lord and Lady Stafford had felt when they asked the factor to pull down their tenant's homes? Had they absolved their guilt with the thought that the people they removed could rebuild their houses somewhere else? She blew a long breath out through her parted lips. If so, then their fight to remain here was futile. She understood now why there had been no legal action taken against Sellar, their petition had fallen on deaf ears.

She crossed her arms and looked out at the township. She recalled the catechist's words as he had preached to them at the mission. Before the factor had read out the names of the first tenants to be evicted, the catechist had instructed them to have faith and to obey the order to move to the coast.

Like the promises made to the Israelites wandering in the wilderness, Lord and Lady Stafford had promised their faithful followers a land flowing not with milk and honey, but an ocean filled with fish and seaweed. But the tenants here were of the land, not the sea. And, they already had milk and honey flowing in abundance. She recalled the tinkers she'd seen sheltering at the harbour. Many families like them had resisted the moves and had been removed from their homes and left to wander the land, denied access to new lots on the coast.

Mhàiri chewed on her bottom lip. What should she do for the best? She decided to make a run for her mother's cottage and would think more about it later. She pulled her plaid over her head and sprinted out the byre. As she dashed through the deep puddles, she held her skirt up by the hem. When she reached her mother's cottage, she threw open the door and hurried inside.

'*A Mhàiri, cionnas a tha thu?*' – Mhàiri, how are you?' Màthair called and threw peats onto the fire. 'It is as well you are here, I was just banking up the fire before bringing this.' She pulled a letter from her pocket and held it out. 'It was brought soon after Cameron left with your father. I offered to take it to you.'

Mhàiri took the letter with her drenched hands. She realised her mistake and popped the letter between her teeth, while she removed her plaid and draped it over a stool by the fire. After drying her hands on her skirt, Mhàiri retrieved the letter from her mouth. She held the paper up. 'Who is this from?'

Màthair raised her eyebrows. 'Not that I get many, but I would say that as sure as hens lay eggs if you open it, you will find out.'

'Perhaps you are right. But it has Cameron's name on it.'

'And yours . . . According to the lad who delivered it and took the payment.' Màthair shook her head. 'And, Cameron is not here to open it, is he? He will not be back until tomorrow night. So, get on with it, so we can see who it is from.'

When Mhàiri still hesitated, Màthair added. 'It could be important.'

'Ah, all right. But put the kettle on first, while I dry myself.'

Mhàiri sipped a warming bowl of nettle tea and contemplated whether, or not, to open the letter lying on the table in front of her. Cameron wouldn't mind, but it felt wrong. She opened and closed her hands and wiggled her fingers above the folded paper, resisting the temptation. But what if Màthair was right? What if it was important?

She spread the letter out on the table and read it out. *Dearest Cameron and Mhàiri,* Mhàiri scanned to the bottom of the page and tilted her head back in surprise. She gestured for her mother to join her at the table. 'It is from Cameron's mother.'

Màthair wiped her hands on a cloth and sat beside her. 'Well, go on. What is the woman saying? I am all ears.'

Mhàiri read out the letter. *'Marta wrote this for me. I am hoping it reaches you. I am also hoping that you have good news to be sending back. Our news is not as good as we had hoped to send. But do not worry. We are well. I am writing to let you know not to follow us yet. Since arriving here, we have remained in the far reaches of Scotland waiting for a ship to be leaving for the settlement. The ship we were meant to sail in left without any of us on it. We were told that there was unrest at the settlement and we cannot leave until it settles. A fight has broken out between the fur traders and settlers, and the settlers have been forced out of their homes for the time being.*

'With so many gathering here, either waiting to board or arriving from ships, there is great demand at the inns for bed and meals. Fortunately, Father found work in an inn. Although he does not earn much, and we have had to use some of the money we had set aside for the settlement, Lord Selkirk has promised us tools and grain if we wait this storm out. We might also be able to buy our allotted land at a low price once we are settled. And that is what we have decided to do. I will write again after we hear word of when we are to sail. With winter approaching, this will not be until the spring.

'We heard news from people embarking from a ship that support for Napoleon is growing again in France, and there are rumours that he plans to return from exile and raise another army. No one knows what to make of this. Marta and Eilidh send their regards and yearn to see you both. I hope this letter finds you both well. Send your reply to the inn at the address below.'

Mhàiri laid the letter down. 'Cameron's family have been delayed in Stromness.'

Màthair smiled. 'Does that mean you will be staying here?'

'It looks like it.' A sense of relief flooded through Mhàiri as if she had been given a reprieve. Perhaps the petition to Lord and

Lady Stafford would work and she would be able to remain in the strath. 'I just hope there is no more word of removals.'

'And I hope there is no truth to these rumours about Napoleon. If he returns to battle, then our men may never get home.'

'And, Cameron might be called to fight.'

2 8

ORANGES AND OMENS

Staffordshire

Winter remained determined not to allow even a hint of spring to show, and the late February wind carried an icy chill. As it was too cold to even contemplate walking outside, Elizabeth strolled through the orangery of her home, with her husband and their eldest son, Lord Gower. Behind them, her lady's maid carried Elizabeth's book and shawl.

Elizabeth stopped and broke a red rosebud from a bush. The bud had started to open, and she held it under her nose and looked out through the wide expanse of glass into the garden. 'The grounds will look stunning this year. The addition of the sunken garden adds such depth to the vista. Shall we sit a while and enjoy the view?'

Her husband nodded and shuffled over and sat on a large white bench. Elizabeth waved for her maid to continue walking and sat beside him. She patted the seat for her son to sit also.

Lord Gower remained standing. 'Thank you, Mama, but no.

Now that we are alone there is something I urgently need to discuss with you and Papa.'

Elizabeth looked up at her son and smiled. 'Good news, I hope.'

Lord Gower placed his hands behind his back and bent his head towards his parents. 'I have received a further petition from the tenants, about the June evictions. It was addressed to me.'

'Dear God,' Lord Stafford said. 'Why are the tenants pestering you with this business?'

'Because they claim no action was taken against Sellar in response to the petition they sent in July.'

'But . . .' Elizabeth held her hands out. 'Surely this business has been dealt with.' After a moment, she recalled what had been agreed. 'I asked Mister Sellar to investigate the tenant's complaints and send his findings directly to me.'

Lord Gower looked skyward, before saying, 'Mama. These complaints were made *against* Sellar. Seven months have now passed. What did the factor say in his report?'

When Elizabeth remained silent, her son said, 'You did receive a reply from him, didn't you?'

Elizabeth turned to her husband, who shook his head and said, 'By damn! No. Apart from his usual correspondence, we have had nothing about this back from him. What do you intend to do, son?'

'I need to reply. And, it looks as though there is substance to some of what the tenants say. With the newspapers behind them, it could look bad for the estate if you were seen not to act on this. But there is more—'

Concerned by the pained look that had appeared on her son's face, Elizabeth said, 'More? More, what?'

George rubbed his face and paced away. After turning around, he paced back and placed his hands behind his back. Standing in front of his parents, he leant towards them and almost in a whisper said, 'On top of the previous charges, the tenants are now accusing Sellar of wilful fire-raising and . . . murder.'

'Murder!' Elizabeth gripped her husband's arm. 'Are these people saying that our factor murdered someone?'

George continued, 'The tenants claim that at least five people died as a result of Sellar's actions. And that one woman died a few days after the evictions as a direct result of the injuries she received when her cottage was set alight while she was still in it. It was only through the good grace of God that her daughter-in-law arrived home in time to remove the old woman before she burned to death.'

'Murder! Fire-raising!' Lord Stafford turned and faced Elizabeth. 'We will be damned if we act and damned if we don't. These are our tenants, but Sellar is our employee. We have to be seen to be looking out for all their interests.'

Elizabeth clenched her fingers, crushing the rosebud. She had to do something to sort out this mess. She looked up at her son. 'Ask the Sheriff to conduct an enquiry into these allegations. If he finds a case to answer against Mister Sellar then the estate will take no offence if this proceeds to trial.'

29

THE SHERIFF'S SURPRISE

Strathnaver

Mhàiri stepped back from the pot of barley broth she'd been stirring and stretched her aching back. She lifted the pot onto the hook above the fire and sat down on a high-backed wooden chair. Cameron sat on a stool beside her, mending their boots. Clad in brown leather breeches, his legs were hunched on either side of him as he tacked a new piece of leather to one of the soles.

Mhàiri repositioned her legs and tried to get comfortable. 'I did not think it possible to get so big-bellied. Anna was never this big.'

'It shouldn't be much longer now until we get to meet this baby.' Cameron looked up and smiled. 'Should we let Maighstir MacCoinnich know that we will be calling on him soon for the christening?'

Mhàiri shifted in her seat. 'Perhaps, I am not sure.'

The nearer the birth loomed, the more she worried about

what would happen to her and Cameron. There had been no word of any further removals, and she wanted to believe that they could remain where they were. But the factor's words haunted her happiness—"*In a few years, all of Strathnaver will be under sheep.*"

Unable to settle, she emptied a shelf on the dresser and placed everything on the table. She filled a pail and washed black ash from each dish. Without turning from her task, she said to Cameron, 'It is near April's end and there has been no more word of removals, either here, or in any of the other townships. Do you reckon our petition to Lord Gower worked?'

'I am not sure, Mhàiri. For this year perhaps we are safe. Lord Gower passed our complaints to Lord and Lady Stafford, and the Sheriff has been informed. We just need to bide our time.'

Mhàiri nodded. She felt a pain in her belly and an urgent need to keep moving. After wiping down the dresser, she returned each dish to its rightful place.

'Sit down. You will wear yourself out.'

'I cannot abide the dirt.'

Cameron raised his eyebrows. 'It is only ash from the fire.'

'Maybe so, but I cannot settle until it is gone.' She paced the length of the room. Cameron was right, she needed to settle. She picked up the book she had been reading earlier. Cameron had brought it back for her from one of his journeys into the hills to meet with the Kildonan men. She stroked the cover. The book was new and had been brought all the way from London. He had bought it from a Kildonan man whose brother worked there on the Military Register. As she flicked through the pages, Mhàiri was startled by a loud rap on the door. She looked up at Cameron, who had already risen from his stool.

Seeing fear flare in his eyes, Mhàiri laid the book down. Rarely did anyone knock. Friends and neighbours tapped and then entered. The knock meant that whoever was at their door would not have a familiar face.

Cameron placed a protective arm around her shoulder. 'Stay there. I will see who it is.'

When he swung the door open, Mhàiri placed a hand on her churning belly and tilted her head; to get a better look at the man who stood outside.

'Ah! It is you.' Cameron held the door open so their visitor could enter. 'Mhàiri, it is the Sheriff-Substitute.'

Concern flooded through her. She wiped her hands down the side of her skirt and stepped forward. 'Sheriff McKid. There is nothing wrong, is there?'

The visitor removed his bonnet. 'There is nothing amiss for you to be worrying about. I am here to talk to you both about the complaints laid against the factor.'

Did that mean their complaint against Maister Sellar was being taken seriously? Or, were they in trouble? Mhàiri's heart raced and she grew flustered. She let out a deep breath and tried to calm her voice. 'Come away in. Cameron, get the Sheriff a seat. You will be having a warming bowl of barley broth, Sheriff McKid?'

'Make yourself comfortable,' Cameron said to the Sheriff-Substitute and pointed to the high-backed chair by the fire.

'A bowl of broth would be most welcome,' Sheriff McKid said. 'But first, I need to ask you a few questions about what you witnessed. You *were* both present during the June evictions?' he asked and glanced first at Cameron and then at Mhàiri.

They nodded.

'Good. Good.' Sheriff McKid sat on the chair. 'I am trying to determine who to take witness statements from. There are a lot of people to be getting through. I have spoken to a few but I am not nearly finished yet.'

Cameron sat beside the man. 'So, you are here to investigate our complaint, a thousand thanks to you for that.'

'I am calling about the complaints made against the factor,' Sheriff McKid replied. 'But there is no need to be thanking me. If Maister Sellar is indeed guilty of the charges laid against him, then if he is not hanged, he will most certainly be sent to Botany Bay. The Sheriff would have come himself, but he couldn't be travelling to Strathnaver at this time. We best get started.' He looked over at Mhàiri. 'You will be joining us by the fire? Then you can both tell me what, if anything, you witnessed.'

* * *

That night, sleep wouldn't come and Mhàiri's thoughts returned again and again to Sheriff McKid's visit. Buffeted by the rising wind, the bedroom window rattled in its casing, and a cold draught seeped into the room. Despite the chill, sweat trickled down Mhàiri's back. She had told the Sheriff everything she could recall about what had happened in her aunt's township on the day of the evictions, including the loss of her baby. Perhaps now, the removals would stop?

Before retiring to bed, Mhàiri had gathered her long hair together at the nape of her neck and twisted it into a single plait. The tightening in her belly had been growing stronger all evening. Between Màthair's and Anna's stories, she understood what the belly pains meant. She had also seen enough births to know what task lay ahead. No doubt the baby would be here in the morning. She closed her eyes. She should get some sleep while she could.

Waking from a doze, Mhàiri clenched her fists as a pain like no other she had ever experienced ripped across her belly and travelled up through her back. She bit on her bottom lip and tried to remain silent. Cameron lay asleep beside her, and she wanted him to remain where he was; he had tasks to attend to in the morning.

When the pain settled, Mhàiri pulled back the blankets and stepped from the bed.

A hand gripped her shoulder. 'Mhàiri, is it the baby?'

She touched Cameron's hand. 'You need to sleep. It will be a while in coming. There is no need for us both to be up. I will wake you when I need you to fetch help.'

No sooner had she closed the bedroom door behind her when another bout of pain engulfed her body. Mhàiri sucked her breath in and wrung her hands together until the attack passed. Realising that she had left it too late to call for her mother and Hattie Bantrach, she groaned. She knelt in front of a large wooden chest, lifted the lid and pulled out a fresh night-dress and two blankets. As she made to stand, another bolt of pain crested through her. A wail rose in her throat and erupted through her mouth. Sweat beaded on her brow and trickled down her back. She pushed her chin down and gritted her teeth.

Cameron appeared behind her, and she turned her head towards him. 'Bring Màthair and Hattie Bantrach. Now.'

After the wave of pain subsided, Mhàiri lifted the blankets and carried them over and laid them on a stool beside the box-bed set into the passageway between the house and the byre. In between the bouts of pain now gripping her, she shook out one of the blankets and spread it over the bed.

A cool hand stroked her forehead. Hattie Bantrach's face smiled at her. Mhàiri screamed. Tears rolled down her face. 'The baby— ' An overwhelming feeling that something was wrong filled her thoughts. She panted. 'Something is not right. The pain— '

Hattie Bantrach rubbed Mhàiri's back. 'Everything is going fine.'

'You are not understanding. This baby. I cannot lose this one too.'

Mhàiri heard her mother's voice; it was as if she was talking from a great height. 'Get yourself away out of here, Cameron. She is nearly there. Let us get you onto the bed, Mhàiri.'

Mhàiri battled against the agony cresting through her body. She dragged herself onto the bed, knelt on the blanket and panted. Bathed in sweat and biting back a scream, she felt an overwhelming urge to get her baby out.

When the next agonising wave ripped through her body, Mhàiri gripped onto her bent knees and pushed with all the strength she had.

CATALOGUE OF CRIMES

London

E lizabeth finished her mid-day meal. She dabbed her lips with a napkin and turned to her husband, whom she had dined alone with in their townhouse. 'I am going to retire to my studio for a few hours. I want to do some more on the painting I am working on. The one of our new jetty up north.'

'Very good, Elizabeth. I will be in my study if you need me. How is the painting coming along?'

'It just needs a few finishing touches and then it will be ready to hang.'

As she rose from the chair the butler tapped on the door and entered. He bowed to Lord Stafford and held out a small, silver tray bearing a single letter. 'This arrived for you from Sherriff McKid, My Lord.'

Elizabeth sat again. When the butler had closed the door behind him, she rubbed her forehead with both hands. 'What now?'

Lord Stafford put his spectacles on and slit the letter covering with a knife. He remained silent as he read. When he finished, he raised his eyebrows and handed it to her. 'Your painting will have to wait.'

Elizabeth scanned the contents. *As you are aware from the tenants' petitions, Mister Sellar, Under Factor, has been accused of behaving with great cruelty during the June removals. Having taken statements from over forty witnesses, and with the evidence now gathered in front of me, I have to say that the extent of his cruelty shocked me to a state of near fainting. It is with the deepest regret that I have to inform you that a more numerous catalogue of crimes perpetrated by any individual has seldom sullied the pages of any precognition taken in Scotland. In point of law, given that the tenants were paid for the timber that was burned, my opinion is that he is not guilty of wilful fire-raising. But, there is evidence to suggest that he is indeed guilty of culpable homicide and criminal oppression. This being the case, the laws of this land call upon me to order his immediate arrest and incarceration for trial.*

Elizabeth's mouth opened in surprise, and she was thankful that she was already sitting down.

* * *

Dornoch

Mister Sellar sat at the table in his prison cell and seethed. As he read back the words on his hastily scribbled letter to Lady Stafford, his face crumpled. He scrunched the paper into a ball and tossed it to the floor, to join his other discarded pages. Unable to settle, he rose from the table and paced the room. Sheriff McKid's interference incensed him, and his dislike of the man now deepened to intense hatred. How dare he attack him in this manner? But he wasn't at all surprised. The man was a scoundrel, a perpetual poacher and his sworn enemy.

He picked up the sheet containing the charges the Sheriff-Substitute had laid against him. As he read through the allegations, his fury rose. He had no doubt that McKid had manipulated the tenants into saying these things to further his cause against him. Once he was out of here, he would have the scoundrel removed from office. Never again would that man be in the position to do this to him. He would make sure of that. But first, he needed to prepare for his trial. Hadn't he led an honourable life? Many worthy names knew him for his sympathy and sense of humanity. Yes, he would draw up a list and have them speak in his defence. There was nothing that could be brought out in court against his character. So, what if he had fathered a bairn to a lass, he had done the honourable thing at the time and acknowledged his daughter.

As a lawyer, he knew how to handle Sheriff McKid's allegations on points of law, but he needed his employer's support. He would have his revenge on McKid. But first, he needed to get out of here. His best chance lay with Lady Stafford.

He took a deep breath, sat down at the desk and picked up his pen. *Little did I know when I last had the honour of speaking with Your Ladyship that I would be communicating with you from such a place as I am now being held prisoner,* he wrote. Pleased by the tone his opening words conveyed, he continued. *Such a conspiracy has been set against me that I no longer know what to think. I only ever strived to carry out my duties as factor to the highest standard I could. As you are aware, my personal enemy, Sheriff McKid, has long held a grudge against me for bringing him to account for his incessant poaching. In all fairness, he cannot be considered unbiased in the interviews he conducted with those tenants who claim wrongdoing by me against them. That this is the case is borne out by his refusal to grant me bail. His hope is to concuss me to ruin. I refute all of the allegations laid against me. As you will recall, I endeavoured to phase the removals of the tenants from my land and allowed them to remain long after the lease became mine. With the help of my father, I am preparing a case for my defence and I trust that I can rely on Your Ladyship to provide every support necessary to me.*

Satisfied with what he had written, he signed and then sealed the letter.

31

RELIGION AND REVELATIONS

Strathnaver

Mhàiri carried her ten-week-old daughter over to Mòrag Mòr's cottage. When she entered, the chair-bound woman stretched out her arms and beamed. 'A Mhàiri, cionnas a tha thu? –Mhàiri, how are you?' she said with delight in her voice. 'My, will you look at that baby. Give her here so I can see her properly.'

Mhàiri placed Caitriona into Mòrag Mòr's arms. 'I would have come sooner, but— '

'Ach! Never mind that. My, she is a bonny baby, Mhàiri. Put some milk on then we can have a good talk. Iain is out seeing Peigi Ruadh.' She paused. 'You will not be hurrying away?'

If she had been, Mhàiri wasn't now. After such a greeting, she couldn't rush away. Unable to leave her home by herself, Mòrag Mòr lived for the visits from her neighbours.

'There are jobs aplenty, I need to be getting on with.' Mhàiri removed her plaid, folded it and laid it on the floor between a stool and Mòrag Mòr's chair. 'But truth be told, a bit of time to myself wouldn't go amiss.'

Gazing down at the baby in her arms, Mòrag Mòr's brows furrowed. 'Iain was refused. He did not get permission from Lord Stafford to marry Peigi Ruadh.'

Mhàiri shook her head. 'Why? When did he hear?'

'The minister called this morning. I do not know what they will do. I don't. Iain has gone to the Mill to see Peigi Ruadh. . .. to tell her.'

'It is not right.'

'Maighstir MacCoinnich was most apologetic, but he said there was nothing he could do. Lord Stafford is not approving any marriages at the moment.'

'Perhaps things will change soon.'

'Perhaps, but Iain is talking about emigrating with Peigi Ruadh. I do not think he is just saying that in anger. I dread to think what will happen to me if he leaves.'

Mhàiri didn't know what to say. She removed the sleeping baby from Mòrag Mòr's arms and tucked her daughter into the folded plaid on the floor. After pouring two wooden bowls of the now hot milk, she handed one to Mòrag Mòr.

Clasping her own bowl, Mhàiri sat on the stool. 'I am not sure if emigrating would solve their problem. It all takes time. Last year it was that Cameron's mother told us they had finally set sail from Stromness. A few months later, we got a letter saying that they had landed and were to be making the journey to the colony. They expected to reach there in November, before the winter set in.' Mhàiri remained silent for a moment and then continued, 'We have not had word from her since. I am concerned.'

'Likely his family will be safe enough. It may be harder for them to send mail.'

'Perhaps you are right. With the winter. Especially if it was a bad one. We should hear soon?'

Mòrag Mòr's head shook from side to side as if she was troubled by her thoughts. 'I wish I could hear something from Micheal. Last year it was that we heard Napoleon had been defeated. Most of the men have returned. But there still hasn't been any word from my son.'

Mhàiri bit on her bottom lip, as if trying to pull her words back. She shouldn't have mentioned her concerns about Cameron's family. Mòrag Mòr had never recovered her strength after the journey to Golspie. Despite her ill health, she never gave up hope that Micheal would return one day.

Mhàiri gazed down at her sleeping daughter. She now understood the woman's refusal to believe that her son was dead. 'No doubt, there are many still to return. It is a worry.' She didn't know what else to say and remained silent.

Mòrag Mòr kept her eyes fixed ahead.

Mhàiri turned her gaze to the fire.

For a few minutes, they sat in silence.

'I had a daughter once,' Mòrag Mòr said with a wistful sound to her voice.

Mhàiri turned her head. 'A daughter? I did not know.'

'Holding Caitriona in my arms, it took me right back.'

'What— What happened?'

Mòrag Mòr let out a deep breath. 'My husband had left for the wars, again. I had two children and another on the way. I was near my time, but the crops needed to be harvested. Time stands still for no man . . . or woman. I had no choice but to gather the crops in by myself. The neighbours helped, of course, your mother for one. But, with your father away as well, she had her own crops to tend to.

'All of us women were drowning in the same peat bog. And, if I wanted my family to eat over the winter, then I had no choice but to climb out of it. Iain and Micheal were only boys at the time but they helped where they could. After they were tucked up at night, I would go out again on my own.'

Mòrag Mòr took a sip of milk and continued. 'Iain took the whooping cough first and then Micheal got it. It raged around the valley like a starving beast.' Her eyes had a distant look and were focussed on the fire as if she were back in her past watching these events taking place.

Mhàiri looked down at her daughter then back up at the woman. 'It must have been difficult for you . . . looking after two sick bairns and trying to get the crops in before the weather turned.'

'It was, but there was no point complaining.' Mòrag Mòr gave a feeble laugh. 'Who would I have complained to?' She bent forward and rubbed her hand over her mouth. 'I collapsed one evening, scything the barley. By the time I came round, my baby was coming. A girl. I wrapped her in my plaid and stumbled down the brae and into my cottage. The girl meowed all night like a starving kitten, but every time I put her to the breast, she sucked for a moment then turned away. By the time the sun came up, she was gone. And, do you know what I said?'

Mhàiri shook her head. She couldn't imagine the horror of losing Caitriona like that. Although she had lost her first baby, she had barely been eight weeks on. And the pain of that loss remained. It was as if a bit of her had left along with that baby.

Mòrag Mòr rubbed a hand over her face. 'I said— It is God's will.'

'I said the same after my own loss. God acts in strange ways sometimes, but it is not for us to question His reasons.'

'But what if it wasn't God's will that my daughter died when she did?'

'What do you mean? Not God's will.' Although Mhàiri knew no one else was present, she glanced around, fearful that someone would hear their words.

'Stuck in this chair, I have time to ponder such matters, Mhàiri. Now I'm not saying that I don't believe God has His own plans for us. I believe he does. When my time comes there will be nothing any man nor beast will be able to do to stop it. But what if? What if things happen that we call God's will but they are actually against the will of God? Could it be that some people are taken before God intends?'

'Surely everything that happens to us is by the will of God. What are you saying, Mòrag Mòr?'

'I cannot help thinking that if my husband hadn't been called to fight then he would have been there. And, if he had been, I wouldn't have had to tend to the harvest alone. It wasn't God's will that took my daughter from me; it was man's will.'

Mhàiri frowned. 'But surely it was God's will that your husband was called to fight.'

'So, you think it is God's will that our men fight in battles that have nothing to do with them? You think that God intended for man to fight man?'

'I do not know. Perhaps. But it is not for the likes of us to say it is not.'

'The minister said, "it is God's will that we are to be removed". You see, Mhàiri, I have had time to ponder the minister's words. Do you really think it serves God's purpose to have us removed from here? That His will is for sheep to have our land.'

Mhàiri shook her head. 'It may be . . . I do not know. Likely it also serves the factor's purpose for us to be removed.'

'These removals are driven by man's desire to make money and own property, *not* God's will. And, to think this is happening while our men are away fighting. Doing their duty to make sure that we *can* remain here.'

'So, why is the minister telling us that it is God's will that we move?'

Mòrag Mòr's face curled in contempt. 'They too take the wages of sin. You see, Mhàiri, even the ministers are driven by earthly greed and are willing to place this above their heavenly souls. And all the while, the factor and the minister are telling us that the evictions are the Lord's punishment for *our* sins. Yes, we should be punished for our sins, but to be cast out of our homes and sent from the land our families have lived on for hundreds of years. It is not only our homes they are destroying. It is our way of living.'

'You shouldn't be saying these things, Mòrag Mòr. Regardless of who benefits, it is God's will that this is happening.'

'Perhaps it is. But it took me to be stuck in this chair to realise that we are being removed from here because of mans' greed. And the greediest one of them all has now been let out on bail.'

'But, the date for the factor's trial has been set. God willing, Maister Sellar will now be punished for his cruelty.'

3 2

ART ATTACK

London

Elizabeth made her way from the art gallery in her home. Startled by the sound of a raised voice calling her back, she turned and hurried up the great staircase.

'My Lady. Ma'am. Come quickly,' a porter from the Gallery called as he raced towards her.

'My goodness, Cantrill, what is it?'

'Come quickly, Ma'am. You best see for yourself,' he said between wheezes. 'I opened the gallery for public viewing not twenty minutes ago.'

Elizabeth lifted the hem of her skirt and followed the red-faced porter through a maze of rooms and into the Old Gallery; the largest of twelve rooms housing her husband's art collection. She followed close behind him as he pushed through the gathering crowd. When she reached the front, she was flummoxed by what she saw and stood for a moment to gather her thoughts. Amongst the symmetry of the paintings adorning one wall, a well-dressed, bearded man stood in front of a Titian, holding a small axe aloft. The painting, *Three Ages of Man*, had been acquired from the deceased Duke of Orléans' collection and was amongst the rarest pieces in this part of the gallery.

The crowd grew silent.

Filled with fury, Elizabeth stepped forward and pointed at the intruder. 'How did you get in here? What is the meaning of this?'

The man continued to stare at the Titian, the axe pointing towards it.

'Have this man removed. Now!' Elizabeth called.

The man lifted the axe as if to strike the painting.

A collective gasp emanated from the crowd.

'Wait!' Elizabeth couldn't risk losing such a valuable work of art. She glanced around. Where was her husband? He would know what to do. 'Cantrill, get Lord Stafford. Make haste!'

Without turning or lowering the axe, the intruder said in a Highland accent. 'Let me have my say and then I will leave.'

Realising that the man was making some kind of protest, Elizabeth hesitated, swallowed and said, 'Very well. Have your say and then go.'

The tall man turned but kept the axe aloft. 'Titian, Rembrandt, Rubens. This gallery has a large collection. How many galleries are there? Eleven, but that is only in this building. What of your other collections? Hmm!'

A murmur arose behind her, but Elizabeth held up a hand, silencing the growing crowd. How did this man get in? She would have to tighten security at the door.

The man continued. 'You raise the rents on your Highland estate so that you can have a picture of a Scottish piper hung amidst your suites of upholstered furniture. And what of your Highland tenants? What are they to hang on their walls? The price of their cattle has halved again. The cattle they rely on to pay you their rents. And what do you do? Do you drop their rents? Indeed, you do not. You raise them. Why? I will tell you why. So that you can purchase and hang a picture of . . . of a starving dog.'

Elizabeth turned her gaze to Fyt's painting. What did this man want? She glanced around, looking for her husband. Seeing no sign of him, she glared at the stranger holding the axe.

The man shook his head and let out his breath in anger. 'A chained and starving dog, no less, with its food placed just out of reach. And you think nothing of hanging this picture while pushing the food further from the reach of your tenants. This picture alone would feed them and compensate for their losses. But instead, you carry on with your . . . your 'improvements'. What do *you* have to say about that?'

Elizabeth continued to glare at the crazed man but remained silent. There had been growing criticism around the country about the heavy-handed manner of her factor during the last removals. Elizabeth had heard much of the gossip and had seen many of the pamphlets and articles condemning her and Lord Stafford. No doubt this man's protest was in response to Mister Sellar's impending trial for cruelty during these removals. She cursed her factor for a fool for placing her in this predicament.

Elizabeth stepped forward. 'You have had your say, now leave.'

The man gave a mocking laugh. 'I will obey your order to leave, just as my family did when you ordered them to leave their home in Strathnaver. Although I know who you are, my face means nothing to you. Let me introduce myself. I am Rob Dunn. My friends lent me these fancy clothes and had a letter of introduction forged so that I could enter here.' The man waved an arm around the room. 'Along with the gentry.'

He shook his head and continued. 'For near a hundred years, my family has paid rent to your family. They paid not just with their hard-earned money but with their lives during battle. I was once proud to call myself one of your fighting men, but not anymore. You see, after two years away I returned from the field of battle to learn that my mother was to be turned out from her home. And all of this after my father had been thrust into a make-shift grave in a foreign land. Despite a promise to your tenants that they would be given tenure of their homes if their men signed up for battle, it seems that your promise has been easily forgotten. You take everything from us and call it improvements. Call it improvements if you like. I call it greed.' He dropped his arms and walked towards the exit, the axe swinging by his side.

The crowd parted as he passed.

Three male servants hurried forward and restrained the intruder. With his arms pinned behind his back, the servants proceeded to march Rob Dunn out the gallery.

As she turned to leave, Elizabeth hesitated. There was criticism enough against her without drawing further attention to the estate. If this man was arrested, then today's events would be publicised in the newspapers and likely used against her. 'Let him be,' she said. 'There is no harm done.'

By the time Lord Stafford hurried into the gallery behind Cantrill, the strange man and the public viewers had already been removed. Elizabeth turned at their approach.

'What has happened, Elizabeth?' her husband said. 'Cantrill tells me a madman is threatening to destroy my paintings.' As he spoke, his head turned left and right, searching for the intruder.

* * *

Later that evening as they dined together, Elizabeth discussed the intruder with her husband. Supping on a bowl of warming cock-a-leekie soup in familiar surroundings, she already felt distanced from the events of the afternoon. 'In truth, although it seemed longer, the whole episode was over in less than ten minutes.'

'Who was the man? You said he was a returning soldier, but—'

'He had been fighting abroad but was returned due to injuries. He said his name was Rob Dunn, a Highlander from Strathnaver. There is not really much more to tell.'

'Was he one of the families removed by Sellar?'

'Now I think about it, yes, he did say that his mother had been removed.'

'But you think it was Sellar's actions that caused this man's outburst?'

Elizabeth had no need to ponder her reply. 'I am certain of it. Mister Sellar's pending trial is widely advertised and discussed in the newspapers. Likely everyone knows of this by now.'

'What are we to do about Sellar?' Lord Stafford peered at her over the frame of his spectacles. 'We cannot be seen to countenance such behaviour. Our estate commissioner is of the same opinion.'

After pushing the now empty soup bowl aside, Elizabeth sipped her wine and contemplated her answer. She laid the glass down. 'I have thought for some time that he should be replaced as under factor.'

Her husband nodded. 'We can no longer have him acting as a factor on our Highland estate. He is too eager by far in his methods, and I doubt he will ever change his ways.'

'Mister Sellar has the best lawyers fighting his case, his father included. For our own sakes, we should continue to support him in this matter. For now. But, regardless of the outcome of his trial, yes, he has to go.'

'In the meantime, Elizabeth, have our lawyer arbitrate to settle this matter out of court. The family who feel they have been wronged can be recompensed. I do not care how much it costs.'

'I agree. This nonsense has to be stopped. We cannot have our home invaded like this.'

33

HARVEST OF HOPE

Mhàiri sat crossed-legged at the side of the field, waiting for Cameron to finish turning the first furrows. As she nestled her sleeping baby into her neck, she watched Cameron's forearms flex as he pushed the plough through the damp earth.

She placed her ear near Caitriona's mouth and listened to her gentle breathing. Whooping cough raged through the strath, and Mhàiri prayed that her daughter would be spared. Satisfied that Caitriona's breathing was regular, she nestled her into her arms. As she did so, the sweet scent of her daughter mingled with the peaty smell rising from the exposed earth. Rich with promise, the sun shone through sparse clouds. Spring had arrived.

Cameron finished turning the last of three rows and laid the plough down. He wiped his forehead with the rolled-up sleeve of his jacket and made his way over. When he had settled on the ground beside her, Mhàiri passed him a jug of oats mixed with milk.

Following a long-held tradition in the strath, he drank the contents of the jug without stopping. Mhàiri held her breath and waited for his reaction.

He nodded. 'The texture is perfect.'

Mhàiri let out her breath and smiled. The omens signalled that a good crop would follow. Cameron had completed the first run of ploughing to his satisfaction. In a few days, she would start scattering the seeds that would feed their family throughout the winter.

Cameron placed an arm around her shoulder and leant his head against hers. 'It is days like this that make life worth living.'

'Hhmm,' Mhàiri uttered and snuggled into him. 'I pray we get to spend many more like it. The nearer the factor's trial dawns the more I believe we will be allowed to remain here.' A surge of hope flowed through her and she tried to swallow the feeling back. Hope that Maister Sellar would be found guilty had lit in her like a smouldering ember, then it had burst into a roaring flame. 'I know I should not be so convinced about the outcome of the trial, but I cannot help believing that the factor *will* be jailed for what he has done.'

Cameron stroked her hair. 'With so many speaking out against him, I cannot see how it could be any other way.'

'Another year has passed without any removals. Do you think it is because people know the factor is to be brought to account? If he is found guilty then surely the removals will stop altogether.'

Cameron stood. 'We better not let our thoughts run away with us, but yes, let's hope it is.' He bent and kissed their daughter's sleeping head and then Mhàiri's lips. 'I best get on. We have a long journey next week. I want this field planted before we leave for Inverness.'

With hope burning brightly within her, Mhàiri nodded. She lay back on one elbow and watched her husband pick up the plough and push it through the damp earth.

* * *

Mhàiri carried her daughter strapped to her back and trekked beside Cameron and her parents as they made their way towards Inverness. The weather had remained clear of rain during the long journey, and they made good progress.

When they finally arrived at her father's sister's house, Aunt Baraball hurried out the door to greet them.

'*Cionnas a tha sibh?* – How are you?' Aunt Baraball called and hugged each of them in turn to her ample bosom. 'A thousand welcomes. Let us be getting you inside. Likely you will be in need of a rest after your journey.' She turned to Mhàiri and held out her arms. 'Give the baby to me and get yourself settled too. There is some broth heating. Help yourself.'

Aunt Baraball cooed over Caitriona and fussed about, settling her guests into her home. Her husband, a small, wiry man brought in peats and banked up the fire.

'Since yesterday, people have been arriving here in droves. There cannot be a bed in Inverness lying empty tonight,' Aunt Baraball said after they had finished eating and the children had been put to bed. Baraball and her husband had six children, ranging in age from three to twelve years.

When talk turned to the trial, Aunt Baraball held up a hand. 'Likely you will be having a long day tomorrow. It is best if you all have an early night.'

Mhàiri nodded her thanks. She could barely keep her eyes open. She lay down on a pallet bed in the back room and was asleep within minutes of her head hitting the generously filled feather pillow.

CIRCUIT COURT

Inverness

The next morning, Mhàiri took a seat on a bench in the courtroom; of the Circuit Court of Justiciary. Cameron jostled in beside her, and they were joined by her mother and father. Aunt Úna and her husband continued to the front and sat in the witness section.

Mhàiri trembled with anticipation. It had been almost two years since her aunt's township had been cleared. It had taken the tenants all this time to bring the factor to trial, but they had achieved it. She settled into her seat and looked around. Despite arriving early, the courtroom had already started to fill. She recognised many familiar faces in the witness section. Over thirty tenants had left their planting unfinished and had travelled from the strath and the new coastal towns to present their evidence against the factor.

When Maister Sellar was brought in Mhàiri was surprised to see a forlorn figure. He sat on a bench and kept his eyes looking downward. His shoulders were slumped and he dropped his chin forward onto his chest. If he was found guilty of murder he could be hanged. A surge of pity flowed through Mhàiri, but she pushed it away.

Màthair leant over to Mhàiri. 'Outside, my sister was telling me that in Brora they are saying that the family of the murdered woman was offered money to stop them bringing their case against Maister Sellar to court.'

'And?' Mhàiri asked.

Màthair shrugged. 'The family refused, of course.'

Cameron held a hand to the side of his mouth. 'If someone was willing to pay not to bring this case to trial then that person must think the factor guilty.'

'It was Lord Stafford himself who offered the purse,' Màthair said, almost in a whisper.

Mhàiri raised her eyes and shook her head. Surely the evidence against the factor was strong. Iain entered with Peigi Ruadh. As the woman sat down Mhàiri noticed a tell-tale swelling of her belly. Although Lord Stafford had refused to allow them to marry, Peigi Ruadh was with child. Despite her dislike of the woman, Mhàiri knew that she would have done the same, had she been refused permission to marry Cameron. She couldn't imagine her life without her daughter. But what would happen to Iain and Peigi Ruadh? The birth of a baby would alert the minister that they were living together as man and wife. They would surely be punished for their sins.

The steeple bell chimed the hour of ten, and the Judge entered. The Clerk of the Court called something in English. Everyone stood, and Mhàiri rose to her feet. After the Judge sat, Mhàiri seated herself.

As the Clerk read out the charges against the factor, Mhàiri looked around in bewildered confusion. The words were in English. Her father and some of the other men could speak a bit of English; from their time spent abroad in the wars and from doing seasonal work in the south, but Mhàiri understood nothing. She sighed with relief when a man stood and summarised the clerk's words in Gaelic.

'. . . is indicted and accused of the crimes of culpable homicide and oppression as mentioned in the indictment pursued against him. The defendant pleads not guilty.'

Mhàiri gripped Cameron's arm, the factor had pled not guilty.

When the Sheriff-Substitute, Mister McKid, rose to present the evidence gathered in his indictment, Mhàiri leant forward and listened closely to the Gaelic summary.

'Mister Sellar ordered the heath and pasture, which the people of the townships relied upon to graze their animals, to be set on fire. The burnings were carried out with such malice and wickedness that it reduced these people to great poverty and distress. Against the practice of the county, mills and barns were destroyed before tenants could remove their crops—'

A member of the defence rose. 'We object to this evidence on the grounds that the Sheriff Substitute has previously shown malice towards the accused.'

After a brief discussion with the judge, the objection was allowed, and Sheriff McKid was asked to sit.

Sheriff McKid hesitated, opened his mouth as if to say something then sat.

Mhàiri's smile faded. What did this mean? She wanted to ask, but couldn't.

The defence challenged the prosecution to prove the allegation of culpable homicide brought against the factor.

A witness for the prosecution took the stand. The woman looked confused by the questions put to her in English and translated into the Gaelic, and then her reply translated back into English for the benefit of the court.

'I don't understand what you mean.' The woman looked about her as if seeking answers in the four corners of the courtroom. 'Your words are not making any sense to me. What are you asking?' she added with a tremor in her voice.

Soon after, the court was adjourned for a recess and Mhàiri listened to the frenzied chatter around her. Sheriff McKid had been silenced, and no one knew what to make of that. Few of the prosecution witnesses had been called, and those who had seemed confused by the questions put to them. Throughout the morning session, Maister Sellar had remained silent and kept his head down.

The trial dragged on through the long afternoon. At six o'clock in the evening, a recess was called, and Mhàiri hastened from the courtroom. She hurried down the staircase and waited outside.

'Ah Mhàiri, you are here,' Aunt Baraball said as she hurried towards her, carrying Caitriona 'How is the trial going?'

Mhàiri held her hands out to take her daughter and shook her head. 'I do not know. I honestly do not know. It is all very confusing.'

The women sat on a bench overlooking the Tollbooth Steeple, adjoining the courthouse. Mhàiri laughed with Caitriona as they watched birds fly down to peck at the leaves blowing on the cobbles. Mhàiri took off her plaid and sat her eleven-month-old daughter on it. She opened out a small folded cloth, containing cheese and dried fruit, and placed it in front her. 'Yum.' Mhàiri said and mimicked eating a piece of fruit.

After putting her daughter to the breast for her fill, Mhàiri wrapped her in a blanket and rocked her until she fell asleep. She hugged her daughter close before handing her to Aunt Baraball. 'I best get back.'

'Leave this little one to me,' Aunt Baraball said as they walked towards the courthouse. 'One more added to my brood isn't making much of a difference. The baby will be asleep anyway, so don't you be worrying or hurrying back. There will be a bowl of something hot for you all when you get in.'

Mhàiri nodded and waved Aunt Baraball off. She remained at the door and watched as her aunt made her way down Bridge Street. When she could no longer see her daughter, Mhàiri turned and made her way up the stairs to the courtroom. What was she doing here? It was all so confusing.

THE JURY'S JUDGEMENT

Not long after the steeple bells rang out the night hour of nine o'clock, the prosecution finished presenting their evidence against the factor. Mhàiri looked around. What was happening? Why had all the witnesses not been called, including her aunt and uncle?

The prosecution explained that they had not called all their witnesses because many shared the same name and township and confusion had arisen over which tenant was being called. While this could have been resolved with time, the prosecution decided not to call these witnesses to prevent the *same* story from being repeated over and over again to the court.

Mhàiri struggled to understand. Surely all the witnesses had a right to be heard? And surely it was a good thing if the tenants all said the same thing?

The defence rose to present their case. Mhàiri strained her neck forward so she wouldn't miss anything and listened to the Gaelic translation.

'The heath that was burned belonged to Mister Sellar. Burning the heath is standard practice.'

'The accused notified the tenants in the previous January

that he had right of entry from May and required the land occupied by them at this time.'

'The accused had waited for the tenants to move to their new allotments but, in the middle of June, finding them still there ordered his officers to evict them.'

The defence continued. 'Mister Sellar had carried out his duties as factor and conducted the evictions in a proper and lawful manner.'

'There is no question of cruelty or oppression on Mister Sellar's part. In truth, he is the victim of a vile conspiracy. The allegations brought against him are designed to undermine the improvements being carried out by the landowners.'

'No homicide was committed. There has been no evidence presented today to show that the old and unwell woman would not have died anyway.'

The defence called several respected gentlemen who, one after the other, spoke of Mister Sellar's good character.

Well after midnight, the judge addressed the jury before sending them out to reach their decision. 'If you are at a loss by the conflicting evidence presented to you, you should take into account the good character of the accused.'

The jury retired.

Fifteen minutes later, the members of the jury were ready to announce their verdict.

Mhàiri gripped Cameron's hand. Their future in the strath depended on a good outcome. She wanted her daughter to laze in the high pasture blowing the heads of dandelions and making wishes. She wanted to take Caitriona to the sheilings in the summer. With newfound clarity, she realised that it wasn't just the tenants' homes that were at stake here today, it was her whole way of life.

The foreman for the jury stood. 'Not guilty.'

Not guilty? A sound grew in Mhàiri's throat and erupted from her mouth, 'Never!'

Her protest joined the rumble growing to a roar around the room. Benches scraped as people stood. Voices called out in protest.

Maister Sellar lifted his head and tilted his beaked nose in the air. Tears streamed down his face.

'Silence,' the judge called and banged his gavel. 'Pray be silent.' Once order had been restored, the judge continued. 'I would have come to the same conclusion. Mister Sellar, you have been sorely wronged. I trust the outcome here today has cleared your good name.'

Cameron put an arm around Mhàiri and pulled her close. A scream rose within her growing to a wail. She swallowed the scream down. It sank to the pit of her belly and lodged there like a boulder, smothering her hopes and dragging her down. Sinking deeper into the bog, she floated downwards— drowning. Grasping on a straw, she dragged herself up and gasped for air. She gripped Cameron's arm. 'Dear God in Heaven, what will happen to us now?'

SWEET SORROW

Hidden from view in the high ground, Mister Sellar leant forward on his horse. He adjusted the eyeglass to better see the flurry of activity taking place on the farm below. As he watched McKid's wife herding a gaggle of sullen children into the back of a battered wagon, his lips twisted into a smile. After settling her children, the woman turned to her husband, who was loading the last of their possessions into another wagon, and said something. The factor cursed that he was out of earshot. He glanced around but couldn't see anywhere closer to move to.

The wagons moved off, setting up a flurry of dust. The factor adjusted the eyeglass and followed the family's slow progress as the wheels clattered across the stony ground taking them from the farm. He watched until he could no longer make out the wagons. Satisfied that his neighbour and sworn enemy had left for good, he tilted his chin into the air and sniffed. Was that the sweet smell of success? If so, it was a very pleasant aroma indeed. Chuckling at his wit, he flicked the reins and trotted down to the farmhouse.

He slid from the saddle and thwacked the horse-whip

against his thigh. Laughing out loud, he strolled around the outside of the two-storey building and imagined with satisfaction the great sense of loss the now jobless and penniless, McKid and his family must have felt at leaving behind their home.

He was surprised McKid had managed to last for so long before accepting that he was ruined. Since losing his position as Sheriff- Substitute, he had survived by selling off the best of his furniture. Well, it had saved McKid from having to cart it away with him today. His smile faded. Perhaps now others would think twice before crossing him.

Although the farm looked run down, the factor contemplated the low price he would get the now vacant lease for. After all, with the money he'd procured from McKid for the recovery of the cost of the damned trial he could well afford it. 'Humph,' he muttered. Whether or not he wanted this farm, he would place a bid for the lease. It would serve as a final sense of closure for the distress McKid had caused him.

His hand clenched around the whip. McKid could not have been blind to the noose that would have awaited had this vendetta against him been successful. He had made the scoundrel pay but he wasn't finished yet. The man had tried to humiliate him and see him dead. Well, he would continue to wreak his revenge on the fool and on the tenants who had spoken out against him. Of greater concern at the moment, despite the not guilty verdict, it looked like his days as factor on the estate were numbered.

On returning home, he made straight for his study. Sitting at his desk, he dipped his pen into the ink and wrote, to Lady Stafford. *As not a mouse stirs here without your knowledge, it is with great satisfaction that I inform Your Ladyship that the estate is now rid of a great nuisance. Having personally witnessed Mister McKid's departure, you can be reassured that the source of the most devious conspiracy laid against you has now been removed. As you know, I showed great compassion and dropped all charges_against him on his agreeing to pay the whole of the expenses I incurred for the lawsuit, because of his gross lies and manipulation of an ignorant group of people to speak out against me. Once I receive these costs and a sum for expenses, I will wash my hands of him.*

If it suits Your Ladyship, it would be an honour for me to be considered for the now vacant position of Sheriff Substitute. As you are aware, I only ever endeavoured to do what was right in educating a slothful and indifferent race towards industry. Not a thing passed me as your factor and I would apply the same strict standards as Sheriff Substitute in order to ensure you with a law-abiding people. To save you the trouble of advertising the tenure, I am also willing to take over the lease of Mister McKid's farm.

Your humble and obedient servant,

37

PEACEFUL PARLOUR

Two Years Later

Strathnaver

I n the manse beside the mission, Maighstir Sage wiped his
mouth with a napkin, pushed back his chair and stood from
the table. The salmon and potatoes he had dined on had suited
his simple tastes well enough. More and more, life in his own
home proved to be to his liking. When his predecessor, Maighstir MacCoinnich, had vacated the manse, he left behind some
of his furniture. The table and chairs had been bought from
Sheriff McKid when he sold off the furniture from his home.
Everything else he had begged from his father.

He made his way through to the parlour and looked at the
hall clock as he passed. There was at least twenty minutes
before Maighstir MacCoinnich was due to call. He settled by
the flaming peat fire, picked up the Inverness Gazette and
scanned the pages.

His eyes grew heavy and he closed them. Having once acted as tutor to Sheriff McKid's children, he knew the family well. It pained him to have witnessed his friend's demise. Doubts about Sellar's actions circled his thoughts. He knew McKid to be an honest man, but had his actions arisen from a personal grudge against the factor? Although Sellar was no longer a factor on the estate and hadn't been granted the position of Sheriff-Substitute, he was still a force to be reckoned with; he held leases for large tracts of land in Strathnaver and in the Strath of Kildonan.

When a knock came on the door, Maighstir Sage opened his eyes and laid the newspaper down.

His sister ushered the minister in and left.

Maighstir Sage stood. 'Many thanks for coming, Maighstir MacCoinnich.' He gestured for him to take a seat and went over to a dresser and poured two generous measures of whisky.

He handed a glass to his guest, who looked at him with furrowed brows and said, 'Why have you asked to see me? Has something happened?'

'Nothing has happened. It is just . . . I hesitated to ask you before, but if I am to take over the care of the people in this parish from you, I need to know more.' He sat down. 'Do you think there was any truth to McKid's claims against Sellar?'

Maighstir MacCoinnich rolled the glass between his palms. After a pause, he leant forward. 'In that case, even if it goes against what some want to hear. Yes, I do believe the allegations had some foundation in truth. The extent of his cruelty, I am less certain about.'

'Yet, you now refuse to endorse the Estate Commissioners statement that moving to the coast is in the parishioner's best interest. For that, I admire your courage. But, why didn't you speak out before?'

'The answer to that question will haunt me forever. My conscience is sorely troubled.' Maighstir MacCoinnich sipped his whisky, as if deep in thought. After a moment, he said, 'I suppose I feel indebted to Lady Stafford. She treats me as a friend, not just as a minister.'

'A friend?' This was the last thing Maighstir Sage expected to hear. 'As I travel around this parish, most parishioners say that Lady Stafford would never force them from their homes. They blame all their present troubles on the factors. That is why so many stay after receiving notice to move. They refuse to believe that she would turn them out of their homes. Do you also believe that your friend has the best interests of our parishioners at heart?'

'I believe her intentions are honourable. And, to be fair, there was no case found against Sellar.'

'Are you surprised?' Maighstir Sage said, his voice rising.

'You have to understand the great poverty that exists in the straths. Before, when demand for cattle was high. During the wars. Well . . . things were different then.'

'I am not unfamiliar with the needs of these people. It is the needs of those who are forcing them from their homes that I am interested in.' Maighstir Sage frowned and shook his head. 'Let us be honest. We might be ministers, but as long as we reside in these parts, we *also* are tenants. If our parishioners can be evicted then so can we . . . and our families. All we know of this life could be gone. Like that.' He snapped his fingers. 'Take your situation. Already removed to the coast. If my thinking is right then, when the tenant farmers are all gone from here, what need will there be for a mission or indeed a church? None of this bodes well for the people or the Kirk.'

'But look how hard the last two winters have been. The crops too poor to see our parishioners through and relief asked for from Lord and Lady Stafford. But you are right. For all that, I can no longer bring myself to support the view that these people would be better off if they moved. Have you seen the hovels on the coast? Granted, there are a few decent houses, but most arrive to nothing more than a shared shed and a scrap of ground.'

'And what about those left to wander? What is to become of them?'

Maighstir MacCoinnich let out a deep breath. 'How can I speak out about any of this? Lord and Lady Stafford employ me. I am certain that they are not being told the full story.'

By the time his guest made to leave it was past ten o'clock. After bidding him goodnight, Maighstir Sage made for his bedroom. Things did not look good at all and there was nothing he could do about it. Any hope he had harboured of helping his parishioners now vanished like dandelion seeds blown in the wind.

* * *

The following evening, a loud banging on the front door disturbed Maighstir Sage from his writing. He rose from the desk and hurried into the hall.

His sister, who had her hand on the latch, turned at his approach. 'What an infernal noise to be making at this time of night,' she said and opened the front door.

A man, the minister recognised as a parishioner entered and removed his hat. The visitor trembled and had a look of terror on his face. 'Maighstir Sage, I need to speak with you most urgently.' The man clutched his cap to his chest. 'A strange thing has happened. A very strange thing indeed, and I don't know what to make of it.'

Despite the late hour, Maighstir Sage ushered him into the parlour. He pointed to a chair and sat opposite. 'What has happened?'

'Well now, this afternoon, I went to pay my rent. My rent was due. The Estate Commissioner was there, but he wouldn't take my money. He said my rent was not being called this year.

He said, "tell everyone that the rest of Strathnaver has been placed under stock".' The man shook his head. 'He also said that those who had not already received notice of removal would be receiving this soon. I don't know what to do.'

'All of the townships?'

The man nodded. 'What will become of us?'

Maighstir Sage rubbed his face. By the sound of it, there wasn't much time left for any of them. As he thought about what he should do, the ticking of the parlour clock grew louder. 'Tick-tock. Tick-tock'.

38

SERVICES AND SINNERS

A s the service in the mission drew to a close, Mhàiri rubbed her swollen belly and shifted in her seat. Now was the moment she dreaded.

The catechist read from a list. The timbre of his voice reverberated across the rafters. 'From within this parish, Seumas MacUilleam has been arrested and charged with sheep stealing. Tòmas Bodhar with poaching deer. Along with their families, they have been evicted. Heed this as a warning. Peigi Ruadh has sinned again in bearing another child while unmarried.'

The catechist's voice continued to call the names of sinners. Mhàiri heard his words as if from a great distance. 'Sin. Sin. Punishment for your sins.'

Her attention was caught by the mention of removals and she leant forward. 'Townships within Strathnaver have been placed under stock. Those who have not already received notice of removal will be receiving this soon.'

* * *

After the service, Mhàiri hurried to the meeting-house with Cameron. When they entered they were met by concerned faces. Mhàiri gripped Cameron's hand and remained by his side. There would be no harvest celebration this year; most of the seeds they had planted had failed to flourish. The weather had been against them. Mhàiri squeezed Cameron's hand. They had other worries concerning them now.

Once everyone arrived, Cameron spoke. 'We have to do something. We cannot stand idly by and let our homes be taken from us. We failed to have Maister Sellar brought to account for his actions, but there must be something else we can do.'

'What can we do against the hand of God?' Fearghas said and placed an arm around his wife, Anna. 'There is nothing else for it, we will have to move. I have a family to think about.'

Cameron nodded and looked at Mhàiri. 'We do indeed have to think of our families. That is why we must fight back. If we want to pass on the ways handed down from generations before us then we have to.'

Anna snorted. 'What good will the old ways be to our children when they have nowhere to live? You heard the catechist. We have to obey the order when it comes.'

'A dark curse on the head of those removing us from our homes,' the fiddler's wife said. 'We should stay where we are.'

'Take heed,' Fearghas said. 'To resist will bring nothing but trouble.'

The fiddler laughed. 'There will be trouble, either way, stay or go. The whisky is the only one I am trusting right now.'

'We are too old to be moving anywhere,' the fiddler's wife said and scowled. 'We are stopping where we are. Anyway, what can we do that we haven't already tried.'

Cameron raised a hand. 'We could petition directly to the Prince Regent. Let him know what is happening. Ask him to intervene on our behalf.'

'And how are we to do that?' the miller said. 'It would mean someone travelling to London and that will cost.'

'We could each give a small amount,' Cameron said. 'Only one person need go. We could approach the Kildonan men in the hills, Rob Dunn, even.'

Mhàiri was surprised to hear Rob Dunn's name mentioned, but if anyone could present their petition to the Prince Regent it would be him. She had heard the story about him confronting The Great Lady in the art gallery of her London home. 'It is worth a try.'

'It is,' Cameron said. 'Those for a petition raise your hand?'

Mhàiri watched some hands go up. She hesitated. It would mean giving out money, and she needed every penny she had just to survive. A few more hands were raised. Anna and Fearghas's hands remained down. Iain and Peigi Ruadh's also.

It looked equal for and against. But the tenants had to do something. What were a few shillings if it meant keeping their homes? She could make do. Mhàiri raised her hand.

* * *

With Cameron and her father away meeting with the Kildonan men, Mhàiri tried to stretch out the little food she had. The frosts would arrive soon, driving the wild animals onto the lower ground. Mhàiri thought of the rabbits, birds and deer that had sustained them through previous winters. She shook her head. A notice had been posted on the meeting-house door, reminding the tenants of the punishment if they were caught poaching and informing them that the watch had been increased. Mhàiri's thoughts turned to the family who had been evicted for killing a deer. Her throat tightened. They had been trying to survive the best way they could. Like they all were.

She placed a handful of wild herbs into the pot of cooling

broth and prayed that it would relieve the children's hunger. She pulled out the cloth tucked into her belt, picked up the pot and carried it down to her mother's house. Her daughter trailed behind her. With the men away it made sense to share what little food they had.

'Ah, Mhàiri, I have made a few oatcakes. Put the pot on to heat,' Màthair said.

Mhàiri rubbed her aching back. 'Another burden on the way but I cannot help feeling excited at the thought of another bairn.'

As Mhàiri and Màthair talked the door opened and Connor entered. He held a rabbit in one raised hand and a turnip in the other. 'Put these in the pot, Màthair.'

Mhàiri felt her face pale. 'What— Where did you get that? Dear God, you will have us all turned out.'

Connor grinned. 'Well, you will never believe it.'

'You stole them,' Mhàiri said.

'I did not.'

'Then explain yourself. Tell me where you got them?'

'Ah, well. I was walking at the bottom of the big brae when the turnip rolled down the hill and hit the rabbit . . . stone dead. What was I to do? I couldn't just leave them there.'

'Connor, mind your lies,' Mhàiri said. Her brother could always make her laugh with his ways, but this was serious. 'If you are caught you won't be smiling then.'

Connor shook his head. 'It is no different than taking berries from the bushes. And, there was no one about.'

'That you know off.' Mhàiri felt her anger rise and she scowled.

'Aw, stop it, Mhàiri,' Connor said. 'We are needing to eat.'

The thought of a succulent rabbit stew had Mhàiri's belly churning.

Her daughter looked at Mhàiri with wide eyes. 'I am hungry.'

Màthair raised her brows at Mhàiri and laughed. 'We will have the rabbit and turnip tonight and feed the evidence to the animals. But no more.'

'Do you hear that, Connor? No more,' Mhàiri said. 'You never know who is watching.'

39

NASTY NOTICE

Caitriona raced after a robin in flight. Mhàiri followed her daughter across the frost-covered pasture. She scooped the three-year-old into her arm and lifted her so that she could watch the bird settle on a shrub of gorse.

'We best get home.' Mhàiri pulled Caitriona close and whispered, 'As Mamó would say, dreaming in the high pastures won't get the cows milked.'

Caitriona giggled and wriggled down from Mhàiri's arms. She ran, hurtling down the brae towards home. Mhàiri laughed as she ran beside her. Below, three horses rode into Achcoil. As the riders came into clearer focus, silver buttons glittered on the jacket of the man on the grey mount riding in behind them. Mhàiri's steps slowed. Dear God, don't let it be.

She picked up her daughter and quickened her step, racing and sliding down the brae towards home. Smudges in the frost on top of a wooden fence whispered of an intruder. Mhàiri stepped through the open gate. When she arrived at the cottage her steps faltered. The berry-laden branches of the rowan tree drooped as if apologising for not better protecting her home. Muddy slush on the path spoke of recent footsteps.

Caitriona cried. Mhàiri shushed her. She lowered her daughter to the ground and gripped her hand. With her eyes fixed ahead, she stared in confusion at the notice posted on her door.

A single word resonated in her head like a slow beating drum; No. No. No... No. No. No.

Notice of Summons Parish of Strathnaver

Lord and Lady Stafford, having determined to lay this place under stock, give notice to the tenants herein that allotments on the coast will be prepared by January next when such person will be informed of the Allotment marked off for him in order that he may prepare to enter it at the Term of Whitsunday first if he so inclines.

Each Tenant who behaves himself to the satisfaction of the proprietors and their factors have permission to occupy their present holdings as pasturage rent-free from Whitsunday 1818 to Whitsunday 1819 in order that those who conduct themselves as aforesaid can have time to remove their property and erect their houses on their new allotment at Invercreag.

Caitriona's cries grew louder. Mhàiri picked her up and nestled her into her arms. Dear God in heaven, why? Why now? Two years had passed since the factor's trial and there had been no word of removals during that time.

Shaking her head, Mhàiri tried to think. Nothing came. She tried again and thought of her mother. She gripped the hem of her skirt and raced down the brae towards her parent's house, her daughter screaming in her arms.

Four riders passed but didn't look down.

Mhàiri glared up at the men and roared, 'Why? Why now?'

The riders continued on their way.

Mhàiri raced past Hattie Bantrach's hovel but couldn't stop to comfort the bowed woman weeping at the door. When she entered her mother's cottage, she tried to call out. She tried to tell her what had been posted on her door. To tell her that she was to move to the coast. No words came. Her body sagged. She gripped her daughter tighter. As if wading through a deep river, she made her way over to where her mother sat slumped forward with her head in her hands staring at the notice of removal lying face up in front of her on the table.

Realisation dawned on Mhàiri. Everyone in Achcoil had received notice to move to the coast.

* * *

That evening, after putting her daughter to bed, Mhàiri settled beside Cameron at the fire. 'Could we take our cattle to that new market at Inverness? We could use the money we save from the free rent to set up somewhere else. We have talked enough about leaving, perhaps now is the time.'

Cameron nodded but didn't reply.

His silence unnerved her. 'What is it? What are you not telling me?'

Cameron rubbed his hands over his face. He stood and stepped towards her. 'Mhàiri, our cattle are near dead. They will not fetch much. Even with the recent rise in price, they are not worth taking to market. Likely they would die in the trying.'

'They have had little or no grazing.' With tears threatening, Mhàiri's voice wavered. 'Why did we have to have such a poor harvest? And last year's no better. We have no choice but to move to the coast.'

Cameron laid his hands on her shoulders and looked down at her upturned face. 'Ha! Free rent if we move to Invercreag without protest. The factor knows fine well we do not have the money to be paying his increased rents. This is all designed to get us to go to the coast without a fight. Well, I for one will not be moving and I doubt many others will.'

Mhàiri stood and collapsed into Cameron's arms. He held her and they swayed together. Their tears mingled. Never had she felt so close to him. Last year she lost another baby. She thought then that her heart would break. But, as she'd looked at her stillborn son, she hadn't said, not even once, that it had been God's will. And neither was them being removed. Mòrag Mòr was right. This was man's doing.

When Cameron loosened his grip, Mhàiri stepped back and wiped the tears from her face with her hands. She tilted her chin upwards. 'The ten pounds from your father, we will use that.'

'We promised not to touch that money, no matter how difficult things got. We have to keep our options open. That money is towards our passages away from here.'

She didn't want to spend the money either, but her family had to eat. She placed a hand on her swollen belly. 'But we cannot risk losing another child. Your parents will understand. Besides, we now need fares for four. We will never be able to save thirty pounds.'

With his hands held to his face as if in prayer, Cameron paced the room. 'We cannot touch that money.' He turned and faced her. 'I will find work. Even if I have to go down the coal-pit at Brora, I will find the money we need to get us through this.'

Mhàiri shook her head. 'You will stay where you are. What good are you to me in Brora? There's no point dreaming, Cameron. If we have to use that money to survive through this winter then that is exactly what we will do. Chances are that even if we did have the money, we wouldn't be able to emigrate. There has been no word of any ships leaving.'

40

CHRISTMAS CHEER

London

Two carriages clattered to a halt on the crisp, frozen ground outside Elizabeth's townhouse. Impatient with waiting for her daughter and her family to arrive, Elizabeth let out a sigh of relief. She dashed out the door and raced down the front steps. A maid followed and placed a fur-lined, hooded cloak around Elizabeth's shoulders.

Charlotte stepped down from the first carriage. 'Mama.'

Elizabeth raised a hand in welcome, but her eyes strayed to the swaddled baby held in the arms of the childrens' nurse who stepped out of the second carriage. She scanned the woollen bundle containing her six-month-old grandson. 'My, how he has grown since I last saw him.'

Her four-year-old granddaughter ran towards her and curtsied. Elizabeth smiled and glanced beyond the girl to fix her gaze upon three-year-old, Henry, the apple of her eye.

'Grandmama,' Henry called and hurtled towards her, laughing. 'Is it Christmas?'

Elizabeth hunkered down and scooped him into her arms. 'No. Not yet. But it will be very soon.'

Flames from the braziers burning outside the entrance lit up the boy's confused face. 'But why is it not? Mama said we were coming to you for Christmas. And now we are here. So, it must be Christmas. Is Uncle George here?'

Elizabeth laughed. 'Yes, Uncle George and the others have arrived.'

'Can I see them?'

'After everyone has been settled into their rooms, we will gather in the withdrawing room for hot chocolate and mince pies. But first, let me show you the entrance hall. The staircase is magnificent.'

Elizabeth led her daughter's family through the large double doors and into the hallway. Behind them, servants unloaded bags from the carriages. It was the fashion again in London to deck the hall with garlands of winter greens, herbs, and coloured ribbons. Elizabeth couldn't contain her excitement as she showed her grandson the decorations that had already been put up.

Servants lined the stairs, watching the family approach. Wide-eyed and open-mouthed, her staff waited for further instructions. Preparations were in progress for the Christmas-eve ball to be held the following evening. When the carriages had drawn up outside, Elizabeth had hurried from the entrance hall, leaving the servants waiting for her return.

'Look,' Henry called to his father and slid from Elizabeth's arms. The childrens' nurse followed Henry as he took in the sights and squealed in delight. Elizabeth's eyes followed her grandson's movements, drinking in his presence.

* * *

At a meal, after her grandchildren were in bed, Elizabeth caught up on her children's news. Platters of goose, swan and beef were placed on the oak sideboard and served at the table.

Elizabeth took pleasure in having her children around her. She picked up her filled wine glass and held it aloft. 'To our new grandson and many more of them to come.' She looked at her husband and then to each of her sons in turn.

Her family raised their glasses in reply.

Elizabeth smiled. '1818 is drawing to a close. Indeed, I wonder where the year has gone.'

'Next year will be equally busy,' Charlotte said. 'There is to be no let-up. The London season will resume again in earnest, Mama. Soon, we will be facing another round of theatre, balls and engagements. We really should finish preparing our spring wardrobes.'

'I would like nothing better than for us to have some trips to shop for fabric,' Elizabeth said to her daughter. 'But, as soon the weather improves, I have to accompany your father north.'

'Why? What has happened now, Mama?' her youngest son, Frances, asked.

'With the Sellar incident finally behind us, we had hoped to continue with the improvements, but at a slower pace.'

'And?' Frances said.

'Mister Sellar and the other sheep farmers are threatening to withdraw from their leases if we don't move swiftly on with the remainder of the removals.'

Charlotte frowned. 'Why?'

'They are losing too many sheep to thefts,' Elizabeth said. 'They no longer want tenants on or near their sheep farms. Put simply, if the tenants remain, the sheep farmers will leave. So, the next phase of removals is set for May. We have much to do to prepare for the tenant's arrival at the coast. That in itself, doesn't present too much of a problem. Indeed, the fishing is proving more profitable than we had expected and we have plans to expand. No, it is the lack of houses that is proving such a headache. It is impossible to build enough before May.'

'But, Mama, what are you to do?' Frances asked.

'I will visit some of the coastal villages. See how things are progressing. But, for now, all I want is to enjoy the Christmas season with my family. After our meal, Charlotte, you must play the piano.' Elizabeth's excitement grew. 'We can select some pieces for you to play at tomorrow's ball.'

4 1

THE SALT SELLER

Strathnaver

A loud wail pulled Mhàiri from sleep. Still not fully awake, she patted her hand around the bed. Finding no sign of her husband, she opened her eyes to near darkness. Cameron had risen early. It could mean only one thing; another one of their animals was ailing. Death stalked the straths and nothing was free from its grasp.

Mhàiri groaned and swung her legs over the side and sat for a moment with her head nestled in her hands. Another wail pulled her into action. 'I am coming. Hold on.' She reached into the cradle and lifted her four-month-old son, Cailean, and laid him to her breast. She sat on the side of the bed and held back her tears. Why was she so tired all the time?

When her son had taken his fill, she laid him in the cradle and stepped onto the cold floor. She dressed quickly. The skirt she had pulled from the chest was too loose. She searched for a belt and tied it around her waist to stop the skirt slipping down.

After wrapping Cailean in a blanket, she tied one end around her shoulder and the other around her waist.

She stacked the fire with peats. When it blazed, she reached into the wooden chest and scooped up a helping of oats. Noticing how low the grain sat in the chest she tipped some back. Hopefully, if she served the porridge with extra milk there would be enough for Cameron and Caitriona.

Connor raced in. 'With Father helping Cameron with the bull, Màthair asked if you were coming down.'

Mhàiri turned. 'Tell her I will be there soon.' After hesitating, she said, 'Would you gather the eggs in for me?' Her brother was good at finding hidden ones, and she could do with some more. 'Do not be climbing too high,' she called to his retreating back.

So, her father was helping Cameron with the bull. It must be bad news. Her concern grew. While she rinsed the bowls in a pail, her mind remained alert, listening. Every sound made her startle. Caitriona clutched onto Mhàiri's skirt and leant against her.

When a shot rang out, Mhàiri lifted her daughter onto a chair and raced outside. In fear of what she would find when she got there, she hurried towards the large barn. With every step, the township retreated further from her vision as if unwilling to bear witness to the waiting scene. She heard the thud of her boots on the hard ground, her ragged breaths and the hens squawking as they scampered out her way. When she entered the barn, her steps slowed.

A musket hung loosely by Cameron's side. He walked towards her slowly shaking his head. 'Nothing could be done for its leg. He had to be put out his misery.'

Mhàiri stared at the bull, who had provided their main source of income and who now lay still on the ground. Blood dripped from the gunshot wound between its glassy eyes and from the sneering slash in its neck. Her father knelt and untied the binding holding the bull's legs together.

'*Mo chèile* -My husband,' she called to Cameron, 'What shall we do?'

As if unable to look at her, Cameron dropped his gaze. 'We will have to leave. There is no other way.'

Tears sprang to Mhàiri's eyes. 'I cannot fight this anymore. I have tried, but I am tired. Perhaps once we get to Invercreag, we might be able to save enough to emigrate.'

Cameron raised his head. 'We still have a few months before we need to move to the coast. I will find work.'

'But, the weather. The worst of the weather is not over yet.'

'I have delayed long enough.' Cameron pointed to the bull. 'At least we won't starve . . . yet. You will have enough meat until I get back.'

With nothing else to be done but prepare the beef to help see them through the coming months, Mhàiri left Cameron and her father to the task. She hung a sign outside the cottage door to let the salt vendor know to call.

* * *

Without Cameron, time slowed. Somehow, the minutes still turned into hours and the hours into days and the days into weeks. Mhàiri sat on the hillside with Cailean strapped onto her back.

She recalled the day she had been lazing on the hillside making dandelion wishes when Maister Sellar had first appeared in Achcoil. Could wishes come true? She hadn't thought then to wish for her family to be secure in their own home. She scanned the horizon, searching for Cameron and hoping that today would be the day he returned. In the distance, she spotted the salt vendor from Brora. Mhàiri hurried down the hillside to meet her. Despite her reluctance, she'd had to have another cow killed.

'*Cionnas a tha sibh?* – How are you?' Mhàiri said to the woman and ushered her across to the barn.

'I am well, thank you,' the salt vendor replied. 'And you? How are you managing?'

From the weight of the large basket of salt she carried, the elderly woman's back was bent forward in a permanent stoop. The wicker basket was covered over with a cloth. The front of which was pulled into a hood over the woman's head and the strap of the basket placed over that onto her forehead. With each step the woman took, her walking stick hit the ground. Tap-tap. Tap-tap.

After buying sufficient to salt the beef and a bit spare for cooking, Mhàiri brought the woman into the cottage and settled Cailean into his cradle.

'What news?' Mhàiri asked. The salt-vendor carried news from the other townships, and Mhàiri was anxious to hear how things were. 'I have only seen my aunt twice since she moved and each time, she told me about the small lots and over-crowding in the coastal villages.'

'Ah, it is not good. It is not good at all. Not so long ago, as I passed through the straths, I knew every face. Now, I meet strangers who do not understand what I say. And everywhere there is the sheep. It is hard to explain the sound of the pitiful bleats echoing across the hillsides where once the silence was broken only by the breeze.'

'And on the coast?' Mhàiri asked. 'How do those who moved there fare?'

The woman tilted her head. 'They manage well enough, some better than others. But it is not the same. It is not like here. Are you to be moving to the coast?'

Mhàiri stood and checked inside the cradle. Satisfied that Cailean was asleep, she sat again. 'Like most others, we have been told to leave. My husband has gone looking for work. When he returns, we will likely move then to Invercreag,' she said with a resigned sigh. 'But my mother and father, they plan on staying here. I do not know what to do.'

* * *

A week later, Mhàiri trudged up the well-worn path to the mill. Caitriona skipped ahead, while Mhàiri carried Cailean strapped into a blanket on her back. Outside the mill house, she was surprised to see the miller and one of his daughters filling two carts with furniture. Five young children and a dog ran around them. Mhàiri frowned and called to the miller as she came near, '*Cionnas a tha sibh?* – How are you?'

The miller's wife stepped out from the cottage and wiped her hands on a cloth. 'I thought I heard your voice, Mhàiri. You will be coming in?'

Mhàiri followed the woman inside. The room lacked its usual warmth. Looking around, realisation dawned. 'You are leaving? I . . . I had not heard.'

'What choice do I have? If I am to plant any crops this year then I best get a move on.' The miller's wife flapped a calloused hand. 'The removal notice was clear enough. Our rent is only free if we prepare our coastal plot in advance of moving.' She grimaced and shifted the kettle onto the hook above the fire. 'One thing is for certain. We will not be lifting any crops here.'

Mhàiri laid her basket down and slumped onto a bench. She opened her plaid and settled Cailean into her arms. Caitriona remained outside with the youngest of the miller's children. Mhàiri could hear their whoops and laughter. 'Children, it is all an adventure to them.'

'They will miss it here all the same when it is gone from them.'

'You will be nearer your daughter,' Mhàiri said and recalled the woman's daughter leaving for the seasonal work on the coast. 'I was going to go that day too. The rents had just risen again.'

'Ah well, it was a difficult time. My daughter is settled well enough now. If you had gone you might have married a fisherman too.'

Mhàiri laughed.

The woman dipped her head. 'It should have been Peigi Ruadh who went that day. But, well, she has always been different. Likely I shouldn't be saying anything, but she always felt left out. She wanted to be your friend.'

'My friend?' Mhàiri thought about the way Peigi Ruadh always seemed to have a smile on her face. The way she had hung around Rob Dunn and then Cameron. Could the girl have been trying to befriend her? 'I did not realise. I am sorry I never made time for her.'

'It is not too late, Mhàiri. It breaks my heart to hear her decried from the pulpit as a sinner. She was not allowed to marry Iain.' A flush crept up the woman's neck.

'They are not the first to be refused, and they will not be the last.'

'It was nothing to do with them marrying,' the miller's wife said. 'It was to stop us from sub-letting our land to them. Well, I do not suppose any of that matters now. I am just thankful she has Iain and the children.'

'Are Peigi Ruadh and Iain going with you?'

'They are staying here. Mòrag Mòr needs them.'

'Of course,' Mhàiri said.

The miller's wife shook her head. 'It will not be like this where we are going. But we have to get the oats and barley planted. I heard that the ground is not good on the coast. Likely there will be rocks aplenty to clear before we can plant anything.' She brushed tears away with her hand and smiled. 'Ach, here am I complaining and I have not asked how your mother is?'

'I am sure she will want to see you before you go. I will let her know you are leaving.' Mhàiri reached into her basket and held out a carefully wrapped parcel of salted beef. Her voice trembled as she opened the cloth. 'Is this enough for some oats? I still have a little barley left.'

The woman took the beef. 'This meat will be a help to us. See the miller when you leave. Tell him to fill your basket. And, ask your mother to come see me if she can.'

Mhàiri nodded. 'When are you leaving?'

'We will take the roof timbers down tomorrow. The quicker we reach the coast the sooner we can start planting.' She gazed around the room, a wistful look in her eyes. 'Ah, well. It is a pity we had two bad years with the crops. Truth be told, I am afraid to take my children to the coast. I heard that typhus is raging there.'

'Typhus. Dear God, what next?' Mhàiri recalled Mòrag Mòr telling her how she had struggled while her husband was away at war. How her children had become ill. How she had lost her new-born daughter.

Mhàiri looked at Cailean. 'Cameron should be back soon. I never thought I would hear myself say it, but hopefully, he will bring back enough for us to emigrate.'

42

WATCHING AND WAITING

Mhàiri pulled the handle of a wicker basket up onto her shoulder and groaned. With Cailean strapped into a blanket on her back, she picked up one end of a wooden tub, and her mother took hold of the other. Between them, they carried their washing down to the river. Anna and Hattie Bantrach carried another tub. Caitriona and Anna's daughter skipped along in front of them.

A gust of wind whipped Mhàiri's hair back. 'The washing will be dry in no time.'

'It is a good wind,' Màthair replied, 'which is just as well with the amount we have.'

Mhàiri laid the tub at the edge of the river and rubbed her aching back. 'This could be the last time we do our washing here. I cannot bear to think about it.'

Her mother raised her eyebrows. 'Then don't. Perhaps, we will not have to move.'

Mhàiri smiled at the thought and filled her tub with water. She rubbed the clothes with soap, working up a good lather. Despite her mother's words, she felt a strong sense of foreboding that something bad was about to happen, and soon. She lifted the hem of her skirt and tucked it into her belt. When she stepped into the tub and trampled the clothes with her feet. Caitriona climbed in and copied her movements. Mhàiri laughed.

She had to keep faith. Had to believe that the removal date would come and go, as it had before. Their petition to the Prince Regent had been met with no response, but Rob Dunn and the Kildonan men were trying to get the removals raised in Parliament.

Anna lifted her daughter into a tub and stepped in beside her. 'Woo, hoo!' she called as her feet met the cold water. 'When I was a child, I watched the women trampling the clothes and couldn't wait to do it. The pleasure has never left me,' she paused. 'But how we are to wash our clothes in the sea. I cannot imagine.'

'We cannot,' Hattie Bantrach said.

Everyone looked at her. 'All that salt,' she said. 'It wouldn't do. In Spain, I had to go inland to find a stream.'

'How did you find your way back?' Mhàiri asked. 'I never could have made that long journey alone.

'Humph!' Hattie Bantrach uttered. 'You would if you were left with the choices I had. When my husband died, I was left alone in a camp full of soldiers. Most in my situation remarried as quickly as they could . . . to the first man who would have them.'

Mhàiri screwed up her face. 'I could never do that.'

'And neither could I, Hattie Bantrach said. 'The second option was even less of a choice. Join the camp followers.'

'Oh, Hattie,' Mhàiri said. 'And you so far from home.'

'Ah well, finding my way back from Spain was the easy option.'

'I have never been to the coast,' Anna said. 'And I have no desire to. The Great Lady won't allow us to be moved to Invercreag. Will she?'

'Why would she empty the straths of her tenants?' Mhàiri said. It does not make sense. All of this is the factors' doing, I am certain of it. When Cameron gets back . . . Well, we are going to bide our time until she sorts this out.'

'Humph!' Hattie Bantrach tilted her head. 'You place too much faith in the Great Lady.'

'Well, I am going nowhere,' Màthair said. 'No matter what that devil, Maister Sellar, says.'

Anna turned quickly to say something and almost tumbled into the soapy water. She righted herself and laughed. 'Paddle faster, Mhàiri. It might bring that bairn on.'

Mhàiri smiled. 'Ah, it might—' Realising that no one was listening, she stopped talking. Her mother and Anna looked straight ahead, and Hattie Bantrach pointed across the heath. Mhàiri froze. A line of bodies snaked towards them. It looked as if a whole farming-township had been cleared. With their plaids pulled tight and their heads bent low, the line drew nearer, and the shapes came into sharper focus.

Most of the women carried children or baskets on their backs. The men looked old, the animals thin. A woman around Mhàiri's age passed, leading a horse pulling a peat basket. Her hair was hidden by a cloth bonnet and her belly was big with child. Following behind her, a man hauled a cart filled to the brim; a pot, a kettle and some blankets protruded out the top.

Mhàiri's vision grew hazy, and the people merged into a line of bonnets, blankets and plaids. In that moment, she saw her own family trudging to the coast. She was that young woman. She shook her head and the vision cleared. She prayed this wasn't an omen of bad things to come.

The white-bearded man on the horse at the front stopped, and everyone came to a halt. The wind whistled through the strath, creating the impression of women howling. Mhàiri stared. What did these people want? Were they going to approach her? She looked over her shoulder and saw her fear mirrored on the other women's faces. She placed an arm around Caitriona and pulled her close.

The bearded man on the horse moved on. The long line of plaids and blankets resumed their slow shuffling steps behind him. The group moved into the distance, and Mhàiri groaned. Dear God in Heaven, what had she done? She should have helped them.

Even if she had greeted them, she would have felt less ashamed. But she had done nothing. Nothing except remain rooted with fear, as she would if she had faced a pack of starving wolves. Drawing in a deep breath, she let it out again. 'We should have offered them food.'

'What could we have done?' Anna said. 'You heard what the catechist said. We will be evicted if we shelter any of the removed.'

Màthair shook her head. 'Even if we had offered to help them, we have nothing spare to give.'

No one spoke. The laughter from before had vanished with the line of shuffling bodies. Try as she might, Mhàiri could not remember what they had been laughing about.

43

PLAYS AND PLANS

Edinburgh

When Elizabeth entered the withdrawing room of her townhouse, Mister Loch rose from his chair and dipped his head. 'My Lady.'

'Ah, Mister Loch, you have arrived. I am particularly looking forward to today's play. I'm an avid follower of the Theatre Royal productions. We have an hour before we leave. If you could talk us through the latest stage of improvements up north, it would be most helpful.'

'Speak up.' Lord Stafford held a hand behind his ear. 'Can you speak up?'

Elizabeth sat beside her husband and gestured for their guest to sit nearer to Lord Stafford's chair. 'I was telling Mister Loch that we are looking forward to today's play, but have time to discuss the latest developments in the north.'

'Ah, good. Good! That is better. It is frustrating not to be able to hear what you say, Elizabeth.'

She patted her husband's arm and continued, 'So, Mister Loch. Now that you've taken charge and Mister Sellar has finally been replaced as factor, please tell us that there will not be a repeat of the debacle we encountered after the '14 removals. You have put all the measures in place that we discussed?'

'Now that we have changed factors surely that should be measure enough.' Lord Stafford said.

Mister Loch ran his hand through his sandy-blonde hair. 'But Mister Sellar suited the estates' purpose well enough at the time.'

'Hmm!' Elizabeth exclaimed. 'Perhaps. But he was too eager by far in his methods. I believe that his replacement is also known for his...erm... enthusiasm.'

'Mister Loch is right. We need someone who can keep order.' Lord Stafford said. 'There is no point taking on some namby-pamby to do the job, Elizabeth. No, it has to be someone who is not in close contact with the tenants and who can exercise their authority.'

'And the lots on the coast . . . are they ready?' Elizabeth asked. 'Are the people who were moved liking it well enough?'

Mister Loch tilted his chin. 'According to Reverend MacKenzie, the tenants are happy with their new lots.'

Elizabeth smiled. 'Good. Good. When I am next up north, I will arrange to visit some of the coastal villages and speak to the tenants myself. I thought they would settle soon enough once they saw their new plots. I am most pleased to hear they have.'

'That, at least, is one worry less,' Lord Stafford said.

'Indeed.' Elizabeth turned her attention back to Mister Loch. 'Are the tenants taking up employment?'

He held a hand to his mouth and coughed. 'I'm giving preference to incomers. If you want thriving villages then you need to draw in new blood . . . English speaking workers from the Lowlands.'

Elizabeth narrowed her eyes and peered at him. 'That is not what we agreed. What about the tenants? Surely that is the reason we are moving them to the coast, is it not?'

Mister Loch nodded. 'There are roads to be built. We also need fishermen, coopers and coal miners. There is plenty of work for the tenants. But for the inns, shops and other commercial enterprises to succeed you have to employ people who *speak* English.'

'Yes, of course,' Elizabeth conceded. 'What you say is true enough, especially for the new shops. Perhaps there may even be a drapers. How exciting.'

'And the new bridges I have planned,' Lord Stafford said. 'We will also have to build more inns. Yes, we need to bring in English speaking Lowlanders for the work associated with all of this. Once the new roads and bridges are up and running business will be booming.'

'I have drafted an advert for the Inverness paper to this effect,' Mister Loch said. 'Along the lines of "preference will be given to strangers". I know it seems harsh but the people from the straths, they want to be all things to themselves— farmer, shoemaker, miller, ploughman, distiller, milkmaid and baker.'

Elizabeth nodded. 'While we need thriving industries and trade within the villages. Yes, for this experiment to succeed we need people who are buying *and* selling.'

'Absolutely,' Mister Loch said. 'Not the bartering system your tenants currently survive on. It will take years to make progress with these people, if at all. How can they work in or contribute to the inns, shops and markets if they persist in bartering their goods and talking in their strange language?'

'No one would understand a word they said.' Lord Stafford pushed his spectacles down and peered at Mister Loch over the rims. 'No, it wouldn't work. You are right. We must ensure all transactions are carried out in English. How else can the new trades flourish?'

Elizabeth thought about her own ancestors. They had spoken in the Gaelic. 'Perhaps once the tenants are removed from the inner straths and hills, their children will flourish and learn to speak English and take on the ways of the world, just as my family had to.'

'If only these savages *would* speak English.' Mister Loch frowned. 'It is barbaric the way they talk and live.'

Lord Stafford nodded. 'I agree with Elizabeth. Once they are removed from the straths, their children will soon forget these idle ways. The new coastal villages will be a huge success.'

Elizabeth didn't like all this talk against her Highland heritage. Despite her immense wealth, were her family also considered savages by some? She looked at the clock and stood. 'Is that the time? We need to prepare to leave for the theatre. Have you had the pleasure of seeing 'The Good Shepherd' before, Mister Loch?'

44

DARK DAYS

A loud rapping had Mhàiri hurrying to the door. Dear God, what was happening? Why would anyone call at this time of night? There was still two weeks until the date set for the removals. Surely the factor hadn't arrived early. Cameron wasn't back yet. How would he find her if she had to leave now?

She opened the door and reeled back. A man stood on either side of her swaying husband. Rob Dunn stood behind them, his eyebrows raised.

Cameron peered at Mhàiri and gave a long, drawn out smile. Anger flared within her, pent-up and now released in a flood. Her husband had been gone six weeks and had sent no word. 'Dear God, he's as drunk as a fiddler and reeks of whisky.' She ushered the men indoors.

'Mhaaari,' Cameron slurred. 'My Dhalling. This is Dòmhnall Beag and Lachlann, from Kildonan. And our friend, Rob Dunn. Give the men some broth.'

Mhàiri gritted her teeth. Broth, indeed. 'Be quiet, Cameron, or you'll wake the children. That's if they aren't already awake.'

Cameron turned his face towards one of the Kildonan men

and raised his eyebrows. 'It is a sad day when a man is unable get a bowl of broth in his own house.'

'I will give these men some broth.' She pointed through the open door to the bed in the recess between the house and the byre. 'But you are more in need of sleep.'

As the men assisted him there, Cameron turned and called, 'Don't be long, Mhàiri.'

After they had deposited Cameron onto the bed the men returned to the main room.

Mhàiri folded her arms and looked at them with suspicion. 'What has happened? Why has my husband returned drunk?'

'I am sorry, but you better ask Cameron that.' The younger of the Kildonan men tilted his bonnet. 'I am Lachlann, and this here is Dòmhnall Beag.'

Dòmhnall Beag shrugged. 'We best be heading. We just wanted to make sure your husband got home.'

'With the removals looming, we thought it best Cameron was with his family.' Rob Dunn smiled. 'Not that he is even aware of what day it is.'

'Perhaps that is his intention.' Lachlann said and held out his upturned hands. 'What can any of us do?'

Mhàiri's realised that she would get nothing more out of these men and her mood softened. 'You too?'

'Our whole township was given notice to leave,' Dòmhnall Beag replied.

As Mhàiri made to close the door behind them, Rob Dunn turned. 'Look Mhàiri, there was no harm in Cameron's intentions tonight.'

Mhàiri frowned. 'What do you mean . . . no harm?'

He shuffled his bonnet between his hands. 'Cameron was in a right state when he arrived at us. He was on his way home, but wanted to ask about setting up a still together . . . to make some money. Well, we liked the idea and got to talking.'

'While you shared a whisky, no doubt?'

'Ah, well,' Rob Dunn said and put his bonnet back on.

After the men left, Mhàiri sat by the fire, deep in thought. Rob Dunn had been fighting to stop the removals in any way he could. She was grateful to him for that. Her thoughts turned to Cameron. She had never seen her husband in such a state before. He must have still been drinking as he made his way back here with the men. Her anger turned to relief to have him home. Unlike her father, Cameron was never argumentative with the drink. She was grateful for that too.

She lifted the candle and made for bed . . . alone. Regardless of what time she went to sleep, Cailean and Caitriona would awaken at the same early hour they always did. Hopefully, Cameron would explain himself later.

The following morning, Mhàiri set to the task of clearing out the clothes chests. While she hoped with all her heart that her family wouldn't be removed, she thought it best to be prepared. Two weeks would pass quickly enough. She opened a chest containing the children's clothes and blankets and sorted through them, laying aside anything that could be unwound or remade.

Cameron rose from the bed in the recess and groaned. He ignored Mhàiri and sat on a chair at the table and cradled his head in his hands.

She filled a small bowl with cooked oats and laid it in front of him along with a cup of warm milk mixed with cow's blood. 'Sup this it might help you feel better.'

When he didn't make any move to eat, Mhàiri sat beside him. 'What is it? What has happened?'

'Not now.' He stood from the table. 'I will tend to the animals.'

'Cameron!' she called.

Without turning, he pulled the door shut behind him.

The next morning Cameron rose early and remained silent

as he sat at the table eating. Mhàiri placed a hand over his. 'Please let me help you. I cannot stand for us to be like this.'

Cameron drew in a deep breath and let it out slowly. 'You are right. We will talk later, once the children are in bed.' He stood and retrieved something from his satchel. He handed it to her and sat back at the table and cradled his head in his hands.

Mhàiri unwrapped the newspaper packaging and stared at a dainty, blue-patterned cup. She placed the dish on the dresser beside the patterned cups Cameron's father had brought back from the Lowlands for his mother.

She stood behind Cameron and folded her arms around him, with his back against her chest. There had been times while he had been gone when she wondered if he would come back at all. She bent so that her mouth was level with his ear. 'A Cameron, mo ghràidh- Cameron, my love,' she said. 'We will make it through this. We will.'

* * *

Mhàiri gathered the children together and made her way over to the meeting-house with Cameron. Apart from the miller and his family, everyone else had remained in Achcoil. This could be the last time they gathered together. She tried not to think about it. Cameron's intention was to emigrate, but Mhàiri's mother and father were set on remaining, so were Hattie Bantrach, Anna and Mòrag Mòr. The fiddler was nearly eighty and his wife was only a few years younger. How would they adjust to living on the coast?

As she arrived at the meeting-house, Mhàiri heard loud voices within. When she entered, her mother lifted Cailean from her and disappeared to show him to Mòrag Mòr.

Connor rushed over and beamed, 'I sang, Mhàiri. You missed it but I'll sing one for you later.'

The fiddler played. He seemed slow and hesitant but

managed to push out a lively enough tune. Mhàiri took Connor's hands and danced a jig with him. Feeling breathless from the exertion, she made her way over to Cameron and laid her arm on his shoulder.

With his head bent close to Fearghas and Iain, Cameron discussed setting up an illegal whisky still with some of the Kildonan men when they reached Invercreag. Mhàiri listened to their conversation and raised her eyebrows. Lord Stafford had already put stills in place for profit. What they were planning was dangerous. Although she was concerned for their safety, she left them to it and went in search of Anna.

She linked into her friend's arm. 'If the time comes that we are forced to leave we will move to the coast. But God willing, we will be staying where we are.'

'Yes, God willing. Fearghas and I will too. And if the worst happens then at least there will be no repeat of the way your aunt's township was cleared.'

Mhàiri remained talking to Anna. Recalling days, they had spent together in the strath.

As it darkened, people drifted away.

After returning home and putting the children to bed, Mhàiri sat at the table with Cameron. 'Soon . . . we will find out soon if we are to leave. But first, tell me what happened while you were gone to put you into such an ill-tempered mood. I need to know, Cameron.'

He stood and paced the room. 'There is plenty of work out there, but not for the likes of us. All the decent work goes to the Lowlanders.' He stopped pacing and rubbed his hands over his face. 'The things I witnessed. I didn't know such horrors were still happening. Stuck here, Mhàiri, we have been shielded from it all.'

His fists clenched and his face darkened, but he turned and sat at the table. 'The sights I saw as I travelled around looking for work. Dear God, we are regarded as buffoons. Lower than animals. There were hundreds of tenant farmers wandering around in search of work. It soon became clear that I was just one amongst many. I saw filthy, bedraggled Highlanders wearing nothing but their kilts, performing for the entertainment of Lowlanders and mocked and jeered as they did so. Dancing our Highland dances while the crowds looked on and laughed. Drink had gotten to many of them.'

Mhàiri took Cameron's hand and listened without interrupting.

'I thought I would have to return empty handed. I had let you and the children down. There was no work to be had for the likes of me in the Lowlands. In the towns, they wanted people for the new factories and I had no experience to offer. The minute I opened my mouth and spoke in the Gaelic, I was brushed aside like dirt on the floor.' His voice broke with emotion. 'I grew lucky.' He opened his hand and threw some coins onto the table. 'I wanted to speak to some of the Kildonan men, to see if they knew what to do. On my way there, I made my way through some land that had been cleared and turned into a sheep farm.'

Cameron lowered his eyes. 'I got work . . . building sheep-walks to keep the sheep safe over the winter.' He shook his head from side to side. 'Mhàiri, I couldn't tell you for the shame of it.' He looked up. 'What will people think if they hear that I have been building sheep-walks?' He hesitated and tears filled his eyes. 'I built the sheep-walks with stones I removed from empty burnt-out cottages. Cottages the likes of us live in.'

MAY MEMORIES

A fine mist rose from the river, casting an unnatural haze over the valley. The distortion suited the day, Mhàiri thought as she trudged beside Cameron and the other towns-folk to the last church service they would attend in the strath.

A crowd had already formed on the hillside overlooking the river and more families made their way to join them: Mhàiri stood beside Cameron, her mother and father, Hattie Bantrach, Iain, Peigi Ruadh, Anna, Fearghas, and the fiddler and his wife, and waited for the minister to arrive. As if shrouded by the loud lamentations around them, the children remained silent. The only person missing was Mòrag Mòr.

The date set for the removals was now less than two weeks away, and Mhàiri hadn't planted anything, either here or on the coast. Her heart thudded. There would be no crops to see her family through the winter.

A gentle breeze blew, and Mhàiri pulled her plaid around her shoulders. Finally, amidst the loud wails of the people, Maighstir Sage arrived and dismounted from his horse. Had anyone escaped eviction? The minister had already vacated the manse and moved back in with his father. He strode over and stood in front of the large group.

He held up his arms and the congregation grew silent. 'My poor and defenceless flock, the dark hour of trial has now come in earnest. Let us pray,

The Lord is my shepherd; I shall not want.
He leadeth me beside the still waters.
Yea, though I walk through the valley of the shadow of death
I will fear no evil . . .'

After completing the prayer, Maighstir Sage raised his voice. 'When it feels like others are fighting against you, you do not have to face the battle alone. Your family will act as your armour, protecting you from your foes.

'When the ground feels fragile, as if it might give way beneath your feet, you are not alone. Your friends will act as your support.

'When you feel as if you are lost, you are not alone. The Lord will help you find your way home.

'Provide the armour your friends and family need to protect them. Support each other to remain strong. Let God guide you. Let us pray for the strength and courage to see us through this dark and troubled time.'

Like the river flowing towards the sea, the tears of the congregation flowed as one with the minister. The land seemed to weep with them, shedding its own tears. It struck Mhàiri that the service felt like a funeral, and in a way it was. The life they had known would be lost for eternity and each and every one of them mourned its passing.

Mhàiri tasted salt on her lips. She raised her eyes and drank in the view that would soon be denied to her. She would carry the image with her until death.

A patchwork blanket formed before her, stitched together from memories.

She recalled birds soaring over the mountains, flying free, swooping and diving.

Breathing in the peaty scent of the soil, she seared the smell to her memory and sealed it in her soul.

She listened to silence, unbroken, and shed shared tears.

She joined in joyful singing.

She breathed in the beauty around her and devoured the scents.

She recalled dandelion days and stays at the sheilings, bees buzzing, birds nesting, births and deaths.

She remembered fire and flames, children crying.

Loud laments, turning to ashes.

Tranquillity and grace taking their place.

And peace descending, transcending the pain.

As if woken from a deep and restful sleep, the world appeared calm, Mhàiri's troubles few. Her burdens light, she looked out over the strath and an overwhelming sense of peace surrounded her.

Beside the still-flowing waters of the River Naver, the voice of the minister grew silent, and people drifted away. As they left, the minister gripped each person's hand and said some parting words, knowing that they might never meet again.

When her turn arrived and Mhàiri bade him a final farewell, Maighstir Sage took her delicate hands between his strong ones. 'God be with you and your family and keep you safe wherever your journey takes you.'

SHIFTING SHADOWS

The cockerel crowed as if heralding in any other day. Mhàiri leant against the open doorway and looked up at the early morning sky. Despite the promise of another sunny day a chill nipped the May air. Regardless of what day it was, there were tasks needing attended to. She pushed away from the door and set to her morning chores.

One job led to another - milking the cows, washing the pails, feeding the hens. Shadows from the past followed her. As she walked through the passage, separating the house from the byre, Mhàiri recalled giving birth to her daughter on the recessed bed, the bed Cameron had been put into when he had arrived home drunk as a piper. When she entered the main room, memories surfaced of the day she properly moved in here, after Cameron's parents emigrated. Her delight at becoming the new owner of the large dresser with the blue painted cups on it hovered mockingly on the horizon, taunting her as she packed the cups into a basket.

When Cameron rose, Mhàiri put on a pot of oats and roused the children. The morning quickly fell into its regular pattern of washing, dressing and eating. She placed a pot of barley broth onto the hook above the fire. Had they got the date for the removals wrong? Everything seemed . . . too normal.

Cameron headed out to the barn to ready the animals for leaving, and Mhàiri lifted the bowls from the table and washed them in a pail. After placing the dishes into a basket, she sat on a bench outside and watched the children running around in play. Her eyes grew heavy, and she fought an urge to drift off. She would continue packing in a minute. She stroked her belly as she counted out the weeks and calculated that she would soon be showing. She had always felt extra tired in the first few months and this time was no different. Later, she would visit Anna; to see how things were with her. And, she would drop in to see Hattie Bantrach, take her some of the barley broth she had—

Iain raced up the brae waving his arms and shouting, 'It has started. '*Seall*– Look.' He pointed. 'Over there.'

Above a neighbouring township, blue-grey plumes of smoke drifted upwards, marring the clear sky. When Mhàiri stood and acknowledged that she had seen it, Iain turned and ran back down the brae.

On shaking legs, Mhàiri hurried to the barn, calling as she ran, 'Cameron. Cameron!' Carrying Cailean and clutching Caitriona's hand, she turned and made her way to her parent's cottage. Cameron followed behind.

A constable rode into Achcoil and pulled to a halt.

Mhàiri stopped and turned towards him.

The constable stood up in the stirrups and shouted, 'Half an hour. You've got half an hour to get out. Take what you want, but do it quickly. Anything left will be destroyed. This land is no longer yours.' The rider rubbed the white stubble on his chin and gave a mocking laugh. 'Why didn't you leave when you had the chance? Ah well, you'll be leaving now whether you want to, or not.' He kicked the horse's side and rode off.

All around Mhàiri turned into bewildered confusion. As if

awoken from a stupor the townspeople moved into action. Sobs mingled with cries for help. Dogs barked, children wailed and cattle lowed.

Mhàiri gripped Cameron's arm and they raced up the brae towards home. Mhàiri placed Cailean in his cradle, and turned to her daughter who was whimpering. 'Sit at the table, Caitriona. Do not move from there until I tell you to. Keep an eye on Cailean. Do you understand?'

Her daughter nodded and sat at the table with her hands clasped between her knees, her eyes wide with fear.

Taking hold of the meal box, Cameron pulled it outside.

Mhàiri knelt by the wall in the gable end and prised out a divot of earth from between the stones. Her hand shook as she reached into the space and pulled out a small leather pouch containing the fourteen pounds they had managed to save and the MacAoidh crest brooch she had worn at her wedding. She stood and tied the straps of the bag around her waist, then tucked the pouch into the waistband of her skirt. She pulled a bench outside and hurried back in to retrieve another.

Cameron lifted the spinning wheel out. He turned to Mhàiri as he passed. 'Clear the dresser, I will take that next.'

Once she had removed the last of the dishes from the shelves, Mhàiri laid them into a basket, beside the bowls and cups she had packed earlier. She dragged the basket out then helped Cameron push the dresser through the narrow door.

Cameron thrust a ladder against the cottage wall and climbed onto the roof. He hacked at the roof timbers with an axe, pushing aside the thatch in his way. 'I'll throw the trusses down, Mhàiri. Give me time then we will gather them together at the gable end.'

Mhàiri remembered about the animals and she hurried to the byre and removed their three remaining cows. They drifted off towards a patch of grass at the side of the hill and lazily grazed on the low stubble. After she had released the horses, goats and sheep, Mhàiri returned to the cottage. The hens squawked and flapped out of her way as she raced past.

She pulled blankets from the beds and tossed them outside. Some of the food had already been placed in cloth bags and she strapped these onto one of the horses. She threw some clothes onto a blanket and tied it onto the other horse.

Mounted figures approached. Maister Sellar, his silver buttons glittering, rode in behind the men. Mhàiri watched as the fiscal, constables and sheriff-officers drew nearer and spread around Achcoil. Some of the shepherds had dogs.

Mhàiri tried to move, but felt as if she were pushing through a thick field of barleycorn.

Time slowed.

Her vision narrowed.

Sounds muffled.

A strong smell of burning thatch and heather was carried in the wind. Mhàiri looked up and followed a line of swirling black smoke as it curled into the air.

Cameron clambered down the ladder and hurried to her side. Mhàiri slumped against him. Taking her by the shoulders, he led her to their cottage. He kissed her forehead and pushed her forward. 'Get the children, Mhàiri, I'll finish taking down the timbers and see to these men.'

Propelled forward, Mhàiri continued towards the open door. As if surfacing from a stagnant pool of water, she gasped. 'The children. Where are the children?' She raced inside and called to Caitriona, 'Hurry. Get outside.'

As she picked up Cailean's cradle and turned to head out the door, a tall, dark-haired man carrying a riding crop entered and blocked her way. Still holding on to the cradle, Mhàiri groaned. Caitriona leant into her and gripped Mhàiri's skirt.

Outside, a dog barked.

'Why are you still here?' the man said. He pushed past Mhàiri and tipped the pot of barley broth onto the fire.

The sizzling sound grated in her ears. The steam irritated her eyes and the stench of peat and burnt barley made her retch. As the man pushed his face towards her, she watched the pores on his red bulbous nose expand.

Random words replayed in her thoughts. The fire is out. Ashes to ashes. Dust to dust.

She stepped back.

She had to get out.

Had to take the children and run.

'Run, run,' the voice of her dead sister called.

'Give that here,' the man shouted and pulled the cradle from her grasp.

'Leave that be,' Mhàiri screamed and hurtled towards him.

Still gripping onto Mhàiri's skirt, Caitriona fell and banged her head against the edge of the open door. Mhàiri grabbed her screaming daughter by the arm. As she followed the man outside, she grasped at the cradle with her other arm and tried to lift Cailean out. When they hurtled out the cottage, Cameron almost tumbled from the ladder in his haste to clamour down. He raced towards them and pulled the cradle from the man's grip. He laid it on the ground and lifted Cailean out.

Rooted to the spot, Mhàiri watched flames flickering at the gable end of their cottage. As the cattle lowed behind her, she watched in bewildered confusion as sparks from the roof timbers which had been set alight settled on the dresser and benches piled beside them.

'Dear God, our furniture. It will burn,' Cameron roared and placed Cailean into Mhàiri's arms. He ran forward and grabbed a basket containing their bowls and dishes. He dragged it away from the flames. As he did so, a blue cup fell to the ground and smashed.

Mhàiri bent to retrieve the pieces, but Cameron shouted, 'Leave it. Leave it be. There's nothing more we can do here. We can come back for what is left.'

She pulled a blanket from a basket. After tying Cailean into it, she strapped the blanket on to her back and tied the ends around her waist. Caitriona clung on to Mhàiri's skirt and wailed. Mhàiri took hold of one of their horses and Cameron took hold of the other and they walked them down to the river. Further upstream, Anna and Fearghas hauled baskets onto an upturned table.

Mhàiri lifted Caitriona and made her way beside Cameron to her parent's cottage. She coughed and held a hand over her mouth. Sweat beaded on her upper lip. She had to fight her fear of the flames. For the sake of the child in her belly, she had to keep going. Everywhere she looked, fires raged. Wood trusses glowed and spat out dark smoke. Her heart thumped and sweat dripped from her face. The widow's hovel was ablaze, her furniture burning beside it. The red flames glowing like demon eyes.

Mhàiri's mother and father stood outside Mòrag Mòr's cottage, with Connor and Hattie Bantrach, while Iain argued with a constable.

Iain gestured to Cameron. 'Help me to get Màthair out.'

Cameron made his way into the cottage behind Iain and Peigi Ruadh. Moments later they emerged, coughing and dragging a blanket between them. Tears flowed down their blackened faces. Mòrag Mòr lay curled up on the blanket, screaming in pain.

As soon as they had dragged the woman clear of the cottage it was set alight. Flames leapt up to join the plumes of smoke, which now rained ash down upon them all.

Mhàiri fought to keep herself upright.

47

DEPARTURE DAY

M hàiri joined the other tenants beside the river and watched the riders thunder off, heading for the next farming-township. She let out a deep breath. A great weight pushed down on her shoulders, and she wanted to lie down. Black smoke rose and settled in dense clouds above Achcoil. The stench of singed cloth and burnt meat made her gag. But she had to keep going. They all did.

'We need to be on our way.' Cameron said and wiped black soot from his face. 'They will be back to make sure that we have left. God help anyone still here when they return.'

Mhàiri helped Cameron gather what remained of their belongings. She was lifting a basket onto their cart when she noticed the fiddler bend over and place his hands onto his knees as if in pain. As she made her way over to him, the fiddler slumped to the ground, beside the few possessions he had been able to save. His wife sat down beside him. Thick smoke drifted towards them from the smouldering fires.

The fiddler coughed and looked up at Mhàiri. 'We are not going to any plot on the coast.'

Mhàiri knelt in front of him. 'You cannot stay here. It makes no sense. You heard what Cameron said.'

She looked over her shoulder. Cameron had finished strapping all that they now possessed onto the carts and was tying them behind their two horses. Iain and Fearghas lifted Mòrag Mòr into a cart and covered her with blankets. It looked as if everyone else was readying themselves to leave for Invercreag.

The fiddler scowled and draped an arm around his wife's shoulder. 'Whether it makes sense or not, I am going nowhere. Let them come back. My home is right here. With my wife.'

'But . . .' Mhàiri said, lost for words.

'Look, lassie, I know you mean well. But, I am near eighty. Even if I made it to the coast, which I doubt, likely I'd die soon after getting there?'

The fiddler's wife nodded. 'We have lived all our days in Achcoil. I never imagined ending them anywhere else. We are going nowhere.'

'We can make room in one of the carts.' Mhàiri stood. 'There is no need for you to walk.'

The fiddler shook his head and picked up his fiddle.

Realising that there was no more to be said, and that it wasn't her place to say it anyway, Mhàiri rummaged through a basket in the cart. Finding a small jug of whisky, she returned and handed it to the fiddler. 'To keep you warm,' she said and made her way over to her children.

Once everyone had readied to leave, the townspeople set off in a line.

Mhàiri's father led the way, followed by her mother.

Hattie Bantrach walked behind them with Connor.

Behind them came Anna, Fearghas and their children. Anna's oldest child had a fever and Fearghas carried the girl on his back.

Mòrag Mòr lay in a cart. Iain and Peigi Ruadh followed it, each carrying one of their two children.

Mhàiri, Cameron and their children brought up the rear. Everyone walked with their animals in front of them.

Following the line of the River Naver, the convoy trudged out of Achcoil. Mhàiri looked over her shoulder at the fiddler. He placed the fiddle under his chin. A lilting tune lifted up and settled above the hill behind him. Shrouded in the melody, the hill appeared to swell as if bidding Mhàiri farewell and the stalks of grass swayed their goodbyes. Mhàiri understood why the fiddler and his wife chose to remain. But for her, it was time to leave. She had to think about her children now, and the baby she carried— had to focus on their future. Bending down, she plucked a seeded dandelion from the ground. She carefully wrapped the weed in a cloth and placed it in her skirt pocket. Were there dandelions on the coast? She would take some wishes with her, just in case there weren't.

Soon Achcoil disappeared from view. Mhàiri looked along the line of bodies snaking their way towards the coast; trudging forward in slow-moving steps. She recalled the day she'd laughed with Anna as they trampled their washing at the riverside and had paused to watch a group making their way north. Shame flooded through her as she remembered her horror when the line had stopped and she had thought they might approach. Now, with her feet shuffling, her son strapped to her back and her daughter at her side, Mhàiri looked at the tenants from Achcoil— all anyone would see would be a long line of plaids and bonnets. At the front, her father rode on a horse, his bonneted head bent forward, the townspeople trudging behind him.

When they neared farming-townships that hadn't yet been cleared, Mhàiri kept her head down, filled with fear and shame. The skeletons of houses and the blackened roof trusses in the empty townships they passed served as stark reminders that others had also been removed from their homes.

'It is the movement, just a little rest,' Mòrag Mòr said, and Iain called to Mhàiri's father to stop.

Leaving her children with Hattie Bantrach, Mhàiri climbed into the cart beside Mòrag Mòr. She laid the woman's head gently onto her lap and stroked her damp hair. While Peigi Ruadh fed and tended to the children, Iain remained at the side of the cart and held his mother's frail hand.

With hazy eyes, Mòrag Mòr smiled up at Iain and then at Mhàiri. 'Ah! That is better. The movement, it was hurting my bones.' Her eyelids fluttered and then closed.

Mhàiri held a bowl of water to the woman's lips. If only Mòrag Mòr hadn't made the long trek to Golspie in such bitter weather. She had never regained her strength since.

Mòrag Mòr opened her eyes. 'Micheal never did come home.'

Mhàiri looked at Iain. Was Mòrag Mòr talking to him?

'Since Rob Dunn's return I've known Micheal was dead,' the woman continued in a rasping voice. 'I never could say it. As long as no one else did, it was as if he was alive.'

Mhàiri continued to stroke Mòrag Mòr's hair.

'Remember, Mhàiri, there is God's will and there is man's will. It was not His will, today. I will meet Him in peace knowing none of this was His doing.'

Mòrag Mòr's eyes grew distant. Mhàiri watched the woman's chest rapidly rising and falling as if each breath caused her pain. After a few minutes, the woman's head drooped. Mòrag Mòr never got to see her son again in this life, but now she could see him in the next. Mhàiri had been surprised to learn that she had known Micheal wouldn't be coming back. She pressed the woman's eyes and mouth closed.

When she raised her tear-filled eyes, Iain nodded. 'I will bury her here in the strath,' he said. 'Màthair would want that.'

After Mòrag Mòr had been placed in a makeshift grave, Iain piled stones above it to mark the spot.

'I will come back,' he said. 'I will place a proper marker with Màthair's name on it, and Micheal's.'

While Cameron prepared the horses to move off again, Mhàiri sat beside Iain.

'I cannot take it in. It does not seem real,' he said.

'I will miss your mother,' Mhàiri said. 'In the months after my sister died, sometimes I would forget she had gone. It would pass through my mind to tell Fionnghal something and then the truth would come flooding back. Each time it was like learning again of her death. I know I'll feel the same about your mother.'

'And this, so soon after losing her home,' Peigi Ruadh said and sat down beside her husband.

Mhàiri laid her hand on top of Betty Ruadh's. Any dislike she had harboured for the woman had long disappeared. She looked around. The low-lying sun reflected off the strath, casting the shrubs in vibrant blue and yellow hues. 'Every morning I wake on the coast, it will be like going through the loss of my home again,' Mhàiri said. 'In truth, I cannot remember much about this morning. It all seems hazy, as if it happened to someone else.'

They moved off again, and Mhàiri trudged forward, placing one foot in front of the other. Time passed, along with the miles.

Night fell.

Under Mhàiri's feet the ground became rockier, and the peaty scent of soil was replaced by the sweet smell of the sea. When they trudged into the cold coastal village of Invercreag, Mhàiri could barely take another step. Her father received directions from a passing fisherman, and the group made their way to one of a long line of sheds which, for a small price, had vacancies for new arrivals.

After leaving the animals in an enclosure, Mhàiri entered a large shed. By the pale moonlight filtering through the windows, she was surprised to see that the shed was already occupied. With nowhere else to go, she had little choice but to settle down there for the night. Tomorrow, they would find out which plot of land they'd been allocated. For now, she claimed an empty space on the floor, and Cameron carried in their bedding.

Mhàiri huddled under the blankets with Cameron and her children and fell into a deep sleep.

48

DIFFERENT DAYS

Mhàiri woke to the screech of cawing birds, the smell of the sea and the sound of someone coughing. She sat up and yawned. Despite what she'd said to Iain after Mòrag Mòr died, she had no difficulty remembering where she was. The large shed was so unlike the home she had left there could be no mistaking the two places, even when surfacing from a deep sleep. Had it really only been yesterday they'd been removed?

People had started to move around. A child cried. Someone coughed. The sound of pots banging and raised voices signalled the start of families making their morning meal. The smell of cooking oats confirmed this. Mhàiri lifted Cailean and rose from their makeshift bed, leaving Caitriona asleep. Her family needed to be fed, and she had best make a start to it.

Against the walls, people stoked fires and they flared into life. Mhàiri settled Cailean onto her hip and rifled through a basket. She retrieved a pot. After adding oats and water, she made her way over. Drawing near, she looked on in horror as a man added lumps of coal to a fire. What was the matter with him? Everyone knew only to burn peat inside?

She reached a hand out. 'Stop! The sparks will catch and set this place ablaze.'

Cameron, who had sat up when she rose, came over and hugged her to him, 'It is all right, Mhàiri. The fire has a chimney. Look.' He pointed to a line of stones extending up from the fire. 'And there is nothing near for the sparks to catch onto.'

Mhàiri stared into Cameron's eyes in bewildered confusion. How could she ever settle here? 'If burning coal inside is part of the new ways here, then I don't like this place. Not one little bit.'

Cameron wrapped his arms tighter around her and pulled her and Cailean close. 'I know, but we have to put up with it. It will only be for a short time.'

When they had finished eating, Mhàiri took a pot of cooked oats over to Anna. Laying it down beside her she said, 'How is the girl?'

'Her fever still hasn't broken,' Anna said. 'Dear God, I hope it isn't typhoid. Can you see any sores, Mhàiri?'

She hunkered down and scanned the girls face. 'There are no sores that I can see. None at all. Hopefully it's just a fever. I will try to get hold of some medicine just in case.'

Anna gripped Mhàiri's hand. 'Could you?' Her voice broke. 'Please try.'

Cameron had gone to speak to Mhàiri's parents about what they should do, and Mhàiri made her way over. After much discussion, it was agreed that Cameron should head out with her to look around Invercreag and see what they could find out about how to claim the lots they'd been allocated and anything else about the village they were now expected to live in.

Outside, the noise and confusion overwhelmed Mhàiri and she gripped onto Cameron's arm. Making their way through a milling mass of people gathered around the sheds, they set off in the direction of the sea, looking for the harbour. Despite the cold wind, the sun warmed Mhàiri's skin.

Soon, they had left behind the sheds and the stink of the

animal enclosures. Clutching on to Cameron's arms, Mhàiri walked along a path above the coastline. The tide was going out, exposing large seaweed-covered rocks along the seabed.

'No boats could possibly anchor here.' Cameron held a hand above his eyes and looked up the coast. 'The harbour has to be further along.'

The wind whipped Mhàiri's hair and she held it back with one hand. If she was to be living here, she would need to start wearing a head-cloth.

Waves lapped over the rocks, and birds swooped and cawed. The smell of the sea and the sights around her couldn't have been more different to what Mhàiri was used to, and she felt a sudden longing to smell the sweet scent of the heather on the hillside.

'So much seaweed,' she said and pointed to a group of children, waist deep in the water, gathering it into large baskets.

Along the coast, women in long aprons and with their hair covered with cloths, prepared fish outside open-fronted sheds. The women's bandaged hands were red and their faces weather-beaten. As they quickly gutted fish and threw the waste into overflowing pails at their feet, they sang together in Gaelic. Young boys, no older than Connor, gathered up the filled pails and lugged them off. Mhàiri looked away. Was this to be her children's fate?

Further along, a man mended a boat. Beside him, a young woman sat on the ground weaving an odd-shaped basket.

Cameron stopped. 'There is no harbour here.'

Mhàiri nodded. 'The whole waterfront is rocks and boulders.' She called to the woman weaving the basket, 'Are you able to direct us?'

The woman stood and stretched her back. 'No doubt, you are new here.'

'We are. Do you know where we should go to find out where our plot is?'

The woman pointed towards a row of cottages. 'Make for the shed behind these houses. You cannot miss it. Likely you will find a queue when you get there. People have been trooping in since yesterday morning. Good luck to you. Likely you will be needing it.'

When they arrived at the shed, Mhàiri and Cameron joined a long line and waited. Finally, their turn came and they stepped in front of a dark-haired clerk seated behind a desk.

'Name, marital status and number of adults who'll be living with you?' the clerk asked and gave out an impatient sigh while he waited for Cameron to answer.

'Cameron MacÀidh. Married. Erm . . . one.'

As if bored by the task, the clerk flicked through a box and extracted a piece of paper. After reading it he noted something on the page and handed it to Cameron.

Cameron studied the drawing. 'What is this?' He passed the sheet to Mhàiri.

The clerk raised his eyebrows and shook his head. 'It is the plan for the house you must build, including the exact measurements for the door, windows and chimney.'

Mhàiri made to speak, but the clerk held the palm of his hand towards her. 'This is not for discussion. Either stick to that plan or don't build at all. We will have none of your hovels in Invercreag. And, you are required to build a separate barn for the animals. The rent will be paid annually. Sign here if you agree.'

After Cameron signed the agreement, the clerk handed him a metal disc with a number scraped onto it. 'Head up to the top of the cliff and look for plot thirty-seven. The number will be burnt onto a wooden post. You can't miss it. Oh, and guard that disc with your life. It proves ownership until you build.'

They headed away from the village and made their way towards the cliffs.

'Look.' Cameron pointed to a large building in the distance.

'A whisky distillery. And behind it, a mill. There must be a river there. And over there, a coal-pit and a road. Do you see the carts on it?'

'But that is not the way we've to go.' Mhàiri shook her head. 'The cliff the clerk pointed to is a good distance away in the opposite direction.'

49

CLIFFS AND COTTAGES

A white-haired and bearded man, walking a cow with a rope tied around its neck, appeared at the bottom of the path leading up to the cliff. He headed towards Mhàiri and Cameron. As he drew level, he stopped and said in a weary voice, 'That is the second time this week I have had to bring this one back. Fortunately, I found her before she wandered too far.'

'I am not surprised she wanders,' Cameron said. 'There is little here for the cattle to graze on.'

'Ah, but it is not like at home. Be warned. Any animal wandering into the shepherd's land over yonder will be impounded, and you will need to pay a hefty fine to get it back.' The man raised his hand and continued on his way.

With the sun beating down on them, Mhàiri and Cameron made their way up the cliff-side path, which grew steeper. Mhàiri looked down at the man with the cow, wondering what he had been talking about. At the top of the cliff, they passed a row of cottages. Some houses had washing blowing on ropes outside, but the lots looked small with little in the way of crops growing. Soon, the cottages disappeared to be replaced with lots with buildings in progress. Continuing on, they reached the empty lots.

'I have found lot thirty-four,' Cameron said. 'Thirty-seven cannot be far away.'

When they arrived at their allocated lot, Mhàiri came to an abrupt halt. Looking around for her new home, she saw only a small stretch of unplanted and bare rocky ground. A barrel sat beside a wooden post containing their plot number.

Cameron opened the lid of the barrel and peered inside. 'Lime . . . for building.'

'They expect us to build a house here, on top of this cliff? I don't like it. I don't like it here at all. The plot is small, bleak and—'

'Barren,' Cameron added.

Mhàiri nodded. 'Oh, Cameron, I do not mean to complain and I know we have no choice but to stay, but I cannot imagine getting any pleasure from living here. Look, there's barely any distance between our plot and the next. I thought we would have a house to live in. A byre for the animals. A stretch of ground to plant our crops. But there is nothing here.'

'We need to let the others know. It will be hard for everyone. At least we are young and still able. I don't know how your parents will manage.'

'Our houses will be close together. It is nothing like we have ever known. I don't think I will ever get used to living like this.'

'And this ground is hard with rocks.' Cameron bent down and scraped the soil with his fingers. 'The soil between the rocks is so sparse it will be unlikely to hold any seeds.'

'What can we do?'

Cameron laughed; a small guffaw that grew louder and built until he roared with laughter.

'What?' Mhàiri asked.

'Well . . .' He took a deep breath. 'There's really nothing funny, but the answer to your question struck me as such.'

Mhàiri raised her eyebrows, urging him to explain.

'The rocks we need to build our house are right here.' He kicked at a large stone. 'They are literally under our feet.'

Mhàiri linked into his arm and smiled. 'Ah, it is not funny, but I do see what you mean. We should look around the village and then head back and let the others know what we have found out.'

Arriving in the village, Mhàiri struggled to take it all in. So many people milled around or hurried past, all of them filled with purpose. Most of the women carried baskets. Mhàiri passed a shop selling milk, eggs, chicken, meat and more. Next to the shop was a blacksmith's and next to that an inn. She bought a small poke of Peruvian Bark, for Anna's daughter, from a street vendor and tucked it into the waist of her skirt.

After stopping to let a horse and cart past, they hurried across the busy road. A woman sold glassware, soap and candles from a cart and shouted in English. Beside her, a boy rolled a large metal hoop and a girl played with a cloth doll. Mhàiri had never seen anything like it. Even the busy harbour on the day Cameron's parents left had not prepared her for this.

* * *

Back in the shed, Mhàiri and Cameron gathered the townspeople together. 'It seems as if anything can be bought in this place,' Mhàiri said. 'The money we have saved towards our passages will soon be used up.'

'If we are to survive here then we need to work. All of us,' Màthair said with a resigned sigh.

Turning her hands over, Mhàiri studied them. 'If the only work I can get is gutting fish, then so be it.'

Her father pointed in turn to Cameron, Fearghas and Iain. 'We can bring the fish in.'

Cameron nodded. 'If we're to bring in a decent catch then

we will be needing at least two good sized boats. And in between that and working, we will also have to build our houses. It would be quicker if we worked together.'

There was a general murmur of agreement, and people tossed around ideas about the best way to do this. 'Wait!' Mhàiri's mother called, raising her voice to be heard above the noise. 'What about Hattie Banntrach? Hattie, you won't be entitled to a plot. You will be staying with us. That's if you want to?'

The widow beamed. 'Of course. But only if you let me care for the children while you all work.'

That evening, overcome with tiredness, Mhàiri slumped against the back wall. Her eyes roamed the shed, scanning for signs of typhus. Fires burned and flared up the chimneys. Memories flooded through her of beating at the flames engulfing her sister. The vision was replaced by a cottage burning, her home ablaze. She closed her eyes and wished that she never had to open them again. Filled with fear for her family, she lay under the blankets. Unlike the night before, when she had quickly fallen into a deep sleep, she drifted in and out of light sleep, her thoughts refusing to settle.

She recalled that fateful day, when she'd been lying on the hillside blowing the feathered seeds off dandelions, when the stranger had pulled his horse to a stop below. Over the years, she'd made many dandelion wishes but they had mostly been for one thing— a family of her own. A family she could raise in the strath, just as her parents and their parents before them had done. It was all she had ever wanted. And, for a long time, in the centre of the picture that had taken root in her mind had been Cameron. Now, she had everything she had wished for, except a home in the strath. Perhaps there would be lochs, rivers and mountains in the Red River Valley. With all her heart, she believed there would be. She would just have to keep going until she got there.

50

TIME TO TALK

The carriage drew to a sudden halt in the coastal village, and Elizabeth waited for a footman to open the door. The smell of the sea and the sound of gulls leant a pleasing quality to the day. She looked forward to hearing how her tenants had settled into their new homes in Invercreag. By all accounts, they had settled well. Despite some criticisms of her actions in the newspapers for moving her tenants from the straths, she was confident that, like the other coastal villages she'd visited, she would be hearing of the benefits these tenants were already experiencing.

The door opened, and Elizabeth stepped out to be greeted by a sea of anxious faces.

A factor, who had travelled ahead of the carriage by horse, bowed. 'My Lady, there is much excitement about your visit.'

Elizabeth adjusted the shawl around her shoulders and smiled. 'I too am pleased to be here. It is one thing to see plans drawn out on paper and quite another to see these plans brought to life.'

'My Lady, I have arranged for you to speak to some tenants and then I can show you around Invercreag.'

Elizabeth nodded and followed him over to a small group of tenants, who stood apart from the larger cluster

The factor waved his arm. 'As none of these natives speak English, I'll translate your questions and inform you of their responses. I trust that meets with your approval.'

The tenants seemed anxious and Elizabeth determined to put them at their ease. She nodded. 'I am pleased to see everyone so well. In concern for your welfare, I had this village built around the industries here. I trust you have all gained employment.'

The factor translated her words and the crowd nodded.

Pleased with their response, Elizabeth singled out a man who looked to be in his twenties. He looked robust and well nourished. 'You there, what do you do?'

'I am a cooper, Ma'am.'

'And do you like this work?'

'I do, but—'

The factor translated his words, cutting him off.

'And your houses, are they to your liking?' she said and pointed to a young woman.

The woman looked around, shook her head and said something. She thrust a sheet of paper towards Elizabeth, containing a drawing of the design for the cottages that were to be built.

Elizabeth scanned the page and passed it to the factor. 'What is this woman saying? Is she unhappy with the design of her cottage?'

The factor shook his head. 'Not at all. She wants to build in the style of the long house she left, including the internal byre. We get this all the time. They say that having the animals inside keeps their families warm through the winter. Once they are settled, they soon realise the benefit of keeping the animals out of their homes.'

Elizabeth nodded. 'And the others, what do they say?'

'They are very happy with their new homes.'

* * *

Mhàiri repeated her words to the Great Lady. 'There is no house. All I have been given is this sheet of paper, some lime and a small piece of ground at the top of a steep cliff.' Mhàiri frowned and rubbed her hands down her skirt. 'With no home, what are my family to do?'

The Great Lady said something to the factor, and he replied in English.

Mhàiri waited for the translation of the Great Lady's words. When none came, Mhàiri repeated. 'How can my family live on the edge of a steep cliff? I have small children.'

The factor raised a hand and addressed the crowd. 'Her Ladyship is happy to hear that you are pleased with your new homes. I have informed her that there are no issues here.'

As the factor led the Great Lady away, Mhàiri stared after them. Her eyes narrowed. The factor had not passed on her concerns. As she watched them depart, she realised that nothing would change. Without the Gaelic, the only words her landlord would hear were those spoken against her tenants.

As if her breath had been sucked from her, Mhàiri's shoulders slumped. Following the breath out of her body was any belief she had tried to hold on to that the Great Lady would help them.

FEELING FEVERED

Mhàiri bent over and gripped the sharp pain in her side. 'Thank you for the dance, Connor, but away you go now and ask Caitriona for the next one. I guess my dancing days are over until this baby arrives,' she added and made her way over to Cameron. She dabbed at the sweat beading on her brow and upper lip.

As she wound her way past the children running around, laughing and squealing, she marvelled at their resilience. She reached the table where Cameron and Iain sat talking and sipping whisky with the two Kildonan men, Lachlann and Dòmhnall Beag.

Breathless and sweating, she rested a hand on Cameron's shoulder to steady herself. He looked up. 'Are you all right?'

'Ah, I am fine. I am getting too old for these fast dances. Well, until this baby arrives.' She sat down at the end of the table beside Lachlann and Dòmhnall's wives.

Cameron laughed and the men continued their discussion.

Mhàiri stretched out her legs and closed her eyes. The fiddle music, playing in the background, reminded her of the fiddler they'd left behind in Achcoil. What had happened to him and his wife? She'd heard stories that some who had been unable to make the journey to the coast had moved into the woods and made shelters there. She hoped the fiddler and his wife had done the same.

Why did she feel so hot? It was as if her body was on fire. The men's voices droned on in the background. She opened her eyes but remained sitting.

'All the good jobs are going to English speaking Lowlanders,' Cameron said. 'If yesterday was anything to go by, then the Great Lady will be unaware of this. Apart from putting our concerns to her in writing there is little else we can do.'

'What good would that do us?' Dòmhnall Beag let out a bitter laugh. 'She is not going to come and build our houses for us, is she? And even if she sent someone to build them, it would take months. Months we do not have.'

'Ah, you are right,' Cameron said. 'Whether we build our houses ourselves or someone does it for us, they won't be finished any time soon. For now, we just have to get on with it. And, there's work available on the boats if we are willing to do it.'

Iain shook his head from side to side. 'We could become fishermen or even miners, but our houses need building and the ground needs to be prepared for planting. How are we to do all that? The seasons won't wait for us before changing.'

'Our days will be long,' Cameron agreed.

'I am thinking of asking one of the coopers to take me on,' Iain said. 'In truth, the work of the men making the barrels has drawn me since we arrived.'

'We might not need to be worrying for much longer,' Lachlann said, causing everyone at the table to stop talking. 'I heard that a ship is to be sailing for North America, and they are recruiting people to go.'

On hearing this, Mhàiri sat up. 'When. Where?'

Lachlann shook his head. 'Sorry, Mhàiri, I don't know. It is just something I heard. But count on it, I will be trying to find out. A group has formed, I will ask about joining. You remember Rob Dunn? He is with the resistance now. He was one of the ones involved in setting up the tenant emigration group.'

At the mention of Rob's name, Mhàiri peered at Lachlann. While she'd sat by, hoping that the evictions wouldn't take place, Rob Dunn had continued to fight against the removals and now he was fighting to help the removed tenants emigrate. She felt a new sense of appreciation for him.

'There is no point in wasting money preparing houses and crops if we are not planning on staying?' Cameron said.

'Ah well, if the rumour Lachlann heard is right then we need to keep what money we have for our passages,' Dòmhnall Beag said. 'And find the rest of the money, and soon.'

Mhàiri grew thoughtful. What Cameron had said was true enough, but they needed somewhere to live in the meantime. They couldn't continue to live in this overcrowded shed. She sniffed her sleeve. The rank smell from the place clung to her. Anna's daughter still had a fever and was growing weaker. It was just a matter of time until typhus hit one of them. Mhàiri's parents needed help to finish building their house. Unlike most others around the table, her mother and father had no intention of emigrating.

She said to Cameron, 'We will help my parents build their cottage, but we won't finish ours just yet. We can stay with them until we board a ship.'

'That would work,' Cameron replied.

'We can do something similar,' Dòmhnall Beag said. 'Two completed houses amongst the rest of us should be enough.'

Mhàiri felt as if everyone was fading in and out of her vision. She touched the back of her neck and felt a searing heat. Her head ached, and she wanted to close her eyes and sleep.

'Ah, that would do fine,' Lachlann said, 'but if there is to be a ship leaving, we will have to find a quick way of earning the money we will be needing in order to board it. Has anyone got any ideas?'

Mhàiri made to stand. The room spun. Everything turned black.

* * *

Someone called her name. Mhàiri opened her mouth to answer but no words came. The effort made her head ache.

'Mhàiri,' the voice called again, but she couldn't find the strength to open her eyes to see who it was. Was it Rob Dunn, back from the war? Why was he covered in blood? And why was he shouting at her?

Blackness enveloped her.

Later, an intense heat raged through Mhàiri's body. It was as if she had been set ablaze, and pain ripped through her belly. She sensed a presence beside her, but couldn't see who it was. Was she dying? It felt like it. Had her dead sister come to get her? 'A Fionnghal,' she called, 'is that you? Are you there?'

Mhàiri opened her eyes but everything appeared hazy, so she closed them again.

Water, was that water? She swallowed the cool trickle of strange tasting liquid in her mouth. She wanted more, but none came. A sharp pain ripped through her, and she groaned. Sweat poured from her body and pooled below her back. Tears coursed down her face. Overcome with pain, confusion and an overwhelming desire to return to Achcoil, Mhàiri screamed.

The next time Mhàiri awoke, she opened her eyes.

Màthair loomed over her, holding a cloth.

'Lie still, lassie,' Màthair said. 'Let me finish washing you down.'

Mhàiri licked her dry lips and made to speak. Where was

she? With a great deal of effort, she managed to force out a single word, 'What?'

'It is a fever, lassie. You rest up, get yourself better.'

Mhàiri nodded. Something didn't feel right, but she couldn't for the life of her figure out what it was. The more she tried to think, the more her mind became a blank. Her eyes closed, and she slipped into a deep sleep.

She awoke again to the sound of clattering pans and loud voices. She sat up and looked around the shed. How long had she been unwell? Days? Weeks? When she pulled the blankets back and made to stand, her hand froze. The answer to the question which had plagued her earlier, rushed towards her, sending her flat onto her back again— she had lost the baby. Her heart ached.

Her mother had said she had a fever. Was it Typhus? Panic flooded through her. 'Dear, God! Caitriona! Cailean!' she called, her voice rising

Cameron appeared at her side and gripped her hands. 'Mhàiri the children are fine.' He dropped his eyes.

Sensing that there was no point in arguing with him that she had lost another baby, she remained silent. At least Caitriona and Cailean were safe and for that she was thankful.

'We need to get you and the children away from this shed. So many here have fevers.' Cameron let out a deep sigh. 'Anna and Fearghas's lassie died.'

'Oh, dear Lord.' Mhàiri said. Tears flowed and she held her hands to her face and sobbed.

'In a few days we will get you moved to your mother and father's cottage,' Cameron said.

'It's near finished . . . That is, if you are up to it.'

52

MONEY MATTERS

M hàiri hung the last shirt over the rope and stood back to watch her washing blowing on the line. The wind was so much stronger on the coast than it was inland and it dried the clothes in no time.

She heard Cameron calling her name and turned. 'What is it?'

'Dandelion is missing. I will search around the other lots. Surely she cannot have gone far.'

Mhàiri held up her hands in despair and made her way over to the barn. Despite her reluctance to come to Invercreag, her life had settled into some semblance of a routine on the coast. The hours had turned into days and the days into weeks and so life had gone on. Her parent's cottage had been completed and all the family had moved in, along with Hattie Bantrach. They'd even managed to build this barn. But still there was no word about any passages to the Red River Valley, and now one of her cows had wandered off.

Mhàiri pulled a strong rope down from a hook on the wall. 'Not again,' she raged and called to Connor and Caitriona who were gathering in the eggs. 'Dandelion has wandered off. Search around and about here and I will go look for her up by the mill.'

After searching for over two hours, Mhàiri and Cameron finally called the search off.

'The longer the animal is missing, the more likely it is that it has been impounded by one of the shepherds,' Màthair said.

'What can I do?' Mhàiri rubbed her hand over her sweating forehead. 'I will have to pay to get Dandelion back. We need the milk. And she is Caitriona's favourite. She named that cow.'

The following morning, Cameron threw a rope over his shoulder, and Mhàiri marched with him to the nearest sheep farm. He carried the four shillings they would need to pay for their cow's release.

Mhàiri walked through the large barn, where the impounded animals were held, looking for Dandelion. With tears in her eyes, she fingered the brooch in her pocket; the MacAoidh crest brooch she'd worn at her wedding. When they spotted Dandelion, Mhàiri removed the brooch and made to hand it to the shepherd.

Cameron put out a hand to stop her. 'We will pay, Mhàiri.'

'But we need that money towards our passages away from here.'

'Make yer' mind up,' the shepherd said. 'I don't have all day to stand around waiting.'

'Then we will have to suffer the loss of the animal.' Cameron turned to leave. 'It is not as if we can take Dandelion with us when we go.'

Mhàiri followed him outside. 'Perhaps we will hear something soon? About a passage.'

'Perhaps,' Cameron said. 'And, in the meantime, we will make do. But we cannot sit around waiting for something to happen. Now that we have a date for the meeting, I am going to join that supported emigration group. The one Lachlann mentioned. I will take Connor with me. The more force we apply the better.'

On returning home, Mhàiri entered the barn and held up the rope. There were other uses it could be put to, she thought and unwound it. After tying one of their remaining two cows to a post, she lifted a bowl and their sharpest knife down from a shelf. She stood in front of the cow and leant her hip against its lower chest. Bending forward, she lifted the knife and sliced a small gash in the animal's neck and held up the bowl. She cut out the sound of the cow lowing and watched the blood trickle into the bowl. Drip by drip.

In the house, she mixed the blood with oats. Scooping out small handfuls, she formed the mixture into flat cakes. After frying the bloody mix in butter, she fried four eggs. There weren't enough eggs to have one each.

'The hens do not seem to be laying as many eggs,' she said to her mother. 'Do you think someone is stealing them?'

Màthair frowned. 'No one would do that. Not even around here. Perhaps the hens are laying under the sheds.'

'Most likely that is what it is, but what a waste.' Mhàiri looked over at the table where Cameron, her father, the two children and Hattie Bantrach waited to be fed. 'But at least for tonight we will eat well.' She lifted the large pan over to the table.

After they had eaten, Mhàiri walked with Cameron down the steep cliff-side path to the sea. The one thing she did enjoy here was their evening walks along the coast. As they made their way past the shed where the lots were allocated, they passed a man and woman making their way from it. Mhàiri stared in surprise to see the red-haired Kildonan woman she had smuggled the whisky with at the sheilings. She waved over.

The woman recognised her and stopped, allowing Mhàiri to catch up.

'*A Ciorstag, cionnas a tha thu?* – Ciorstag, how are you?' Mhàiri said. 'Have you moved to Invercreag too?'

'We are not allowed to. Apparently, we are not of good character. There is no lot for us here. Not that I am surprised,' Ciorstag said.

Cameron shook his head. 'Not of good character.'

Puzzled why Ciorstag would be turned away, Mhàiri asked, 'Did you get caught smuggling the whisky?'

'Likely it would have been better if we had. When the officers came to remove us, we refused to go.' Ciorstag pointed a thumb at her husband. 'Alasdair threw a pot of cold oats over an officer, before he could tip it onto the fire.' She laughed. 'And I threw the piss pot. So, it is no surprise to hear that we are not welcome.'

'What will you do?' Mhàiri said with concern. Ciorstag and Alasdair would be left to roam the land. At least they had no children. Her thoughts turned to Iain. He too had been refused a lot on the grounds of not being of 'good character'—due to living with Peigi Ruadh and having children with her out of wedlock. Fortunately, a minister had agreed to marry them, and they were given the plot reserved for Mòrag Mòr—for a higher rent than everyone else.

Ciorstag pointed up the coast. 'We found a cave. There is a large space at the back. It is high enough up that the water doesn't come in . . . even when it's raining. We are fine enough.'

'Dear God, you're living in a cave? But—'

'We are not the only ones. And we only use it when we're here to ship our whisky along the coast. We get by well enough, mainly by stealing a sheep or two. It's not as if the shepherds don't have enough. And, as long as we are careful going in and out the cave, no one will even notice we are there.'

Mhàiri shuddered. She couldn't contemplate living inside a cave. It made her appreciate all the more what little she had.

'Don't worry about us.' Alasdair placed an arm affectionately around his wife's shoulder. 'We are not stopping. Like many others, we are waiting to hear about the ship that's meant to be sailing for North America. We need to stay nearby until after the meeting.'

'I plan on attending too. We can go together,' Cameron said.

After bidding each other well, Ciorstag arranged to meet with Mhàiri again. 'I will watch out for you,' Ciorstag said. 'We're setting up a good business, smuggling tea, tobacco and brandy in and getting the whisky out along the coast. You should join us. No need to agree now, but think about it. There is money to be made. Enough to get you away from here.'

Mhàiri watched the woman leave and rolled her eyes at Cameron. 'Ciorstag has never been caught, yet.'

53

TEA TIME

Mhàiri grimaced and almost spat out the hot, tarry liquid. 'It is strong,' she said to Ciorstag and rested the cup on her knee. 'So, this type of tea is popular?'

'It is. And with the new inns and shops along the coast catering to the Lowlanders we've no trouble selling it on.'

Two weeks had passed since she'd met up with Ciorstag again. Mhàiri had agreed with Cameron, not to get involved in smuggling brandy, whisky or tobacco. Now, Ciorstag was asking her to help sell tea on.

Mhàiri stared into the fire deep in thought. 'I do not know, Ciorstag. Everyone is being watched closely.'

'It isn't as if you haven't smuggled before. Granted, the profits for tea aren't as high as they were, but it still pays well.'

Mhàiri hesitated. When she had set up the stills at the sheilings she'd thought the risk worthwhile to take Maister Sellar to court. But now, they only had to bide their time until they could leave. Was it worth the risk? Cameron had built a chimney into the gable end wall. A pot, suspended at the side on a movable metal arm, held soup. And, the kettle had been placed onto a metal plate at the side of the fire. Everything was different on the coast.

Reaching a decision, Mhàiri lifted her cup and sniffed the contents. I am not sure what to make of this tea but if the Lowlanders like it then I will help to sell it on.' She looked up. 'Have you heard anything of the emigration meeting about the ships leaving?'

'Nothing, but it is not for the want of trying. If there is anything happening, we will hear about it as we go around the villages. Have the men finished their boats?'

'They have readied one. But there isn't a lot of wood around. With so many building, the cost of wood is higher than ever. It looks like it will be a never-ending task to get the other one finished. We've used all the wood we had. Even the carts have been broken up.'

'You don't have time to wait. You'll be needing money now. Cameron and your father should take a share in one of the fishermen's boats.'

'They can't afford to, Ciorstag.'

'They can now.'

'A thousand thanks to you, Ciorstag. The money from the tea will certainly help. With no crops in the ground, we need to earn. The men thought about setting up a still, but it seems nigh on impossible to do that without getting caught. Even working the small stills, we couldn't produce enough to make it worth our time.'

Mhàiri stood and stretched. 'Standing all day gutting the fish is playing havoc with my back. But, sore back or not, I'd best make my way there.' She held out a hand and wound strips of cloth around her fingers, to stop the salt nipping the cuts.

Connor rushed in, interrupting their conversation. 'Anna's ready to leave. She sent me to fetch you.'

'I will catch you later, Ciorstag,' Mhàiri said and hurried out the door. With leaden steps, she made her way over to Anna's plot. Connor ran ahead, but she couldn't summon the energy to keep up.

Anna hurried towards them. 'Oh, Mhàiri, I know I said we wouldn't be leaving until tomorrow but everything's ready and there's no point in delaying. It looks like there is a storm coming.'

Mhàiri held her dearest friend in a tight embrace. 'Wouldn't it be better to wait until the storm has passed? Why do you have to rush away?'

'We have to leave before it comes.'

'I understand, but that doesn't make parting any easier.'

Anna had tears in her eyes. She stepped back. 'I have no family here. Fearghas has family of sorts in Caithness. At least we can plant in the strip of land we will be renting there.' She swept a hand around the rock-covered ground which sloped down to the top of the high cliff. 'Since my daughter died, I haven't been able to settle. Neither has Fearghas. You've seen how it has changed him.'

Mhàiri nodded. She'd seen the growing anger in Anna's husband, and heard it too. He'd become argumentative and had distanced himself from the other men.

'We tried, but we are farmers. We are of the land, not the sea,' Anna said. 'We are going back inland. Even if I'd been able to settle, I cannot risk staying. When the winds come, I am not able to let my son out for fear of him being swept off the cliff. The slope is so steep. I will not risk losing another child to here.'

'And the seeds we plant,' Fearghas said arriving beside them. 'The wind sweeps away what little soil there is and our seeds with them. We need to get going Anna. You've lingered long enough.'

Mhàiri linked into Anna's arm and walked with her to the cottage door. 'If we hadn't planned on emigrating, I would have done the same myself. Still, it is hard to be going our separate ways.'

'We have been given no choice,' Anna said. 'The people from our township, spread all around when once we lived so close, like family. It saddens my heart. And this house,' she added. 'Even if we had been able to stay, there's no time to do what is needed. I know some have built a barn but, with working all day, we never would have found time before the winter was upon us.'

Returning alone to the fisheries, Mhàiri kicked a stone, sending it clattering along the hostile, cursed ground. Her dearest friend had gone, and she would miss her. Though it had only been five minutes since Anna and her family had departed it already felt like forever.

Why? Why had their lives been torn apart like this? If she didn't secure a passage abroad, she wouldn't be able to stay on the coast either. What life would her children have here? They would be no better than servants, handing back whatever money they earned on rent and food. Mhàiri looked up at the darkening sky and shivered. Anna was right, there was a storm brewing and it looked like it would be a bad one.

Mhàiri's eyes were drawn to the notice posted on the door of the receiving-clerk's shed.

£20 reward for any information leading to a conviction for sheep theft.

5 4

SEA STORM

That night sleep wouldn't come. Mhàiri lay there thinking. The wind had whipped up a storm so fierce she thought the roof would be blown off the cottage. Rain clattered down, and the waves crashed relentlessly against the rocks below. The howling wind shrouded the cottage in regret and created an eerie sense of foreboding that something bad was about to happen.

Mhàiri tried to shrug the feeling off. Was it a reaction to her dear friend leaving? Although she had known Fearghas all her life, Mhàiri no longer trusted him. Since his daughter's death, something about him frightened her. She hoped Anna would be all right. Losing her had dug a deep hole in Mhàiri's life, one that might be plugged but never filled. Or had it been Ciorstag talking about smuggling tea along the coast?

A loud crash sent Mhàiri leaping out of bed.

Cameron sat up and rubbed his eyes. 'Mhàiri, it is only thunder. Get yourself back into bed.' He held out his arms and cradled her into them. 'Shush, try to sleep. If this continues the children will be up and then we'll wish we had slept.'

Mhàiri snuggled into him, relishing the closeness of his body. When his lips settled on hers the storm growing inside blotted out the one outside.

* * *

By the following afternoon the weather had settled, leaving a crisp freshness to the air and the sun peeked through grey clouds. Although one of their boats was ready, Cameron and her father had never sailed before and had arranged for one of the fishermen who had been brought up from Aberdeen to take them out. The fishermen had told them to prepare for a long night— it was never certain when and where they would get a good catch.

Cameron and her father made their way down to the shore. The boats had already been pushed out into deeper water by white whiskered and bearded men, who waited for the fishing crews to climb aboard.

Mhàiri giggled as her mother and Hattie Bantrach sat on a large rock and removed their shoes and socks, as the other fisher-men's wives did. When they had finished, they hitched up their skirts and tucked them into their belts. Following the lead of the fisherwomen, they carried the men out to the boat on their backs. Mhàiri regarded her mother and Hattie Bantrach as old, but watching them lumber through the water towards the boats, she realised now how young they were; neither of them yet forty-five. If it hadn't been for Mhàiri's sore back, she would have carried Cameron out to the boat herself. She couldn't risk her husband spending a night at sea with wet feet.

Mhàiri remained with the women, watching the boats sail out. When the vessels became blots on the horizon, she turned and made her way to the fisheries, where she would spend the next few hours sorting and gutting fish. As she took a place at the table, a woman with her head bent caught Mhàiri's attention and her heart skipped a beat. Was that Anna? When a stranger looked up, Mhàiri felt a stab of pain. Of course, it couldn't be Anna, her friend had gone. She missed her, likely she always would.

Engrossed in the mournful Gaelic songs the women sang, Mhàiri was startled by loud shouts. After dropping the knife onto the table, she followed the women to the source of the disturbance.

Two sheriff officers marched Alasdair, towards a cart. The man squirmed and struggled. 'Get off me, leave me be,' he roared.

Ciorstag reached out to grab her husband. An officer pushed her back, and she screamed.

Mhàiri looked around the growing crowd. What was happening?

A shepherd rode in on a grey horse and sat upright in the saddle. 'That's him all right.' He pointed to Alasdair. 'That is the man I was telt was stealing ma' sheep.'

A loud gasp rose from the crowd, and Mhàiri's hand leapt to her mouth.

The officers bound Alasdair's arms behind him and thrust him struggling into the cart.

'Transportation would be too guid for him. Let that be a warning to you all.' The shepherd called and rode off behind the cart which carried Alasdair.

When Ciorstag's legs buckled, Mhàiri ran forward and grabbed her. Holding the weeping woman under the arm, she guided her up to the cottage and sat her on a chair.

Ciorstag moaned. 'I have to get him out. I have to. I need to go to Dornoch. Someone must have told on us.'

Mhàiri held the woman and rocked her. She had been thinking the same thing. Who would have claimed the £20 reward by informing on Ciorstag's husband? Few knew of their existence. Her thoughts turned to Peigi Ruadh. Could she have? Mhàiri shook her head and said, 'What can you do? What can any of us do?'

55

LOST LAMBS

Mister Sellar lifted his wine glass and swirled the remains of the dark liquid before gulping it down. 'A bunch o' thieves,' he said to the shepherd. 'Good for you catching that man. I don't know how many sheep I've lost.'

'Aye, but for every scoundrel we catch there will be another to take his place,' the shepherd said.

Mister Sellar filled his glass with wine and offered a refill to his guest, who held out his glass and said, 'I'm fair stuffed. That was a braw meal. The lamb was succulent. I dinnae ken how your housekeeper does it. She aye puts out a guid meal.'

'After the poor yields we've had the last twa years, this year produced a bountiful crop o' potatoes. I agree, tonight's were particularly tasty. It is not just the sheep these folk are stealing. Lord and Lady Stafford have had tae put constant patrols in place on the coast tae stop these beggars helping themselves tae the shellfish. Even with the patrols, they try every trick they can tae steal the fish. They want everything, an' they're not likely tae work for it when they can take it for nothing.'

The shepherd shook his head in despair. 'They give nae

thought to the cost o' their thievery to us who are trying to earn an honest living.'

Mister Sellar swirled the wine around in his glass. 'Perhaps we should be more forgiving o' these poor unfortunates, but if we don't come down heavily on them, then…. I have nae doubt at all that we will be the ones living in fear. If we make even one concession we may as well say goodbye tae our stock.' The blood-red wine settled and he laid the glass down.

'Aye, you are right. And while our Cheviot sheep have settled here well enough, the profits are no as guid as we'd first expected. I've no time for them that want to steal from me. No, I canny afford to just give my stock away.'

Mister Sellar chortled. 'Imagine even thinking that we would tolerate them stealing our sheep. That man will remain in jail without a doubt, he may even hang. An' many more scoundrels like him will follow before long.'

'Aye, there is no shortage o' informers now that we've offered up a reward.'

'It is money well spent,' Mister Sellar said. 'And we are going tae have that Tenant's Emigration Society declared illegal tae. Lady Stafford doesn't want her tenants emigrating.'

'Aye, they won't be forming again in a hurry. We should round up the ringleaders anyway, before they think o' another way to get by without earning.'

'These barbarians will do anything tae get out o' doing an honest day's work. Drink up an' I'll refill your glass. Have you been back down tae the Border country lately? I'm thinking o' looking for another farm. Now that I'm married, I need a bigger house.'

The shepherd chuckled and Sellar joined in.

56

THREAT OF THUNDER

After depositing Cameron and her father onto the fishing boats, Mhàiri watched Hattie Bantrach and her mother, laughing and chatting together as they trundled back through the water— the weight of their wet skirts slowing them down.

Reaching the shore, Hattie Bantrach held out her hands, palms upward. 'In all the time I spent abroad in the wars, I never saw anything like it.' She guffawed again. 'Women carrying grown men on their backs. I don't think I will ever get used to seeing that.'

'Ah, but it is not as if we aren't used to carrying such a weight,' Mhàiri said. 'All these peats we've carried.'

'And the soil we've lugged up that cliff,' Màthair added.

'Ah yes, that too. A woman's work, eh?' Mhàiri frowned. 'With Ciorstag gone, I cannot see us having the money to get the other boat finished.'

Hattie Bantrach nodded. 'Cameron and your father should soon be able to take their boat out on their own. Things should get easier after that.'

Mhàiri looked up at the darkening sky. 'I hope so.' So far, the threatened storm had held off. 'I hope the weather doesn't break.'

$$* * *$$

The weather, which had started out dismal, grew bleaker by late evening. Rain lashed against the windows as if trying to get in, and the howling of the wind surrounded the cottage with an eerie sense of foreboding. Mhàiri shivered and held her hands towards the fire. 'Cameron and Faither should have returned by now,' she said to her mother. 'The boats should have come back in.'

Màthair picked up her shawl. 'I can't sit here any longer. I'm going down to see if there is any sign of them.'

'Hold on.' Mhàiri grabbed her plaid from the back of the door. 'I'm coming with you.'

When she stepped out the door, the driving rain lashed at her. She gripped onto her mother's arms. Watching where they stepped, they made their way down the steep cliff-side path, heading towards the sea. The wind whipped Mhàiri's plaid, and she pulled it tighter around her.

By the time they reached the shore, a large group had gathered. Mhàiri recognised Dòmhnall Beag and Lachlann's wives, and made her way over. Huddled together in the lashing rain, none if the women spoke; their eyes remaining fixed on the horizon.

Waves crashed over the rocks and pounded onto the shore. The sky darkened, but the women remained. Mhàiri clung onto her mother's arm and looked out across the sea, searching; watching for any sign of the fishermen's boats. The rain lashed against her, and the wind howled a loud lament. The rain turned into a torrential downpour, stinging Mhàiri's face. But still, she remained. Watching. Scanning. Searching. Rooted there, unable to move away.

A boat appeared on the horizon. Mhàiri made to run towards it, but her mother pulled her back. 'Wait. Wait until it is nearer.'

The fishing boat lunged upwards with every wave, before crashing down again. Mhàiri gripped onto her mother's arm and prayed that the boat wouldn't crash into the rocks. One moment the boat was there and the next it was gone. A feeling of dread flooded through Mhàiri. 'Dear, God. Let it not be!'

'Likely the other boats will have taken shelter,' Dòmhnall Beag's wife shouted above the raging storm. 'There is no way any boat will be landing here tonight. It would be senseless to try.'

Still shaken by what she had seen, Mhàiri prayed that the woman was right. It made sense, and she clung to the idea that the men had taken shelter. 'Likely you are right,' she said, and her mother nodded.

The women drifted off home, to wait.

At first light, Mhàiri and her mother made their way back down the cliff-side. The storm had settled, but the sky remained filled with dark clouds. Mhàiri walked beside her mother, among the debris washed onto the shore, and stared out to sea. Praying, watching, listening, but there was no sign of any boats.

'Likely they will have taken shelter further down the coast,' Màthair said. 'It could be time enough before they return.' Placing her arms around Mhàiri's shoulder, they made their way home.

* * *

Mhàiri looked out the window, again. The rain had stopped, and the sun peeped through the sky, promising a clear day. Mhàiri sat beside her mother and took her hand. 'The boats must have taken shelter right enough. They should be returning soon—'

The door swung open and Iain beckoned to them. 'Come quickly. Two boats are coming in.'

Mhàiri jumped up from the stool and raced through the open door, her mother following behind her. Mhàiri hurried down the cliff-side path. Blind to the slope beneath her feet, she stumbled and righted herself. Careening down the hillside, she slid and stumbled until she felt soft sand beneath her feet.

Ahead, four men pulled in a boat. Behind them another boat waited to come ashore. Breathless, Mhàiri held a hand to her mouth and scanned each fisherman who climbed over the side and jumped down. She stretched her neck and raised her head, searching for Cameron and her father.

She gripped her mother's arm. 'I don't recognise any of these men, do you?'

'That is not Niall or Cameron's boat,' Màthair said and ran towards the second boat, which was now being pulled ashore.

Two fishermen hauled a body over the side and dropped it into waiting arms. Recognising Cameron, Mhàiri raced forward.

A hand grasped her arm and pulled her back. 'Wait, Mhàiri, give them a moment. Let them bring Cameron ashore.' Her mother held on to her, while her eyes continued to scan the boats, searching for her husband.

The men carried Cameron's body up the steep path, Mhàiri walked beside them, glancing over her shoulder at her mother who remained behind, still waiting and watching.

Cameron opened his eyes. 'Mhàiri—'

Mhàiri stroked his ashen face. 'Ah, we are just getting you home.'

Cameron winced and sucked in his breath. Blood seeped through the blanket swaddling him.

Mhàiri's heart raced and her head spun. She tried to focus on the fact that her husband had returned. Although Cameron seemed badly injured, he was alive. The men carried him into the cottage and laid him face down on the box-bed in the main room. When the blanket was pulled back, Mhàiri reeled at the sight of a large, gaping blood-covered wound on his back.

'Dear God, what happened,' Hattie Bantrach asked.

'He got thrown in the storm. We need to get that wound cleaned,' one of the fishermen said.

Brought back to her senses, Mhàiri filled a bowl with hot water, while Hattie Bantrach ripped a cloth apart. Together they cleaned Cameron's wound and, with the help of the fishermen, settled her writhing husband into the bed.

Mhàiri pulled a stool over and sat beside him. '*A Cameron, A ghràidh*- Cameron, my love.' she said and clutched his clenched fist. 'You made it back, you are safe now.'

57

GRIEF AND GOODBYES

Mhàiri stood near the edge of the cliff, scanning the coastline. Spotting her mother below, knee-deep in the water, she tucked the hem of her skirt into her waistband and raced down the steep cliff-side path. At the water's edge, she braced herself and waded into the freezing sea. Two weeks had passed since the fishing boats had gone missing, and every day had been an agony of waiting. Nine boats had gone out, only three had returned. Mhàiri's father had not been on any of the ones that had taken shelter and returned.

Reaching her mother, Mhàiri placed an arm around her shoulder 'Come on, Màthair, you can't stay here. Let's get you home and warmed up.'

Her mother turned to her with vacant eyes. 'Shh!' She held a finger to her blue lips. 'Listen. Niall is calling me. *'A Catriona'*. Do you hear him?' She tilted her head up. *'A Niall, mo ghràidh*– Niall, my love,' she called back and made to wade further out. 'Where are you?'

The wind sighed, and Mhàiri joined in its weary lament. She trudged through the water, pulling her mother behind her towards the shore. Tears threatened but she bit them back.

What was the point in crying? She'd cried all the tears left in her and was dried up, empty. She had to stay strong. And, she had to get her mother dried and into bed; the same as she had had to do yesterday, and the day before, and every day before that.

Màthair kept her head turned, looking back over her shoulder, staring at the sea; her eyes clouded . . . distant . . . empty. Her voice hoarse, as she continued to call, '*A Niall, mo ghràidh*– Niall, my love!'

Mhàiri kept a firm grip on Màthair's arm and led her up the steep path, all the time hushing her mother as if she was a child. On reaching home, she called to Hattie Bantrach to put the broth on to heat.

'Is she all right?' Hattie asked, her voice filled with concern. 'She cannot keep doing this.

'I got to her this time, but we will have to keep a closer watch on her. Bring a little whisky. She is frozen to the bone.'

In the bedroom, Mhàiri stripped off her mother's wet clothes and settled her onto the bed. She rubbed her with a dry cloth until her teeth stopped chattering. After Mhàiri covered her with blankets, Hattie Bantrach spooned whisky into Màthair's mouth.

Mhàiri changed out of her own wet clothes. She placed hot stones, wrapped in a cloth, around Màthair's feet and went to fetch a bowl of the warming broth. By the time she arrived back, her mother had fallen asleep. Mhàiri made to return to the main room to sit with Cameron, but stopped. She laid the bowl on a chest and sat on the bed.

She pulled a tendril of greying hair off her mother's pale face. Although she likely couldn't hear her, Mhàiri spoke anyway. 'You were always the strong one, Màthair. It pains me now to see you like this. All my life, I have relied on you and marvelled at how good you were at everything you did. There seemed nothing you couldn't do, and do it well.'

Mhàiri felt a twinge of guilt at not having helped her more.

She had brushed aside helping on the grounds that her mother could do any task better than she could. Memories competed for a place in her thoughts. Feeling an overwhelming desire to be close, Mhàiri lay down and stretched out beside her. Her mother stirred, but didn't wake.

How could Mhàiri keep her safe? It was only a matter of time until she waded too far out. Mhàiri thought of the hard life her mother had led. Her husband had been away on and off for ten years, fighting in wars that had nothing to do with him. But it had been a matter of honouring the Great Lady. Like all the men in Strathnaver, her father had done his duty. Many hadn't returned: Hattie Bantrach's husband, Mòrag Mòr's son, Cameron's brother.

Mhàiri winced as a thought occurred to her. A sharp pain stabbed through her chest. Cameron had been torn between emigrating and staying with her. With his brother dead, and as the only surviving son, he must have felt a sense of responsibility towards his family. Mhàiri had never acknowledged this, and Cameron had never said. Despite this, he had chosen her before them. She had never thanked him for staying, or told him that she understood his desire to emigrate as well.

She now also understood her mother's pain; it was as if she had finally reached the end of how much she could take. Mhàiri wanted to close her eyes and snuggle into her. She wanted to close her eyes to it all and keep them closed, but she couldn't. She had the children and Cameron to look after, and Màthair. She couldn't give up. It had been her father's time, and no amount of weeping would change that. It was God's will. But that didn't stop her missing him. Living with him had been like living with two very different fathers; the sober, gentle, loving one, and the wounded, drunken, argumentative one. She had loved them both.

Mhàiri felt as if the hole that had been torn in her heart when they had been removed from their home had been ripped further open. Time and more torments here would continue to pull the hole ever wider, until one day there would be nothing left but a large gaping space where her heart had been. Just like Màthair, gone would be the rhythm of her life, no longer putting out its own steady beat.

* * *

Mhàiri stood at the graveside and dropped a handful of salt and a clod of earth onto the makeshift coffin. 'Ashes to ashes, dust to dust.' She missed Màthair. Anger stirred. Why did she have to leave her now, of all times? With her father gone her life had felt empty. And now you too, Màthair, she thought and raised her eyes upwards. At least Cameron was showing signs of recovering. He remained bed-bound but seemed to be gaining strength every day. Dear God, how long could she continue to manage without Cameron working?

The surviving boats had managed to find shelter when the storm had broken, but ten men had perished, never to return. She didn't want to think about her father out there, at the bottom of the sea, lost and cold. That's not how she wanted to remember him.

Màthair never rose from her bed again. As she had withered away before Mhàiri's eyes, like an apple left in the hot sun, Mhàiri had been unable to do anything to stop it. Now, no one could move her parents again. They were together, and Mhàiri would carry their memory with her, always.

Hattie Bantrach stood beside Mhàiri, with an arm around Connor. Mhàiri looked down at her brother. He would soon be twelve and had started work, gathering in the seaweed. But the work was hard and the hours long. What would become of him, and Caitriona and Cailean? What future was there for any of them here? The land here was useless for farming. There was little hope of growing crops to feed a family over the winter.

The boulders were so large that even when they had removed enough to build their house and barn, the ground spewed out more.

There had been no mention of the events that had brought Màthair here, or of the life she had led before being removed from her home in the strath. It was as if none of the removals had happened, as if Achcoil had never existed. Sadness crept over Mhàiri, invading her bones and making her limbs heavy.

The long procession moved away from the burial plot and made its way down to the shore. Mhàiri shuffled beside them, gripping on to Hattie Bantrach's arm. Today they were also burying the memory of the fishermen who had been lost at sea. Someone said a prayer for the lost souls but most of his words were drowned out by Mhàiri's own thoughts. She tried to focus. Tried to listen to his words. What was the man saying? 'Remember. Fishermen. Eternity. Rest in peace. God's will.'

Mhàiri recalled Mòrag Mòr's words, the day she had first taken Caitriona for her to see. There was God's will and there was man's will, but for the first time, Mhàiri realised with a clarity that had previously evaded her, that she also had a will of her own. Regardless of the will of God or man, she could make decisions about her life, and she intended to. But first, there was something she had to do.

RETURN ROAD

Strathnaver

Mhàiri had wanted to make the long journey back to Achcoil to visit her sister's grave alone, but Connor insisted on going with her. When Hattie Bantrach and Cameron had added their viewpoint to the discussion that it would be better if Mhàiri had someone with her, she knew she had lost the argument. Now, as she approached her old township, she was glad to have Connor beside her. She stopped in front of her parent's home and looked around. Everything looked the same, but different.

'*Seall*! Look.' Connor pointed to the cottage. The house and the byre at the end were missing their roofs and weeds grew around the empty building.

'And, look there. Isn't that where the rowan tree was?'

Mhàiri looked around the place that had once been so familiar. Water trickled on its way along the River Naver, just as it always had, but what she remembered of Achcoil was gone. She looked out over ground that had once been so familiar and saw only sheep. Hundreds of white-faced sheep, baaing and bleating their indignation at the intruders who had dared to disturb them.

Leaving the sheep to graze in peace, they made their way inside the desecrated shell, which had once been their home. Reflected in the sun glinting through the open roof, Mhàiri faced the ghosts from her past. She watched Màthair stooping over the fire stirring a pot of barley broth - Her father walking through the open door, carrying an armful of peats - Hattie Bantrach, visiting and staying to tell tales of her time away in the wars.

Mhàiri walked to where the front door should have been and leant against the frame. As she looked out across the empty township, she recalled the day she had watched the women passing through, making their way to the coast to work on the fish. She had thought then about going with them. What would her life have been like if she had? She shook her head to clear the thought. Dear God, what was she thinking? Her time with her parents had been short enough without wondering what if and about what could have been. Regardless of whether she had joined the women, or not, nothing would have changed. Her family would still have been forced from their home. And if she had left then, likely she would never have married Cameron. Although he was showing signs of recovery, he remained wracked with pain and still couldn't walk around without assistance. What was to become of him? He was a proud man who wanted to provide for his family. He wouldn't survive being an invalid.

Mhàiri turned. The millstone still sat in the middle of the floor, where their fire had once been. She knelt and stroked the large, cold stone. She remembered the night her sister had arisen from their bed and had lain beside the fire to get warm.

On hearing Fionnghal's screams, Mhàiri had jumped from the bed and beaten the flames with her arms.

'Do you remember Donaidh Dròbhair coming to collect the cattle?' Connor asked, interrupting her thoughts. 'And us laughing as we raced to gather in the barley stalks?'

Mhàiri stood. 'Do you remember packing to go to the summer sheilings?'

'Ah, and swimming down at the river. I still miss it here, Mhàiri.'

'Me too. And Fionnghal and Màthair and Father.' She gripped Connor's hand. 'At least we have each other. Come on. Let's get on with what we came here to do. It will take about an hour for us to walk to the cemetery, and I want to get there before it gets too dark.'

Arriving at the back of the crumbling mission hall, Mhàiri looked around in surprise. Although she hadn't thought it possible, her heart sank even lower. 'Dear, God, where is the cemetery,' she said to Connor and sank to her knees.

He stood beside her open-mouthed. 'The stones are missing. What have they done with the stones?'

A deep wail built within Mhàiri, and she gave vent to it. Of all the things that had happened here in the name of progress, the removal of the stones marking the graves affected her the most. Surely no one could be so heartless as to do this. Rising to her feet, she searched for any sign of her sister's resting place.

Unable to find where their sister lay, Mhàiri and Connor gave up searching.

'We might not be able to find exactly where Fionnghal is, but we can spend the night beside her,' she said. 'We can shelter here and set off for home in the morning. It's as well our mother and father aren't here. At least they were spared seeing this.'

That night, wrapped in her plaid and with Connor snuggled beside her, Mhàiri couldn't sleep. She shouldn't have returned here. Why had no one warned her? Dear God, she couldn't carry back the news of the desecrated graves to the others. She should have realised that nothing would have been as it was. It was as if no one had ever lived here.

Lying there, ghosts of the past haunted Mhàiri's thoughts. On the journey here, there had been times when she had felt like turning back. But she had known that she had to keep going. Her eyes closed, and her thoughts drifted. As he had promised, Iain had returned to his mother's grave a few months before and placed more stones there. Mòrag Mòr hadn't survived the journey to Invercreag. But she would be pleased that Iain and Peigi Ruadh were now married and had built a home together. Iain was still working as a cooper and had settled into the life on the coast.

She felt guilty for suspecting Peigi Ruadh of informing on Ciorstag's husband for sheep stealing. It had been Fearghas who had claimed the £20 reward money. No wonder Anna and Fearghas had hurried off. Although she wanted to, she couldn't feel anger towards them; the money would help them set up a new home. After the death of his daughter, Fearghas had changed. Hadn't they all?

Mhàiri recalled the first night she had spent in the hut on the coast. But now, in her thoughts, the hut transformed into a dark cave. Shivering shadows flitted around the walls. A dog barked in the distance, and fear flooded through Mhàiri. She tried to move, but couldn't. The shadows stretched and grew larger. A shape appeared at the entrance to the cave, blocking the light. Someone was coming. It was unsafe here. She had to get Connor out, but her legs wouldn't move.

'Mhàiri.' Someone called to her, but she couldn't see who it was.

'Mhàiri, wake up!'

She opened her eyes to see Connor's startled face. She sat bolt upright. 'Connor, what is it?'

'You were dreaming. Are you all right?'

'Dreaming? Ah, I am fine. You are right. I was having a bad dream. You go back to sleep. We've a long trek in the morning.'

Connor nodded and settled back down, but Mhàiri still felt disturbed by the dream. What did it mean? She hadn't even been aware of falling asleep. She felt like giving up, just as her mother had. Was it possible to die of a broken heart? Was that what had happened to Màthair? Mhàiri didn't want to face any more hardship. She could remain here in the strath—never be moved. She had been happy here. Memories competed for a place in her thoughts—laughter at the summer sheilings. Snuggling inside her home throughout the hard winters. Peat-stained faces washed away by the arrival of spring. The autumn harvests. Visions of her children surfaced, intruding into her thoughts. She saw her daughter's tear-stained face, after she'd tumbled over and cut her knee while running too fast. She thought about the pleasure her son took in everything around him; the way he smiled at the buzz of the bees, the cawing of the birds, and her gentle kisses. And, she thought about Connor, and his gentle, loving ways. She recalled him returning from the cliffs carrying gull's eggs for her, his face beaming.

She couldn't give up on the children. She had to keep going for their sakes. Even if it meant living without her parents— and her strath. Cameron needed her too. The wound on his back would heal. His pain would go. She couldn't give up on her family, wouldn't give up.

Her thoughts turned to her sister and a pain pierced her chest. It had been her fault that Fionnghal had died. Why hadn't she acted sooner? Despite what she told everyone, she hadn't been asleep before she had heard her sister scream. She'd heard her slip from their bed that morning but had been too warm and sleepy to get up to see to her. She had blocked that memory out but it had always simmered there at the back of her mind; taunting her, teasing, threatening to surface. When her sister had first screamed, Mhàiri had frozen, unable to move. Only when Fionnghal screamed again had she darted from the bed and started to beat at the flames. If she had acted sooner, her sister might still be alive. It was only when Màthair had rushed in and snuffed the flames out by wrapping Fionnghal in a blanket that Mhàiri had stopped beating at them.

Why hadn't she thought to smother the flames? Why hadn't she risen straight away? 'I am sorry, A Fionnghal,' she whispered. 'I'm so, so very sorry.'

TALL TALES

Invercreag

After returning to her cottage on the coast, Mhàiri wrapped a shawl around her shoulders and sat on a chair beside the fire. Hattie Bantrach brought her a bowl of broth, made with nettle, dulse and dandelion leaves, and sat on a stool beside her.

As Mhàiri sipped on the broth, she told Hattie what she had seen at Achcoil. 'I wish I'd never gone back.'

'Then you would never have known. Perhaps it is for the best that you saw the strath as it now is, or you might always have been hankering to return there.'

'Ah, maybe you are right. But, despite what I saw, I will still always have the strath of my memories. I had the most disturbing dream while I was there. It was as if demons had invaded the place. All I wanted was to leave as soon as I could.'

Caitriona glanced up from her knitting, and Mhàiri fell silent. There was no point in going over things. What was done was done. Cailean sauntered over and rested his head on Mhàiri's lap. She stroked his hair. 'Are, you tired? Come on. Let's get you to bed.'

Later, as Mhàiri sat with Cameron, Connor hurried through the door. 'Dòmhnall Beag and I got work moving stones. We're working with some of the Kildonan men to clear the ground for a new stretch of road. There's about ten of us. And, I've to go back tomorrow. I'm to be paid, Mhàiri.'

As he reached out to hang his jacket up, Mhàiri gripped his hand and turned it over. 'Will you look at these hands, they are covered in blisters. Come and I will grease them for you.'

'I am fine.' Connor pulled his hand from her grip. 'A few days and the skin will toughen up. Dòmhnall Beag said so.'

Mhàiri raised her eyebrows. 'That may be so, but I'll grease them for you anyway.'

* * *

The weeks passed, and the days fell into a semblance of a routine for Mhàiri. She placed a pot of potatoes on to boil and called out to Connor to bring some herring in from the barrel in the barn.

While she waited for him to return, Mhàiri brought in a basket of peat.

Cameron sat on a chair by the fire. 'I missed the smell of burning peats,' he said. 'But, like you said when we first arrived, there is nothing that can't be bought here.'

Mhàiri laughed and looked over her shoulder at him. 'And nothing tasted the same cooked on a coal fire either.' She wrapped her arms around him. Cameron was recovering his strength and the wound on his back had started to scar over. Although the scars remained red and raw, they would improve with time, and ointment, she thought. 'Take your' shirt off Cameron MacÀidh and I'll get the paste for your back.'

'Any excuse, Mhàiri. Can you not wait until we are abed before you strip me of my clothes?'

Mhàiri rolled her eyes. 'Though I can't deny it is working, this paste smells foul.' She screwed up her face. 'If I never smell it again it will be too soon.' She rubbed the concoction onto his back, massaging the scars with her fingers.

'Mhàiri—'

'Hmm?'

Cameron swallowed.

She dipped her fingers into the paste and spread it over his puckered flesh. 'What is it?'

'Do you remember the day we sat on the hillside? The day we were trying to decide when to marry—'

'The day you promised to build me a new bed because I refused to sleep in your parent's one.' Mhàiri laughed and rubbed the paste into his skin. 'And you did build it Cameron, and I knew nothing about it until we returned from seeing your parents off.'

'Do you remember what you asked me that day? About the scars on your arms.'

Mhàiri stilled her hands and stared down at the puckered flesh on her arms and then at Cameron's back. 'I— I showed you my scars and asked how you could want me.'

'And do you, Mhàiri? Do you still desire me, now that I have scars?'

'*A Cameron, mo ghràidh-* Cameron, my love,' she said. 'How could I have even thought to let such a thing worry me? Of course, I do. You were right in what you said.'

Connor came in with the fish, halting further discussion.

* * *

Days passed and nothing much changed. Mhàiri continued to spend her days gutting and preparing barrels of fish at the fisheries, while Hattie Bantrach looked after Caitriona and Cailean. Although Mhàiri missed her parents beyond words, life went on. Connor continued to help build the new road with the Kildonan men and stashed away almost every penny he earned. He began to spend nights away and, although Mhàiri was concerned for his safety, she stopped asking him where he had been when he did choose to come home.

They hadn't heard lately from Cameron's parents— the last letter they'd received, through Maighstir MacCoinnich, had been three months before Mhàiri buried her mother. On the day of the funeral, she'd given the minister a letter for Cameron's family telling them about her parent's death, but she hadn't found it in herself to tell them about Cameron's injury.

Although she continued to add money whenever she could towards their passages abroad, there still hadn't been word of any ship sailing to the Red River Valley. Mhàiri had all but resigned herself to staying here. But winter would soon be upon them. How would they survive it with no crops and Cameron not working?

SEASHELLS AND SURPRISES

Mhàiri followed Caitriona and Cailean as they meandered bare-footed along the sandy beach. The sun shone down on her, on one of the rare free hours she had. The red-cheeked children gathered sea-shells into woven baskets, calling out to her whenever they picked one up.

'Yes, I see it,' she called to Caitriona. 'Ah, that is indeed a lovely one, Cailean.'

As she continued to call to them, Mhàiri's mind drifted. She soaked up the sights and inhaled the fresh salty smell of the sea. Her back ached from the long hours spent gutting fish. She wondered if she would ever get used to it. And Cameron—

'What have you got in those baskets?' A stiff-backed bailiff said as he approached. He pulled the basket from two-year-old Cailean. 'And yours,' he said to Caitriona and tore it from her hands.

Caitriona trembled and her eyes widened in terror.

Cailean screamed, and Mhàiri lifted him into her arms. She gripped her daughter by the arm and pulled her close. 'Shells. It is only sea-shells the children are gathering.'

The man tipped out the baskets and kicked the scattered contents across the sand with his boot.

Mhàiri held back her anger. She looked down and turned to leave.

'Where do you think you are going? Wait there until I say you can go. I need to check each of these shells. You are not allowed to take shellfish. Be warned if I find even one live one amongst this lot, I will have you arrested for theft.'

'They are children, they wouldn't know if there was a live one in them, or not. And, anyway it was just empty shells they were picking up.'

'I will be the judge of that,' the man said and continued to scan the shells. When he was satisfied that there weren't any mussels or shell-fish, he grunted and set off calling threats behind him. 'Be warned. I have my eye on you. If you are gathering mussels for the fishing without paying, I will soon find out.'

Mhàiri bit on her bottom lip and picked up the empty baskets. Making her way home, she passed a line of sheds. A bonnet-clad, young man stepped out from behind one. 'Are you all right, Mhàiri? I saw what happened,' the man said and removed the bonnet from his head.

'My God, Rob Dunn, you gave me a fright. I'm fine. Just angry at that man for upsetting the children. I need to get them home.'

Rob Dunn replaced his bonnet, pulled it low over his forehead and walked beside her. 'How is Cameron? I heard he is improving.'

Mhàiri turned her head. How had he heard that? 'Every day he is gaining more strength.'

'But he is still not working?'

Mhàiri dipped her head. She didn't know how much longer she could manage without Cameron earning. 'The Fife miners have been to see him, to discuss him starting at the coal-pit.'

'The coal-pit,' Rob Dunn's voice rose in anger. 'You do know of the conditions there,' he said between clenched teeth. 'If you thought the fishing was dangerous, it pales to nothing compared to working down the mines. Look over yonder at that harr. It is coming off a mine. It is another explosion waiting to happen. Four died in the last blast.'

Mhàiri shifted Cailean into her other arm. 'What choice do we have? It's not as if we have any say. And it will be another few weeks, at least, before Cameron will be well enough to start.'

'Look, if it is money you need, I can get you some.' Rob Dunn rubbed his beard. 'To see you through until Cameron secures other work.'

Mhàiri shook her head. 'We will get by.'

He took her hand. 'Come with me into the mountains, Mhàiri.'

Mhàiri stared at him, wide-eyed. 'Please, Rob—'

'Cameron too. I meant both of you. To help in the fight. The more there is of us the better. We get by well enough, and we don't have to work all day to fill a landlord's purse. How long will it be before that boy in your arms is out there, waist-deep in the water, gathering seaweed for a pittance?'

What he said was true, and the thought of fleeing from the coast tempted Mhàiri. What kind of life would her children have here? They would be no worse off hiding out in the hills. But, a different set of problems would likely be waiting for her there. She wanted her children to be safe, but she also wanted them to be free. 'Thank you for your offer of help. Perhaps one day we will consider moving to the hills. But we can't give up yet. We plan to emigrate.'

Rob Dunn let go of her hand. 'Although the Emigration Society was declared illegal and prevented from meeting, we are still continuing our work to secure low-cost fares for anyone who was evicted from the straths.' He raised his brows. 'The fares could now cost as little as three pounds each.'

'Three pounds?'

Rob Dunn grinned. 'That is the real reason our meeting was declared illegal. Rest assured, the fight will continue until we secure passages for anyone who wants them.'

'You always had strength and courage, Rob Dunn. You've never stopped fighting for the tenants.'

'Nor will I. But watch out for Connor MacNiall. He is mixing with those out to harass the shepherds. Have your brother take care. There are plenty like Fearghas Mac Uilleam who will tell.'

As they passed the shed where the lots were allocated, Rob Dunn stopped. 'I best be getting back, Mhàiri.'

She nodded and pointed to a notice pinned to the door.

£70 Reward Offered

Reward offered for Alasdair MacIllEathain, husband of Ciorstag, sometimes residing in the Parish of Kildonan. Stands accused of theft of one sheep from Messrs Reid and escaping from Dornoch Prison. In the name of the most noble Lord Stafford and the Association Against Felons, a reward of seventy-pounds is offered to any officers of the law or other persons who apprehend the said Alasdair MacIllEathain and lodge him in any of His Majesty's Jails on which the reward will be duly paid.

Description of Alasdair MacIllEathain - Aged about 25years, 5 ½ feet in height. Light brown hair, grey eyes. A little freckled in the face. Generally, wears a blue or green tartan coat.

. . .

Mhàiri stared at the poster and shook her head in disbelief. 'Ciorstag's husband had escaped.'

Rob Dunn, who had made to move away, turned and winked. Think about what I said, Mhàiri, about joining us in the hills. Talk to Cameron. We need all the help we can get. And, I'm sure Ciorstag and Alasdair would be pleased to see you both again.

61

NEW DAY, NEW DREAMS

Elizabeth's Highland Castle

E lizabeth folded the Edinburgh Gazette and laid it on the table. 'Oh, dear,' she said to her husband as they relaxed together in the morning room of the castle drinking tea. 'The price of kelp is predicted to fall again. We need to do something.'

'Falling, again!' Lord Stafford pushed his spectacles back onto the bridge of his nose with his forefinger. 'And so soon after the price of wool falling. Coal is still turning a profit though, isn't it?'

'For the moment, yes, but I'm not sure for how much longer.'

'There are still many developments in progress.' He adjusted the blanket on his knee. 'We should see the results of these soon. With more bridges and roads opening up, we'll soon have better means of moving our produce. And most exciting of all is that the bridges will also increase the range of my new postal service.'

'Hmm,' Elizabeth uttered. She didn't want to broach the subject with her husband, but she had to. There was no getting out of it. 'That is as may be, but the new sheep farms aren't providing us with the rents we expected. I'm not sure the sheep have proved the success we'd initially hoped for. Although the estate is producing vast quantities of wool, the price we get is lower than it first was. It seems that the more everyone produces, the cheaper the wool becomes. Mister Sellar and some of the others did well enough from their Cheviots. But, as an experiment, I would say sheep farming isn't proving particularly successful. Granted the rents have risen, but we now have less people paying rent, and the sheep farmers, including Mister Sellar, are struggling to pay the agreed amount. We need to find another means of making the land profitable.'

'So, the sheep farmers may move out?'

'They are not saying that, yet. But—'

'Fishing shooting and hunting lodges, perhaps?' Lord Stafford tilted his nose and sniffed.

Much to her surprise, her husband had reacted with enthusiasm. It was as if he had already thought this through. 'Lodges, you say?'

Stafford's face brightened. 'Yes, lodges for the gentry to holiday in. The deer are bountiful, and the stunning landscape, with its lochs, hunting and fishing. Why, many of the Lowland gentry would jump at the chance to pay to come here to fish and hunt. I think we should have our estate commissioner look further into this.'

Elizabeth thought about what her husband had said. He was right. 'How exciting! Yes, many of our London friends would also holiday here, particularly for the hunts and the fishing. Yes, have Mister Loch look into it,' Elizabeth stood. 'If you don't mind, I think we should go out in the carriage later . . . to see how your latest bridge is progressing. Perhaps we will see the ideal place to situate our first hunting lodge?'

Elizabeth made her way towards her study. How long would her husband be able to continue making the journey north? The new jetty helped, but for how much longer?

* * *

Later that afternoon, as she journeyed through the straths with Lord Stafford, Elizabeth looked out the carriage window. The view had changed. Gone were the townships with the grey-blue peat smoke curling from the cottage roofs. Gone were the cattle, goats and horses grazing on the high pastures. Gone were the people gathering in their crops from the fields or cutting peats. Gone were the children playing on the hillsides. And, the missions and churches lay abandoned, rundown and forgotten. The only signs of life were the incessant baaing of sheep and the occasional sight of a shepherd and his dog.

'How desolate the vista looks,' she said.

Lord Stafford pushed his spectacles further up his nose and peered out the window. 'Desolate? It looks little different to me. But imagine how it will look with more roads and bridges.'

Elizabeth nodded and looked out across the strath, imagining the hunting lodges that would replace the shepherd's cottages, the forests and deer which would replace the sheep. The image was more soothing. Her thoughts turned to her forefathers, The Clan Chiefs. These days have gone, she realised. Times have changed. And so had she. She was of the nobility now and married to the richest man in the country.

Although she had been raised a Lowlander, her Highland estate had always drawn her to it. She had mixed roots, but as she looked around, Elizabeth came to the cold realisation that regardless of her ancestry her family was now more English than Scottish. Her children and grandchildren were now her main focus. She adjusted the wrap around her knees and smiled at the knowledge of the legacy she would leave them.

62

DECISION DAY

Invercreag

Connor hurried through the cottage door, his face alight, and his eyes sparkling as bright as the spring day. He grabbed Mhàiri's hands and twirled her around.

Taken by surprise, thoughts raced through Mhàiri's head. 'What is it? Connor, what is going on?'

'There has been word of a ship. It's to be leaving for the Red River Valley.'

She looked into his smiling face. Had she heard right? 'Did you say that there is to be a ship leaving? Where did you hear that?'

'Rob . . . Rob Dunn told me, and he's arranged for passages for us. It leaves in five weeks. You've to get the money to him as soon as you can.'

Mhàiri hesitated. 'Leave. Leave now?' How could she leave? Cameron was working in the coal-mine. But, he had a hacking cough which had been brought on by the dust. Would he survive the journey?

'There are more people than places. Rob Dunn said if you want the places you will have to be quick about it.'

Mhàiri stepped backward and, holding her hand behind her, caught hold of the chair. She slumped back onto it and stared at Connor. After all this time, it was finally happening. They'd managed to get a passage, but at what cost? And for it to happen now, when she no longer had any desire to leave . . . couldn't leave.

63

FINAL FAREWELL

Mhàiri lifted the hem of her best skirt and climbed the steps of the ship bound for Stromness. Cameron, their children and Connor climbed the steps beside her. Once there, they would wait on the Hudson Bay ship that would take her family over to the Red River Settlement. Dòmhnall Beag, Lachlann, and their wives boarded behind them.

As people pushed past, Mhàiri kept hold of her children's hands, and they joined the crowd which had gathered on deck. She leant against the side and looked out at the coastline. Cameron placed an arm around her shoulder, and Caitriona and Cailean held tightly on to her skirt. Connor climbed up on the ledge and looked over the side.

Pinned to Mhàiri's plaid was the MacAoidh crest brooch. She stroked the metal centre, and felt the small red stones. The brooch had been handed down through the generations. Mamó and Màthair had worn it on their wedding days and Mhàiri had worn it on hers. One day, Caitriona would wear it too.

When the ship started to move away, Mhàiri lifted Cailean up. She waved to Iain, Peigi Ruadh, Hattie Bantrach and the others who had come to see them off. Hattie Bantrach had refused to make the long journey. Iain had also decided to remain, along with Peigi Ruadh, and their children. The widow, Hattie, would live with them. Mhàiri would miss her friends, but Iain was earning well as a cooper and had settled into the new way of life on the coast.

She scanned the crowd, but could see no sign of Rob Dunn. The offer to help with the resistance had never really been an option for Mhàiri; she had her children to think about. But, once again, Rob Dunn had fought back on behalf of the evicted tenants, helping them when they had been unable to help themselves. Like many Highland men, the war had changed Rob Dunn, or had it? Despite his experiences in battle, he had remained strong, had remained good. And, he swore to keep fighting with the others living in the hills until the law gave back this land to the tenants who had been removed. Deep within her, Mhàiri knew that even if it took many years, they would succeed.

Someone on shore started singing a familiar lament, and the song was taken up by those on board.

Mhàiri, Cameron and Connor joined in—

Land of our fathers, carried with us in song,
Land of our fathers, it's where we belong,
Weep not for wanting, all ours is yours.
Land of our fathers, filled with happy hours
As long as we have you, we will have plenty
Land of our fathers, for all, not just the gentry.

When the land grew distant, Mhàiri let Cailean down and made to move away, but she stopped and turned. She placed an arm around Connor's shoulder and remained with him and Cameron, watching the coastline fading away along with the way of life she had once known. The life her children would now never have.

Although she couldn't bring an uninjured Cameron to his parents, she was at least bringing him to them. He had insisted that he was well enough to make the long, hazardous, journey, despite a near constant cough. Mhàiri was also bringing their grandchildren to them. She looked down at Cailean and Caitriona, who both gripped on to her skirt. She rubbed her belly. And a new one on the way.

Tears fell at leaving behind her parents, but they were now resting in the land they had loved and would never have left. At least they have that, she thought. She prayed that their resting place would remain undisturbed and that they would never be moved again.

Mhàiri dried her tears with the back of her hand. There was no going back now; nothing could be as it once was. Life consisted of nothing but dead dreams. She removed a cloth from her pocket, opened it and gently lifted out the dried dandelion she had picked as she had left her home in the strath. Should she use her last dandelion wish to ask to return to Strathnaver one day? But what would she be coming back to? Nothing would be as she remembered. The only way now was to look forward— and to keep looking forward.

As the ship sailed onwards, Mhàiri tossed the dead dandelion into the sea and turned towards her future.

GLOSSARY OF SCOTTISH
TERMS USED

Bannock – a simple bread-like dough. Made from grain and cooked on a flat iron plate.

Birl – turn quickly.

Bonnie – beautiful.

Brae – hillside or slope.

Byre – a barn or cowshed.

Ceilidh – traditional Scottish social gathering. There are many forms: music, storytelling, poetry, dancing or just talking.

Clachan – a small village.

Clod – lump of earth.

Crowdie – a soft, crumbly Scottish cheese.

Drover – a person who moves livestock (mainly cattle) over long distances.

Factor – an agent within the management structure of a Scottish estate.

Feared - Afraid

Griddled – (or girdled) food cooked on a heavy, flat iron plate.

Ken – know.

Lassie – a girl or young woman.

Lugged – carried a heavy load with great effort.

Peats – cut out from mossy, boggy ground, dried and used as fuel. Has a distinctive 'peaty' smell.

Plaid – a long piece of woollen cloth. Often in a checked pattern (tartan).

Sheiling (or shieling) – a hut, or collection of huts situated in the hills or mountain pastures, used for summer grazing of cattle.

Spurtle –a wooden spoon. Used for stirring porridge, soups or stews.

Strath – a wide, shallow, river valley.

Thatch – a roof covering of straw or similar material.

Twirl – spin.

ABOUT THE AUTHOR

SHEENA MACLEOD

Sheena lectured at the University of Dundee where she gained her PhD. She now lives in a seaside town in Scotland. She is a member of the Scottish Association of Writers. Her father grew up in a Gaelic speaking crofting community, which gave her her passion for Scottish history. When not writing Sheena loves to spend her time by the sea with her dogs.

Follow Sheena on her website: https://www.sheenas-books. co.uk

ALSO BY SHEENA MACLEOD

If you've enjoyed this book please consider leaving a review on your favourite ebook platform.

HISTORICAL FICTION

Reign of the Marionettes

HISTORICAL NON-FICTION

So, You Say I Can't Vote!

Printed in Great Britain
by Amazon

32620334R00182